"It's more than...friendship between us, Erik. Isn't it?"

He breathed the word, "Yes."

Suddenly Evie didn't feel so bold. She whispered, "I'm afraid."

"So am I."

And then she sighed. "But I don't think...I can stop it. I don't think I *want* to stop it."

His eyes were still closed. "You should stop it."

"No. Don't say that."

"I have to say it."

"No—"

"I have nothing, Evie. Nothing to give you."

She covered his lips with her fingertips. "Shh. You have everything. Everything that matters...."

Dear Reader,

Welcome to Silhouette **Special Edition**...welcome to romance. This month we have six wonderful books to celebrate Valentine's Day just right!

Premiering this month is our newest promotion. THAT'S MY BABY! will alternate with THAT SPECIAL WOMAN! and will feature stories from some of your favorite authors. Marking this very special debut is *The Cowboy and His Baby* by Sherryl Woods. It's the third book of her heartwarming series AND BABY MAKES THREE.

Reader favorite Christine Rimmer returns to North Magdalene for another tale of THE JONES GANG in her book, *The Man, The Moon and The Marriage Vow.* The wonderful Joan Elliott Pickart continues her newest series, THE BABY BET, in Special Edition this month. *Friends, Lovers...and Babies!* is book two of the MacAllister family series. Also in February, Pamela Toth introduces the Buchanan Brothers in *Buchanan's Bride*— it's the first book in her series, BUCKLES & BRONCOS. Sharon De Vita's *Child of Midnight* is her first for Special Edition, a passionate story about a runaway boy, a caring woman and the renegade cop who loves them both. And finally, Kelly Jamison's *The Wedding Contract* is a marriage-of-convenience story not to be missed!

So join us for an unforgettable February! I hope you enjoy all these stories!

Sincerely,

Tara Gavin
Senior Editor

Please address questions and book requests to:
Silhouette Reader Service
U.S.: 3010 Walden Ave., P.O. Box 1325, Buffalo, NY 14269
Canadian: P.O. Box 609, Fort Erie, Ont. L2A 5X3

CHRISTINE RIMMER

THE MAN, THE MOON AND THE MARRIAGE VOW

Published by Silhouette Books
America's Publisher of Contemporary Romance

For my sister, Beverly Jordan,
who always loved a good fairy tale

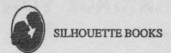 SILHOUETTE BOOKS

ISBN 0-373-24010-4

THE MAN, THE MOON AND THE MARRIAGE VOW

Printed in U.S.A.

Books by Christine Rimmer

CHRISTINE RIMMER

is a third-generation Californian who came to her profession the long way around. Before settling down to write about the magic of romance, she'd been an actress, a sales clerk, a janitor, a model, a phone-sales representative, a teacher, a waitress, a playwright and an office manager. Now that she's finally found work that suits her perfectly, she insists she never had a problem keeping a job—she was merely gaining "life experience" for her future as a novelist. Those who know her best withhold comment when she makes such claims; they are grateful that she's at last found steady work. Christine is grateful, too—not only for the joy she finds in writing, but for what waits when the day's work is through: a man she loves who loves her right back and the privilege of watching their children grow and change day to day.

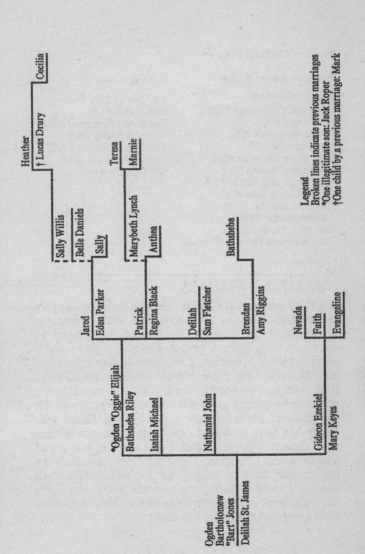

Heather
† Lucas Drury — Cecilia

Sally Willis
Belle Daniels
Jared
Eden Parker — Sally

Teresa
Marybeth Lynch — Marnie
Patrick
Regina Black — Anthea

Delilah
Sam Fletcher
Bathsheba
Brendan
Amy Riggins

"Ogden "Oggie" Elijah
Bathsheba Riley
Isaiah Michael

Nathaniel John

Nevada
Gideon Ezekiel — Faith
Mary Keyes — Evangeline

Ogden
Bartholomew
"Bart" Jones
Delilah St. James

Legend
Broken lines indicate previous marriages
*One illegitimate son: Jack Roper
†One child by a previous marriage: Mark

Chapter One

At first, the sound was like the crackle of static from a radio turned down very low. Vaguely irritating, but nothing to be concerned about.

Evie ignored it. She sat straighter in the old wooden pew. She listened more attentively to Reverend Johnson's sonorous, singsong voice as he ran down his list of announcements.

The minutes ticked by. Evie began to feel more confident that the indistinct noise was gone. She relaxed a little. She allowed herself to enjoy the crystalline quality of the late-morning light that poured in through the windows on either side of the double rows of pews. She admired the flower arrangements, mostly glads and iris, that adorned the altar. And she registered the slight shifting of the big man, Erik Riggins, who sat on her left; he was leaning toward the boy on his other side and murmuring, "Sit still, Pete. Or else," in a tone of strained fatherly patience.

Evie smiled. Everything was fine. Normal. Good.

But then she frowned. Everything *wasn't* fine. Not really. She could actually *hear* the sound now, as if a mischievous hand had reached out and turned up the volume just a little.

Just enough that she was forced to acknowledge consciously that there *was* a sound.

Evie stared hard at the reverend. She listened intently to what he was saying.

"And please," the reverend solemnly chided his flock, "we need more volunteers to run the booths at Septemberfest, which is going to be held on Main Street as always and looks as if it will be bigger than ever this year. Every merchant and businessman in town will be involved, not to mention all of the local volunteer associations. We want our church's part of the proceedings to be a rousing success. So do join in. Time is flying. The big day is Saturday, the ninth, which is only three weeks away now. Anyone who can give us an hour or two, be sure to let Nellie Anderson know as soon as—"

Crackle. Hiss. Snap. Pop. The sound would not be ignored. It had slithered right over the threshold of Evie's conscious mind and wouldn't go away. Now it grated, demanded, *insisted* that she give it credence.

Evie was forced to block it. She drew in a long, slow breath. She brought up the wall inside her mind.

The sound stopped.

That's that, Evie thought with a tiny sigh.

The reverend had finished the announcements. "And now, let us take a moment or two to reflect in song. Please turn in your hymnals to hymn number 213. 'Softly and Tenderly.'" There was the rustle of turning pages. The reverend instructed, "All rise."

Evie stood, as did everyone else in the small church. At the piano, Regina Jones, who was the wife of Evie's cousin Patrick, began to play the sweet melody. Along with everyone else, Evie started to sing.

She made it halfway through the first chorus before she realized that the sound was back. The wall, which had always worked before, had not worked this time.

Evie sang louder, though sweat broke out on her upper lip and her heart pounded hurtfully under her ribs. Yes, the sound was back. And growing.

Around her, fifty voices were raised in the final chorus, "Come home, come home... Ye who are weary, come home..."

By then, much louder than the music, was the sound. The sound of someone suffering. Someone crying out. Wordless. Alone. In silence. A sound that only Evie could hear.

"Please be seated."

Around Evie, everyone settled back into the pews.

Her arm brushed Erik Riggins's briefly as they sat. And that was when Evie knew that the awful, screaming, needful sound was coming from him.

None of my business, she instructed herself silently. *I will not interfere...*

Evie tried to keep her eyes to the front; she put everything she had into listening to the reverend as he launched into his sermon on the meaning of the Twenty-third Psalm.

But the soundless noise was so painful. So relentless. It seemed to shoot off the man beside her like tiny slivers of exploding glass.

Before she could stop herself, Evie turned and looked at him.

She saw a big man with wide, thick shoulders and muscular arms. His large, rough hands rested stiffly on his knees. She studied his profile: a tender mouth and a hawk-like nose, bronze-colored hair that could use a good trim.

What she knew of him scrolled through her mind.

He was newly returned to town. A brother of Amy Jones, another of Evie's cousins by marriage. Evie had heard from someone in the family that his wife had died. And there were children: the blond boy on his other side. And a girl—no, *two* girls.

Erik Riggins felt her watching him. Slowly, like a hawk on a high crag annoyed by some slight movement way below, he turned his head and met her gaze. He did not smile. His eyes were gray—storm-cloud gray. He looked ... far away. And sad. But perfectly calm.

However, the way he looked didn't mean anything. The sound didn't really exist anyway. Not on any level that any ordinary person could hear.

But Evie heard it. She knew that his outer calm meant nothing. Less than nothing. Inside, he was screaming, crying out ...

She couldn't take it. She did the forbidden thing. The thing she'd sworn never to do again.

She lifted her hand and laid it over his.

The sound ceased.

Sweet, so sweet. That moment of peace. Though the reverend droned on and a fat fly buzzed against the windows, trying to get out to the summer world beyond the glass, to Evie, right then, there was silence.

Pure, complete silence. Silence as sweet as water from a mountain spring.

Water. Yes ...

Evie closed her eyes and imagined the purest of soothing water, flowing through the palm of her hand and into the man beside her.

The hand beneath her own went lax. She felt his big body slump a little, in what she sensed was profound relief.

Evie sighed as she let it flow, let the imaginary water go into him, easing the loneliness that can eat a person alive, soothing the agonies that no one knew he felt.

But then he shook his head. The hand she covered with her own went as cold as stone. And the imaginary water fled back, like a river at high tide, into her own body, where it churned and roiled, without direction—hurting her with the very *wrongness* of its flow.

Right then, he snatched his hand away.

"Oh!" The word escaped Evie before she could stop it. She closed her mouth immediately, so no other sound could get out and betray her further.

Her stomach ached. She clutched it surreptitiously, trying not to let anyone else know her distress.

But the man beside her knew. He was still looking at her, *glaring* at her, really, through eyes that were now the color of a frozen mist over a storm-tossed sea. It seemed to her that his expression was one of disbelief—and distaste.

Shame and embarrassment made her face flame. Oh, would she never learn?

Erik Riggins was still glaring at her, no doubt telling himself that Evie Jones was a brazen woman who made passes at men she hardly knew—and in church, no less!

Her cheeks burning hotter by the moment, Evie managed to whisper, "I...uh... Sorry."

That seemed to be enough for him. After the briefest of nods, he pointedly faced front once more.

" 'My cup runneth over,' " the reverend quoted with sonorous feeling. "What a wondrous image..."

Somewhere outside, a robin was singing. And the boy on the other side of Erik Riggins let out a long sigh, no doubt eager to be out in the summer morning, yearning to be playing ball or swimming in the river not too far away.

Evie sat very still until the clutching nausea in her stomach slackened and finally passed away. Then she drew her shoulders back and made herself breathe deeply.

She spoke silently to herself. *It's all right. It's over. Just put it from your mind. . . .*

Yes, she'd broken her own vow to herself; she'd reached out and touched when she had no right to. She wasn't pleased with what she'd done. But it had happened. She would put it behind her—and she'd keep a little tighter rein on herself in the future, that was all.

And as far as the way Erik Riggins's silent cry had scaled the wall, well, it had been a fluke. Nothing more. It would never happen again.

She would look at the bright side. After all, things could be worse. If the man beside her still cried out for help in his heart, at least she could no longer hear him. And a couple of swift glances at the people sitting nearby left her reasonably certain that no one else had noticed her odd behavior.

It had been an insignificant incident, really. And it was over. She'd thank the good Lord for small favors and leave it at that.

After the service, Evie sought out Nellie Anderson to offer her help for Septemberfest. She found the church's tall, gaunt volunteer secretary out on the patchy slice of lawn between the steps of the church and the sidewalk. Nellie stood with her clipboard high and pencil poised, casting piercing looks at the members of the congregation as they filed out into the sunshine. The technique seemed to be quite effective. As Evie watched, more than one person stepped over and volunteered a little time behind a counter during the September street fair.

With a tight smile on her thin lips, Nellie scribbled on the clipboard. Then she looked up, this time at Evie. Evie smiled at the older woman.

"Ah," Nellie said. "Evie Jones. Can we count on you to lend a hand, too, dear?"

Evie nodded. "But I won't be able to help out in a booth. I'll be working behind my own counter that day."

"Ah, yes. That *interesting* store of yours."

Though Nellie Anderson was one of the few people around who could make the word "interesting" sound like a criticism, Evie didn't take offense. "Why don't you drop in some time?" she suggested. "I'll show you around."

Nellie's pinched expression relaxed a little. She seemed pleased to be invited to the shop. "Well, I just might do that. Thank you, dear."

And then Nellie blinked. Her face went blank as she stared beyond Evie's shoulder. Evie glanced back to see what it was and found herself looking at Erik Riggins and his son, who both seemed to be staring right back at Nellie. But only for a moment. Then, as one, the boy and the man cut their eyes away. They moved on by.

Evie gazed after them for several seconds, thinking that Erik Riggins had the broadest shoulders she'd ever seen. And that his hair had gold lights in it when it caught the sun.

But then she drew herself up short. What was the matter with her? She simply had to put the Riggins fellow completely out of her mind.

She turned to Nellie again.

Nellie seemed embarrassed. Her bony hand went to her throat and she coughed, a nervous sound. "Oh, my. Excuse me. I...where were we?"

Evie couldn't help wondering what was going on between Nellie and the big man with the rough hands. But then she reminded herself once more how she intended to forget all about Erik Riggins. Speculating about him and Nellie was no way to do that.

Nellie had collected herself enough to prompt, "You were saying you can't take a booth?"

"Right. Wishbook will be open that day. But maybe I could call around for donations. Or bake a few things, if there's going to be a bake sale."

Nellie scribbled on her clipboard. "Good, good. I'll get in touch with you about the calls you can make. And how about if I put you down for, say, two cakes and ten dozen cookies?"

It was a lot of baking, but Evie didn't hesitate. She said yes. She really did want to help out. She'd lived in the small town of North Magdalene for almost a year now, and she was doing everything she could to make it the true home she'd always longed for. That included lending a hand at community events.

"Lovely, dear. Thank you," Nellie murmured sweetly, and looked beyond Evie's shoulder again, eager to capture her next booth-manning victim before the poor soul could escape.

Ten minutes later, Evie arrived at her store. She found her uncle, Oggie Jones, waiting there for her.

She spotted him before he saw her. He was sitting on the wrought-iron bench to the right of the door, a cloud of cigar smoke ringing his grizzled head. He'd propped his favorite cane, a stick of gnarled manzanita, at his side.

Oggie appeared to be staring at a pair of buildings across the street—the Hole in the Wall Saloon and the Mercantile Grill. Both buildings had burned down almost two years before. It had taken eighteen months to rebuild them. And now they were open for business once more.

Evie thought that Oggie looked contented. And well he should. Both businesses were Jones family enterprises—very successful ones, too.

Evie stopped for a moment on the sidewalk, looking at Oggie, feeling warmth and affection move through her, washing away the last of the jitters from her unsettling encounter with that Erik Riggins fellow.

As if he could feel her gaze—and the love in it, too—the old man turned his head and looked at Evie. Through the cloud of smoke, she saw his wrinkled mouth stretch into a grin.

"There you are, gal. Been waitin' for you."

She moved to stand before him. "Hello, Uncle Oggie. We missed you in church."

He let out a wicked cackle. "I show up for the marryin's and the buryin's. And that's just about as much organized religion as a bad old fool like yours truly can take."

Evie rolled her eyes to indicate her disbelief. "You're hardly a fool, Uncle Oggie."

"But you do admit I'm bad?"

She wrinkled her nose at him. "I'm not going to answer that."

He puffed on his cigar and wiggled his bushy brows at her, then he stared off across the street again. "I been sittin' here ruminatin' on how if we don't watch it, all of Main Street is gonna be Jones owned."

Evie chuckled. "We're close, but not there yet. There's still Lily's Café and Santino's Barber, Beauty and Variety, and Swan's Motel and—"

Oggie waved his cigar. "Evie, honey. It ain't as if I don't know who owns what around here. You gonna invite me in?"

"Could you put out the cigar?"

The old man's sigh was deep and resigned. "Hell. You bet." He used the tall, sand-filled ashtray that Evie had conveniently set at the end of the bench, then he grabbed his cane and followed Evie through the door into the dim interior of her shop.

After taking a minute to close and lock the door behind them, Evie led her uncle around the shadowed groupings of furniture and clothing, past the button cabinet and the carnival glass display and the big, antique brass cash register that sat on a glass-fronted case in the middle of the room. Behind her, she could hear the old sweetheart huffing and puffing, his cane tapping the hardwood floor as he hastened to keep up with her.

They went through an archway and a short hall at the back, and then up the narrow stairs to Evie's apartment above the shop.

Evie got the old man settled into a big chair in the living room and turned on a window air conditioner to cut the growing heat of the day. Next, she made sandwiches and brewed some coffee—when Oggie came to visit, no matter what time of day it was, he always liked a good, strong cup of coffee with mountains of sugar in it.

After the coffee was made and she'd served him, Evie asked him if he had something special on his mind. But Oggie only asked wasn't he welcome, even without a reason to call.

Though she sensed evasion in his reply, Evie assured him that he was always welcome. As they shared the simple lunch, he told her a story or two of long ago, of growing up in Kansas. He spoke of his wonderful mama and his cruel daddy. Oggie said his mama had adored his daddy, in spite of the meanness in his daddy's soul. Thus his mama's gentle heart was broken when his wicked daddy died.

Oggie talked a little about his brothers, too, though not much. He only mentioned his youngest brother, Gideon, one time. But one time was enough.

"Is that it?" Her appetite gone, Evie set her half-finished sandwich on the battered steamer trunk that she used for a coffee table. "Have you heard from my father?"

Oggie's black eyes were fathoms deep. "Sometimes, gal, it's like you really *are* psychic."

Evie absently brushed away the few sandwich crumbs that had dropped onto her antique silk dress. She wanted to cry. And she couldn't help thinking how carefully she'd chosen the dress that morning, humming and feeling good and thinking that she was headed off to church in her new hometown, where every face was becoming familiar to her— and everyone thought of her as an ordinary woman named Evie Jones.

"I've explained to you, Uncle Oggie," she said tightly. "There's nothing psychic about me. I know how to read people, that's all. My father taught me. And he was a pro."

Oggie shook his head. "Whatever you say."

"It's the truth, Uncle Oggie. I am *not* psychic."

Oggie put up both hands. "Hey. Am I arguin'?"

She drew in a long breath. "I'm just telling you, all right? My father taught me everything. You don't know the... tricks he uses. You hardly knew him, after all."

"Gal, he's my brother. I knew him."

"You know what I mean. You lost track of my father when he was ten or eleven, you said."

Oggie couldn't resist correcting her. "Twelve. He was twelve, the way I remember it. Gideon was five and I was fifteen when poor Ma went to her reward. They farmed all of us boys out to foster care. I did my level best to keep in touch, even after I was grown-up and on my own. But then Giddy ran off. He was twelve, then, like I said. And I was twenty-two. I tried to track him down, but then the war came. And after I got back from France, his trail was as cold as yesterday's flapjacks."

"Fine. And it's been fifty years since then."

"More'n that, I'm sorry to say."

"So take my word for it. I know him better than you ever did. Gideon Jones is a cheat and a swindler. He finds out a person's dreams and desires and hopes and fears. And he *uses* what he finds out."

"But—"

Evie wasn't finished. "As I said, he knows how to read people and he taught me how to read people, too. I turned out to be good at it. Very good. And that's all there was to the *famous psychic,* Evangeline."

Oggie was watching her. He said very softly, "Gal, don't let bitterness get its teeth in you."

Evie glanced away. "I'm trying, Uncle Oggie. I'm doing my best. Most of the time, I do pretty well. But sometimes, when all that old garbage comes up, it's hard, you know?"

"But I don't really get it. I don't really understand why you're so sensitive about it after all this time."

"Uncle Oggie, I—"

He cut her off, intent on making his point. "No, I'm serious. I read some of those articles about you. I can't believe it was all a fake, those lost people you found and the sick ones who got well after you—"

Evie couldn't take anymore. She stood. "Please, Uncle Oggie. Please." She turned away from him, away from the light that flooded in the window at his back.

"Come on, now," Oggie said from behind her. "It's ancient history, that's all I'm sayin'. It's time you let it go."

Evie spoke in carefully measured tones. "I *want* to let it go. Honestly. I want to be just an ordinary person." She turned, and made herself face him. "That's why I hope you've remembered your promise. I hope you haven't said anything to anyone here in town about who I was and what I did all those years ago."

Oggie fiddled with the head of his cane. "I don't get it. I don't see what you did that was so bad. You really did help people. And if there was anything dishonest about it, well, you were only a child. A child who was used. It wasn't one damn bit your fault."

"Uncle Oggie." She made herself look right into his eyes. "I'm grateful to you. You came and found me in Santa Fe last year, when everything was going so wrong for me. And you brought me here with you and you helped me to start over."

"How many times you started over, gal?"

She pushed the uncomfortable question away with a wave of her hand. "Please, Uncle Oggie. I'm just Evie here, and I like that. I've got you and all the family and you all treat me like I'm one of you."

"You *are* one of us."

"Look. I just want to know. Have you kept your promise to me?"

"Hell, gal."

"Evangeline is gone. She doesn't exist. She hasn't existed for fifteen years. That's how I want it. So answer me. *Have* you kept your promise to me, Uncle Oggie?"

He sighed. "Yeah. I have. No one in this town knows about your past but you and me—or if they do, I ain't the one they heard it from."

Relief made Evie weak. She sank to the flowered, overstuffed sofa once more. And then she asked the question she really didn't want the answer to. "And was I right, then? Have you heard from my father?"

"Gal..."

"Uncle Oggie, please. Just tell me what you heard."

Oggie studied her for a moment, and Evie did her best not to fidget under his sharp regard. Then at last, he leaned forward in the soft chair, grunting at the pain in his aged joints as he did it. He felt in a back pocket and pulled out a card, which he held out to her across the steamer trunk.

Evie saw that it was a postcard with one of those silly pictures of dogs playing poker on the front. She took the thing gingerly and looked down at it as if one of the dogs might come alive and bite her. Then she made her numb fingers flip the card over. It was addressed to Ogden E. Jones, General Delivery, North Magdalene, California.

There was a brief message in a scrawl Evie knew like she knew all her own darkest secrets.

> Hey, big brother. How you been all these years? Lately, for some reason, all my thoughts turn to you. Keep in touch now, you hear?

There was no return address.

Evie felt numb. She looked up at her uncle. "He knows I'm here."

Oggie snorted. "It's a definite possibility. Can't see any reason for him to send me that otherwise, after all these years when I ain't heard a word from him."

She looked down at the card again. "It's postmarked Las Vegas."

"You think maybe that's where he's livin' now?"

Evie shook her head. "Knowing him, Las Vegas is just what he wants us to assume."

"Maybe so."

Evie handed the card back to her uncle. "I had hoped maybe he wouldn't find me here."

"Yeah. So did I." Oggie stuck the card in his back pocket once more. "But maybe we were wishin' for the impossible. I suppose I ain't a hard man to find, if you're lookin'. I've lived in this town for over forty years. And I ran a bar for most of that time. I know lots a folks all over the western states." Oggie regarded her solemnly. "I didn't want to show it to you. But I felt I oughtta."

"I understand. And you did the right thing. I needed to know."

Oggie said nothing for a moment, then asked wearily, "Does this mean you'll be pullin' up stakes on us?"

Evie sank back into the deep cushions of the couch, rested her head and looked at the ceiling. She thought of all the years she'd been running. Sometimes it seemed that everything she had, she'd earned on the run. She'd never finished high school, but she'd managed to earn her G.E.D.

And she was a hard worker. She'd saved her money. Three years ago, in Santa Fe, she'd finally opened a shop of her own.

Such a lovely little shop. But she'd pulled out of it quickly, losing a bundle on her lease. All because a reporter from the *New Mexican* dug up all the old tales about her and plastered them all over the newspaper. The story had been picked up by the wire services—and her father had found her once again.

She thought of this beautiful little town. And her new shop that she loved. And the people here. Her family. Not since she and her sisters had gone their separate ways had Evie known real family close by like this. She hadn't realized how much she missed the contact, the closeness with others of like mind and heart, until she'd found it again.

In his chair on the other side of the steamer trunk, her uncle was silent. It was one of the many things she loved about him. He could drive you crazy with talking, but when the time came to be quiet, Oggie Jones knew how.

Evie lifted her head and looked at him.

And that was when he spoke. "Giddy's an old man now, gal. An old man like me. And you're a grown woman in the fullness of your strength. Here, you got your people all around you. Here, you ain't alone."

"I was just thinking the same thing, Uncle Oggie."

"Maybe here you're meant to discover that an old man doesn't have any power over you that you don't give him of your own free will."

"You don't know him."

"Tell me you'll stay."

Evie's throat felt tight. She swallowed. And then she nodded. "You're right, Uncle Oggie. It's time I quit running. It's time I put the past away."

Chapter Two

Two days later, on Evie's thirty-third birthday, both of her sisters called early in the morning while she was sitting at the table savoring her second cup of coffee.

Nevada, the oldest, called first. Nevada sang "Happy Birthday" in that rusty contralto of hers and then she chatted a while about her life in Phoenix and her talk-radio show, Honeymoon Hotline, that was getting such high ratings. Before she hung up, Nevada promised she'd take some time off real soon to visit the town where her baby sister seemed to be settling in so contentedly.

Faith, Evie's middle sister, called next from the huge Queen Anne-style mansion in the bay area where she'd been the housekeeper for about ten years now. Faith was much more reserved than Nevada, so Evie did most of the talking during that conversation. Evie told Faith how Wishbook was doing. She talked about Oggie and her cousins and their spouses and children and how much she loved living in such a great little town.

Before Faith said goodbye, she too mentioned coming for a visit soon. Evie said she'd love that.

When the calls were over, Evie sat, her chin on her hand, wondering if she should have mentioned the postcard Uncle Oggie had received.

But what was the point? Faith and Nevada had nothing to do with the postcard. It had been aimed at Evie, just as all of their father's energies had been directed at his youngest daughter, ever since the day he'd discovered how imminently exploitable she was. Over the years that they lived with him, Gideon had never had much time for his other two daughters—except to heap abuses on them when either was foolish enough to get in his way or go up against him.

The way Evie saw it, there was really nothing her sisters could do. To tell them about this latest contact from Gideon would only worry them—or worse, make them think they should rush to her side to protect her.

And protect her from what? Nothing, really, but a cryptic note from an old man—a note that hadn't even been addressed to her.

No, Evie thought, as she stood at the sink and rinsed out her coffee cup. She was staying put this time and she was going to handle whatever came up herself. When her sisters did come to North Magdalene for a visit, it would be strictly for her pleasure and theirs.

Evie hummed as she took her shower and donned another of her favorite flowered silk dresses. She brushed her long red-brown hair and pinned it up loosely. As a final touch, she wore the single strand of pearls that she'd discovered under a pile of junk jewelry at a flea market a few years before.

Still humming, she descended the stairs to her shop. Once there, she dusted a few display cases and straightened things up a little. And then it was time to switch on all the lamps, unlock the door and turn the Open sign around.

There were lots of tourists in town, strolling up and down Main Street, soaking up the atmosphere of an authentic gold-rush town. Business was good. Within an hour after opening, Evie had sold a set of ivory napkin rings, four antique bottles collected from local mining sites, a lovely maple-topped bin table and two silk dresses very similar to the one she was wearing herself.

At a little past noon, there was a lull. Evie got out the light lunch she'd prepared before coming downstairs. She sat down to eat at a little secretary near the front door.

She was halfway through her Camembert and crackers when the bell over the door told her she had more customers. She looked up as two children came in: a round-cheeked blond cherub of five or six and behind her, a slightly older girl with thick bronze-colored hair and the faintest dusting of freckles across her nose.

Evie knew immediately who they were: Erik Riggins's girls. Her heart gave a silly lurch inside her chest as she thought his name; she almost choked on a bit of cracker. But she recovered. Their father wasn't even with them. And really, she hadn't even *thought* of the man since the incident in church two days before. Just the sight of his children shouldn't bother her at all.

Evie downed a little iced tea to wash away the cracker. The older girl carefully shut the door. The younger one, her baby-angel's face lit from inside with frank delight, moved a little deeper into the shop.

"Ooh, Jenny," the little one sighed. "It's so pretty. Like a magic place."

"Becca," the older girl, instructed. "Don't touch anything."

Becca stuck out her lower lip. "I won't. You know that. I'm behaving myself, just like you said."

Evie slid her chair back and stood. "Hello. May I help you?"

The older girl, Jenny, moved a step closer. "Are you Miss Jones?"

"I am. But please call me Evie. Everyone does."

Becca, the little one, spoke up. "It's rude to call grown-ups by their first names. Our dad says so."

"Hush," Jenny said in the tone of a miniature mother. "It's all right if the grown-up gives you permission."

Becca's nose wrinkled in perplexity. "It is?" She looked at the only grown-up in the room—Evie—for confirmation.

"Yes," Evie said. "I'm sure your sister's right."

Becca thought about that. Then she grinned. "Well. Gee. Good. I'm Becca and she's Jenny and guess what?"

"I don't know."

"It's our dad's birthday today. He's thirty-three years old."

That news sent a shiver through Evie. *Born on the same day, in the same year, as I was . . .*

Which meant nothing. Less than nothing. A meaningless coincidence, and that was all.

So why did it seem such a significant thing?

"Umm, isn't that nice?" Evie knew that she sounded utterly inane.

"I don't know," Becca said, "Thirty-three is pretty old."

Jenny nudged her sister, no doubt fully aware that Evie must be pretty near that ancient age herself. "It seems old to us, since we're just kids," she said tactfully, then moved on to the real issue. "We came to buy our dad a present. We heard that you had nice things here."

"*Different* things," Becca elaborated. "Things that are special. Do you?"

Evie smiled at that. "Hmm. Well, of course, I think so. *I* own the place. But *special* has a different meaning for everyone. Tell you what." She lifted her hand in a gesture that took in the whole shop. "Why don't you look around and see if there's anything that catches your eye?"

Becca liked that idea. "Okay." Her round face a study in anticipation, she headed for the child's bed in a corner that Evie had covered with a bright quilt and piled high with dolls and stuffed animals. Her sister's voice stopped her in her tracks.

"Becca. It's for Dad. Not for us."

Becca sighed. Her small shoulders slumped. "I know that." Dutifully, she returned to stand by her sister.

Now both girls looked at Evie expectantly. "We thought maybe you could help us choose," Jenny said.

Evie felt distinctly uncomfortable at that suggestion. And then she immediately wondered what was wrong with her. After all, helping people choose gifts was a major part of owning a shop like this. But for some reason, the thought of helping to find something "special" for Erik Riggins bothered her no end. She recalled the way he had looked at her in church—with disdain and disapproval. She didn't think he'd like the idea that she'd been instrumental in the choice of his birthday present.

However, she had a job to do, and do it she would. Evie was pleased that her voice betrayed none of her apprehension when she agreed, "Certainly. Perhaps you could give me a few hints." She recalled again the feel of the man's big, rough-skinned hand beneath her own and remembered another detail about him that she'd heard from someone. "He's a house painter, isn't he?"

"Um-hmm," Jenny confirmed. "But we don't want to get him anything do to with that. We want to get him something nice, something to keep forever and ever."

"Yeah," Becca said, joining in. "It's got to be so special. So he'll never forget us, even when he's as old as Granny Tilda and can't hardly remember anything anymore."

"Granny Tilda's our great-grandmother," Jenny explained. "She's ninety-three."

"And that's *really* old, even for a grown-up," Becca said.

"Hmm," Evie said, since she still had no ideas about what to suggest. "Help me out some more, all right? Tell me his hobbies, the things he enjoys doing when he's not working."

"He likes to paint pictures and draw things," Jenny said.

Becca added, "And he does cally—cally—"

"Calligraphy." Jenny provided the word, then began looking around a little. She picked up a snow globe of a fairy princess in a wintry fairy glen and turned it upside down to watch the snow fly.

"Jenny," Becca chided. "Remember what you said. It's for Dad. Not for us."

Reluctantly Jenny put the princess back on top of the display case by the cash register.

Recalling that she was supposed to be coming up with some "expert" suggestions, Evie started toward the shelves and drawers of stationery and craft supplies along the back wall. "I do have a few artist's supplies over here."

"He *has* all that stuff," Becca announced. "We don't want to get him more of that."

Evie had moved past Becca when the child spoke. She stopped and turned. Her eyes met the child's eyes.

Beautiful eyes, Evie found herself thinking. *Soft and sweet and just a little bit sad. . . .*

The longing rose in Evie, to take that sadness into herself, to know it—and to understand. She felt herself opening, relaxing, letting herself hear the things that couldn't be heard, see the things that no one else saw.

Evie knew what was happening. And there was a split second when she could have put up the wall. But she didn't. Those beautiful eyes were too full of need.

And inside Evie, something was melting.

Reality shifted. The shop faded into shadow.

It was another time, another place. And in that time, Becca's blue eyes were red with tears. She sobbed in loss and wounded anger.

"Mommy. I want my mommy. She can't be gone. She said she was better. She was home. With us. She promised never to go away again. She crossed her heart . . ."

Erik Riggins was holding the child in his big arms, rocking her so gently, kissing her spun-gold hair.

"I know, honey. She didn't want to go away. But it's just the way it happens sometimes. People die. She loved you so much. So very, very much . . ."

The vision faded, melted to nothing. The shop came into focus again.

And so did Becca, as she was right now, her eyes clear and bright, her expression concerned. "Uh-oh," Becca was shaking her head. "You don't look so good, Miss Jones."

Evie blinked to clear her sight.

"Maybe you better lay down or something," Becca said.

Evie sucked in a deep breath and managed a wobbly smile. "I'm fine," she said, grateful beyond measure to hear that her voice sounded almost normal. "Just fine."

Becca smiled back, reassured.

"Becca." Jenny's voice, a few feet away, was charged with hushed excitement. "Becca. Come look."

Becca hurried to join her sister.

Jenny was peering into a display case right by the register. "See?" Jenny said. "See that?"

"Oh!" Becca said, and nothing more, a sound of childish satisfaction and delight.

"Gold," Jenny said. "And with all those pearly colors, like the inside of a shell. He would love them, wouldn't he?"

"Oh, yes," Becca whispered. "Oh, so pretty. Oh, yes."

A few feet away, Evie closed her eyes and took a few more deep breaths. As soon as she was positive she'd regained a firm hold on her composure, she approached the girls.

"Have you found what you're looking for?" She was pleased when her voice came out crisp and businesslike.

"I think so." Jenny pressed her index finger against the glass. "It's those. Right there."

Evie looked where the small finger pointed, at a Deco-era fountain pen and pencil set of gold with mother-of-pearl and jet inlays. The set, in perfect condition, was nestled in its original black velvet case.

"Could we look at them?" Jenny asked reverently. "Up close, I mean?"

Evie glanced at the tiny price tag. It was turned facedown. Jenny had no idea that the set cost two hundred dollars—which was certainly a great deal more than what these two children had to spend.

But still, Evie observed her own rules of etiquette for the situation. Evie never told a customer the price before the customer had either asked for it, or said the magic words, *I'll take it."*

Evie nodded. "I'll get them out for you." She slid behind the counter, unlocked the case with a key that she kept in the register and brought out the velvet box, which she held tipped up for a moment, displaying the beauty within.

"The price tag!" Jenny exclaimed.

"Excuse me?"

"It fell." Becca pointed to the space behind the counter, where Evie stood. "Down there."

"Oh." Evie turned the pens so she could see them herself. Sure enough, the tiny tag was gone. She shrugged. "I'll get it." She handed the velvet case to Jenny and then knelt to look for the tag. She found it right away, and reached for it. But then, at the last minute, she couldn't quite make herself pick it up. She straightened again without retrieving it, even going so far as to slide it beneath the display case with the toe of her shoe.

"Well," she said when she was facing the girls again. "It must have slid beneath the case. But it doesn't matter. I know the price, of course."

The girls hardly heard her. They were admiring their find.

"Gently, gently," Jenny chided her sister. She held the velvet case in cherishing hands as Becca lovingly stroked the barrel of the pen.

"They're perfect," Jenny said.

"Yes," Becca concurred. "Perfect." She looked up at Evie, then nudged her big sister. "We have to give her the money, Jenny."

"Okay." Carefully Jenny set the precious pen set on the glass counter and reached into the pocket of her worn plaid dress. She removed a red plastic coin purse, snapped it open and emptied it onto the counter.

Evie hid a tender smile as two sets of small hands got busy keeping the change from rolling onto the floor. Once the coins lay still, the girls set about flattening out the three one-dollar bills and stacking the change into neat piles.

"There," Jenny said with satisfaction when their fortune was in order. "Seven dollars and thirteen cents. How much do we owe you?"

"Well, let's see." Evie turned to the cash register. "That's six-fifty for the pen set." She quoted the preposterously low price without batting an eye. Then she checked her sales tax schedule, which was taped to the face of the register. "And forty-seven cents tax, for a total of..." She pushed down the old-fashioned keys in one stroke. The bell rang and the drawer slid open. "Six dollars and ninety-seven cents."

The girls watched solemnly as Evie collected their bills and their change and put them in the proper compartments within the cash drawer. When she was done, one shiny dime, a nickel and a penny remained on the counter. Evie scooped them up and extended her hand. "Your change, miss."

Jenny snapped open her change purse and held it out. "Thank you, ma'am."

Evie dropped the change into the purse. "Would you like that wrapped?"

"Is it extra?"

"No. It's a service to my customers, when I have the time—and when I know that their purchase is a gift."

"Could we pick the paper?" asked Becca.

"Of course. Right this way." Evie led them to the wrapping area, by the hall that led upstairs. They chose a red plaid, very close to the plaid of Jenny's worn dress, only bright and fresh and new.

Just as she finished wrapping the pen set, something else occurred to Evie. "What about ink and pencil leads?"

"Ink and pencil leads?" Jenny repeated. The two girls exchanged glances.

"They'll be needed," Evie said.

Jenny, her awareness of how their cash had dwindled plain on her face, asked cautiously, "How much?"

Evie thought fast as she realized that the prices were going to be clearly marked on the boxes. "Well, of course they come free of charge, when you buy a pen and pencil set."

Jenny looked doubtful. "They do?"

"Absolutely," Evie lied once more and didn't feel the least bit guilty about it. "But remember. That's only one bottle of ink and one box of pencil leads." She tried to sound uncompromising. "After that, your father will have to buy his own."

Becca whispered something to Jenny, then Jenny said, "Okay. We'll take the free ink and the pencil leads, too."

"Wrapped in this lovely plaid, just like the gift, am I right?"

The girls looked at each other again and nodded in unison. Then Becca said, "Yes. Thank you...Evie." Her shy smile was a beautiful thing to see.

Evie wrapped up the leads and the ink, and then walked them to the door, where she stood watching after them as they headed off toward the turn to Pine Street. She felt good all over, warm and happy and full of a special, thoroughly self-indulgent satisfaction.

It took several hours for the glow to fade a little. Then she scolded herself, told herself how foolish she was. She could never expect to make a living here if she developed the habit of virtually giving away high-ticket items to children she hardly knew.

And selling a two-hundred-dollar pen set for a fraction of its value wasn't all she'd done. She'd also let down her guard, opened herself to Becca in the old, forbidden way. She'd *spied* on Becca's mind, witnessing Becca's suffering at what had probably been the lowest point of her young life. Evie shouldn't have done it. She had no right.

And yet in Becca, she'd seen herself. Evie had lost her own mother when she was only five.

Maybe that was part of the reason—that special sympathy she felt for the girls—that she had trouble making herself feel all that bad about what she'd done. The warm glow
of happiness refused to go away—at least not until the next
morning when she went to turn the Open sign around again
and saw Erik Riggins waiting outside the door.

Chapter Three

He was dressed in painter's overalls, which led Evie to suspect he must have taken time off from a job to be there when she opened up. He did not look happy—and the scowl on his face only deepened when he caught sight of her beyond the window as she peered at him anxiously over the top of her Open sign.

For a suspended few moments, they regarded each other. Evie used those moments to breathe deeply and put up the wall inside her mind. She was taking no chances this time. This time, the pain he hid from the rest of the world wouldn't come flying at her like invisible knives.

She moved out of his line of sight to unlock the door. Then, before she even had a chance to zip behind the counter where she could have pretended she was safe from him, he was inside.

Evie froze where she stood as the bell tinkled and the door swung shut behind him. They stared at each other again, like fighters squaring off before the first punch is thrown. Evie thought once more how big he was, an imposing man with a working man's hand and a sad face. He dwarfed her shop, made it seem overcrowded with delicate, unnecessary things.

He was the one to break the hostile silence. "I want to know what the hell you're up to." His tone was pure antagonism, yet he reached up and doffed his painter's cap as he spoke.

Evie was touched, in spite of herself, by the odd combination of courtesy and belligerence. She found herself staring at his hand, which clutched the cap so tightly. There was a faint spattering of whitish paint on the back of that hand. And there was paint in his hair, too. She could see it, a fine film of it, now that the cap was gone, on the strands that the cap hadn't covered. He *had* interrupted a job to come here and confront her.

She felt... such tenderness as she thought how he must work long, hard hours, to care for his children, to make sure they were fed and clothed. And she remembered, though she shouldn't have let herself, the vision of him, holding Becca so tightly. She recalled how he had rocked the child, reassuring her that her mother had loved her, though she was gone now from the earth.

Oh, the warmth inside her was a lovely thing, the need to reach out to this man so very strong...

"What are you staring at?" he demanded.

Evie stiffened. The wall was slipping. What in the world was the matter with her? She had to stop indulging herself, stop allowing herself to be moved by this person she hardly knew.

She threw the wall back up again. She imagined she had ice water in her veins, a stone for a heart.

Then, her defenses in place once more, she spoke in a voice like autumn's first frost. "I'm sure I don't have any idea what you're talking about. There is nothing the matter with me and I am up to nothing. Nothing at all."

He glared at her a bit, as if the force of his scowl might break her, then he marched toward her. With a gasp she couldn't quite stifle, Evie fell back out of his way. But he didn't touch her, only blundered on by, to the register, where he yanked a familiar black velvet box from his pocket and slammed it down on the glass case there.

He stepped away from the box, and then gestured at it with his balled-up cap. "Is this yours?"

Evie absolutely refused to be ruffled. She made herself stand very tall and kept her chin high. "It was. Until yesterday when I sold it."

"*Sold* it?" His tender mouth grew hard, it curled in disgust. "*Gave* it away's more like it."

"No, I did not give it away." She sounded so patient. So reasonable. She was proud of herself. "Your daughters paid for it, fair and square."

He grunted. "Fair and square. Sure. I know how much money they had between them. And even an idiot could tell that pen set is very fine. So unless they held up the Hole in the Wall before they came in here, they didn't have anywhere near what they needed to pay for it."

Evie's heart was beating faster. All right, maybe she'd used bad judgment in selling the pen set for such a ridiculous price. But he was acting as if she'd committed a *crime*, for heaven's sake.

This time, when she spoke, her voice was downright icy. "This is my shop. *I* set the prices here."

"Lady, you look smart enough to me. I think you know the value of your own merchandise."

"Of course I do."

"So that means you gave two little girls something they couldn't even come near to paying for. What are you after?"

"Nothing, I—"

"Look." He glanced away, then met her eyes once more. "I've got no time for women. I've got three kids to raise."

Evie felt her face grow warm as she remembered again the incident in church. He thought she was *after* him. "You think I was trying to, umm, get your attention?"

He seemed as embarrassed as she was. "Were you?"

"No. No, I certainly was not."

He stared in her eyes for a moment, as if trying to measure her sincerity. At last, he shrugged. "Well, I had to ask. From the way you acted in church, I wondered. Though I couldn't see any reason why someone like you would be interested in..." He swallowed. "Hell. Never mind. If not that, then what?"

"Well, I—"

He didn't let her finish. His gray eyes were stormy again. "Don't make up any pretty lies. I know what."

"You do?"

"Yes. Charity." He uttered the word with bottomless disgust.

"No, I—"

He cut her off again. "I don't take charity. And neither do my kids."

Evie could feel the cold weight of his pride then; a wounded pride, the pride of a responsible man with money troubles. "No." She spoke with some urgency, all at once really wishing that he might understand. "It wasn't charity. Not at all. It was..." She ran out of words. How could she explain? How could she make him understand that it had been her own birthday present to herself? She had done it to see them smile. To see two little girls glowing with pride at the fabulous gift they'd give the most important man in their lives.

"I want the real price." It was a command. "I'll pay the difference. Here and now."

Evie shook her head. "That isn't necessary. I've already told you I—"

He cut the air with his cap. "The price. Now."

Evie bit her lip and hesitated, wondering if she should just let it go. Let him pay her the money. But that seemed wrong. Beyond her instinctual certainty that she would be taking money he couldn't afford to lose, she didn't *want* the money. Because it really *hadn't* been charity. However she'd lectured herself afterward for giving her merchandise away, she felt in her heart that she'd been paid in full.

She couldn't do it. She *wouldn't* do it.

"The price was what they paid for it," Evie said. "Six dollars and ninety-seven cents, including tax. That is all I have to say on the matter, so if you don't care to purchase anything, I'd appreciate it if you'd please leave now."

"I'm not leaving until I've paid what I owe you."

"You owe me nothing."

"The hell I don't."

This was going nowhere. Evie decided to end the exchange in the most expedient manner she could think of. She stuck her chin in the air and started walking. Her intention was to march straight to the back of the shop, through the hall and up the stairs to the safety of her rooms. Then, since he'd have no one to argue with, Mr. Riggins would be forced to go back to working like a dog to support his family and she could get on with her life.

But it didn't quite turn out as she planned, because before she could get past him, Erik Riggins stuck out his hand and wrapped his big, paint-dusted fingers around her arm.

And that was when it happened. Something terrible and wonderful and totally impossible. In that split second, when his strong hand closed over her arm, the shop began to spin, as if the very walls had suddenly come alive around them. They stood still in the center of a shifting, whirling world.

And within the spinning, a bolt of physical desire rocked Evie, shook her right down to her toes. It was full-blown desire, a woman's desire, dangerous and marvelous. Such desire as Evie had never known.

And in the charged air around them, colored lights seemed to swim and pop, bursting open to reveal centers of shimmering gold. Images flashed among the lights.

Evie saw herself and this man, naked, their bodies entwined on a couch in a light-filled room. He called her name. She clutched him close, her pale hands splayed across his bare, muscled back...

And then the room was gone, the lovers vanished. She saw a red bird in a cloudless sky. There was a woman, a woman with Becca's eyes. Smiling in a dazed way, staring in wonder at the red bird overhead, the woman stepped off a curb and into the path of a large white delivery van. The driver slammed on his brakes, but it was too late....

Next she saw Nellie Anderson, a slightly younger Nellie Anderson. Nellie's eyes were hard and bright, but her heart was full of pain. "If you marry him, I have no daughter," Nellie said.

And after Nellie, she saw her own father, looking old and ill—even older than he'd looked a year ago in Santa Fe, when he'd found her there. His dark eyes were feverishly bright as he leered down at her in some dim, forbidding place.

"Everything's gonna be just fine," her father said. "Soon's you see the light. Soon's you and me go back into business together again. Everything'll be like it used to be. You just wait and see...."

"Sweet heaven. What *is* this?" Erik Riggins whispered on a ragged breath. Through all the spinning and the lights, his voice came through to Evie as if it were inside her own head.

Something on the end of the counter near Evie's elbow suddenly dropped hard to the floor, crashing to bits. In the same way, several books slid from their shelves. All over the shop, things rattled and shifted in place, as if shaken by a minor quake or a sudden fierce wind.

Evie heard all of this happening around her; she separately registered each individual sound. But she couldn't move. She was frozen in place like someone slammed by a powerful, long-lasting electrical shock. And she could see Erik, see the stark bewilderment in his eyes. He didn't seem to be able to move, either.

And then slowly, the colored lights and shifting images faded. The spinning world grew still.

Evie became aware of her own breathing, of the feel of her blood as it coursed through her veins. She knew then that she could move again, yet she remained perfectly still.

Erik moved instead. With great care, he released her, peeling his fingers away one at a time, as if he had to be careful, as if getting away too fast might land them right back in another incident like what had just transpired.

Finally, when he'd taken his hand away finger by finger, he dropped his arm and stepped back.

Evie's mouth was dry. Her skin felt hot. She leaned against the counter a little, because her knees were shaking so badly.

"What the hell is going on?" His voice was raspy, more of a whispery croak than a true sound. All his anger and belligerence were gone. He looked baffled, totally stunned. "What *was* that?"

Evie didn't reply. She *couldn't* reply. Not right then.

"What *happened?*" he demanded, more strongly than before.

Still, she said nothing. She had nothing to say. No answers to his questions. In a life of out-of-the-ordinary experiences, nothing precisely like that had ever happened to her before. Always, once Evie put up the wall in her mind, nothing could get through.

And yet, with this man, the wall was as nothing. Twice now, he had overridden all her defenses.

"I asked you." He spoke once more, pure bewilderment in his deep voice. "What was that? What *happened?*"

Evie stared at him, shaking her head. She felt weaker as each second passed. Her hands shook and her stomach felt queasy. "I told you. I don't know. I just don't know."

She looked down. She saw that he'd dropped his cap. It lay behind him. And her feet . . . her feet were damp. Littering the floor nearby were shards of glass. It took Evie a moment to piece these clues together.

Then she understood. The object that had dropped from the counter and broken had been the snow globe of the fairy princess that Jenny had admired the day before. The tiny, forlorn princess, flung from her miniature, snow-globe world, lay facedown, one of her wings bent, beside Evie's right foot.

The sight of the princess was simply too depressing. Evie couldn't just leave her there. She put a hand on the counter to steady herself and knelt to retrieve the tiny figure.

But, sinking to her knees was a foolish thing to do. She was far too weak by then. She got down there and wrapped her clutching fingers around the sodden princess—and then she had no idea how she was going to stand up again.

Her stomach churned, and the world went fuzzy around the edges. She felt drained, right down to her soul, something she hadn't felt in a long time. Not since those last years with her father, when she often expended immense amounts of energy in exercising the strange talents she possessed.

Evie closed her eyes and commanded her legs to straighten. "Oh!" She didn't even know she'd uttered the word aloud as she opened her eyes and discovered she'd done it; she was on her feet once more. But the room still looked fuzzy.

Evie put her tongue between her teeth and bit down hard. The pain cleared her head a little. Using the counter for balance, she managed to remain upright—though how long she was going to be able to stay that way she couldn't have predicted.

"What is it?" Erik Riggins was saying. "What's the matter?"

She lifted her head and made herself look at him. She saw honest concern in his eyes. "I . . . please. I'm very tired. If you would just—"

"You look awful. Your skin is gray."

"Please. Just go."

But he didn't move. "You're ill."

"No." She turned from him and groped along the glass counter, telling herself it wasn't that far upstairs, she could make it if she went very, very slowly. "No, I'm not ill," she said over her shoulder. "I'm only...tired. Very tired. If you would just go away now..."

"God help us," she heard him murmur behind her.

"Exactly." She sighed.

She felt cold. And the world had recommenced spinning again. But this time there was nothing supernatural about it. Evie was about to faint.

But then she didn't faint; not exactly. It was more that her legs lost all their strength.

"Oh!" she said again as she started to sink to the floor.

She didn't quite get there. Strong arms scooped her up. She landed against a broad chest. She felt warmth and strength—and the deep, steady beating of a powerful heart, *his* heart. She blinked and looked up at his face as it swam above hers.

"You caught me," she whispered, amazed.

He looked down at her with soft eyes, eyes full of concern. Evie felt as if the sun was shining on her, warming her, filling her, so that the cold and the weakness were fading away. She smiled back at him.

"Where to?" he asked.

Evie didn't care. She could have stayed there forever, held safe and warm in Erik Riggins's arms. Still, somehow, she managed to instruct him, "My apartment. Upstairs, through the hall there." She pointed to the back of the shop.

Without another word, he turned and carried her, as if she weighed nothing, through the shop to the hallway and up the stairs. At the small landing there, he hesitated. She reached out and pushed the door open onto her minuscule foyer. He spotted the big, soft couch in the living room. He strode to it, nudged the steamer trunk/coffee table back a little with his leg and laid her down with great care, as if she were delicate and breakable and infinitely precious. Evie reveled in such treatment—and she had to restrain herself from clutching for him when he gently moved away.

Then he was standing once more, looking down at her. "I'll call and get you in to see Will Bacon right away." Will Bacon was the practical nurse who ran the local medical clinic. "Where's your phone?"

"No." She struggled to sit up a little against the arm of the couch. "I'm all right. I really am. It's only a . . . a momentary weakness. You don't have to worry about me. I'll be fine."

He studied her, his big head tipped a little to the side. "You do look better."

"I am," she said earnestly. "Much."

He looked at her some more, then shrugged. "All right. But you should probably rest for a while."

"I will."

"And I'll bet you're thirsty. *I* sure am. I'll get you some water."

He was right, of course. Evie's mouth felt papery, it was so dry. Still, she heard herself protesting, "No, really. I don't need—"

But he was already turning, spotting the arch that led to her small kitchen and heading for it. She sat up a little more, as she heard cupboards opening and closing, then the water running.

He returned in less than a minute, the promised glass of water in his hand. He knelt at her side, the movement smooth and graceful for so large a man. "Here you go."

Evie took the water and drank it down. It felt like heaven, so cool and fresh. When she was done, he held out his hand. She gave him the glass. He turned to set it on the trunk behind him.

She watched him, her eyes wide and wondering. He could be so harsh, yet there was great gentleness and simple human kindness within him, too. Most men, after what had happened down in the shop, would have gotten out of there as fast as they could. Not many would have waited around to ask questions. And even fewer would have dared to touch her a second time—let alone have caught her up in capable arms, carried her right up the stairs and then run to fetch her a glass of water.

"Thank you," she said. "I'm feeling really good now. Just as good as new."

He was studying her again. "Are you sure you won't let me call the clinic?"

"No. It's not necessary. As I said, I'm just fine."

His gaze was on her lips; he was watching them move as she talked. She dipped her head a little and captured his glance. They looked at each other. She could see his concern for her in his expression. And yet his brow was not quite so furrowed as before. He seemed almost... relaxed now.

"I'm sorry," he said.

She frowned. "For what?"

"When I grabbed you like that, downstairs. I scared you to death, didn't I?"

Evie started to tell him that *he* hadn't scared her at all. But then she stopped herself as she realized what was going on inside him.

He was busy forgetting. He was making excuses for the incredible thing that had occurred between them. He was *normalizing* it. By tomorrow, he would only remember it as an uncomfortable moment when he had grabbed her arm.

Over the years, Evie had watched the process happen time after time. Under ordinary circumstances, people tended to do one of three things when confronted with the unexplainable: they sought to discredit, to destroy or to deny. And Evie was always grateful when they chose denial. Of the three, it was by far the least painful for her.

"*Didn't* I scare you?" Erik asked again, seeking her complicity in his denial.

Evie made a small sound that he could take for agreement if he wished.

He took her hand. "Look." His voice was kind and matter-of-fact—and every bit as warm as the fingers that were wrapped around her own. "About the pen set—"

She waved the hand he wasn't holding, in which she still clutched the bedraggled fairy princess from the broken snow globe. "Please. I wanted Jenny and Becca to have the set, so I sold it to them cheaply. It doesn't have to be a big deal. Can't you just let it go?"

Gently he released her hand and stood. "Sorry. I can't do that. I'm just . . . not made that way. How much?"

She could see he wasn't going to leave it alone. So she confessed in a whisper, "Two hundred dollars." And then she spoke more strongly, "But your daughters already paid me—"

"I know, I know." He chuckled, a wry sound. "Six dollars and ninety-seven cents." He took some bills from his pocket and dropped them on the steamer trunk. "That should cover it."

She looked at the money, and still didn't want to take it. "Erik, I . . ." And then she was meeting his eyes again, blushing, realizing that she'd just addressed him by his given name for the very first time. It seemed a huge milestone.

And yet totally appropriate. Because everything was changed between them now.

It really didn't matter how Erik chose to rationalize what had passed between them. The bare truth was that the two of them had touched on a deep and turbulent level; they were strangers no more. Now he spoke to her gently, he touched her with care and he looked at her as if she were someone who mattered to him.

"Erik." She said his name once more, enjoying the sound of it. And then she remembered about the money again. "Listen, I really don't want—"

"Shh." He actually put a finger to his lips. "Rest now. And don't worry. My girls have taste. That is a fine pen set. I know it and you know it. It'll be worth a hell of a lot more than two hundred in a few years." He started for the door to the little foyer and the stairs that would lead him down to the shop.

She couldn't resist reminding him, "Don't forget to take the pen set with you—now that you've paid for it."

He paused to glance back at her. "I won't. Don't worry."

And then he was making for the door again. She couldn't quite bear for him to go, so she said, unnecessarily, "It's on the counter."

This time he stopped and faced her fully. There was a faint smile tugging at his mouth. "I know."

They stared at each other.

"And your cap..."

"My cap?"

"It's on the floor, near the cash register."

"Thanks." They looked at each other some more. Then he remembered a question to ask *her*. "Do you want me to lock the door to the street?"

She considered, then decided, "No, no. I'll go down in a few minutes. As I said, I really do feel fine."

"Just take it easy, all right?"

"I will."

"Take care of yourself... Evie."

A warm flush of pleasure spread through her at the sound of her name on his lips. The very last traces of cold and weakness were washed away.

"I will, Erik," she promised.

A long moment elapsed.

"Well," he said. "I should go."

"Yes. Of course. Goodbye, then." Evie made herself stop looking at him. With a sigh, she stretched out on the couch once again and closed her eyes.

After another long moment, she heard him go out the door.

Chapter Four

At home that night after his children were in bed, Erik Riggins sat at his drafting table in the big upstairs room he'd claimed as a studio. He set the drafting table at a low slant and he did some experimenting with the fine fountain pen his daughters had given him for his birthday.

In free script, he began to write out the lyrics to the hymn, "Softly and Tenderly." The words flowed, the nib scratching satisfyingly across the sheet of smooth bond paper.

When he'd completed the first verse, he sat back in his chair for a moment and stared at the words. The song had been one of Carolyn's favorites. And in church Sunday, when everyone stood and started singing it, the melody had pierced him like a lance.

Just being in that particular place was hard for him. Carolyn had loved that old church so. But the song made it worse. A thousand times worse. The song had brought it all back, all the pain and the misery, the emptiness, the loss.

But then, when the pain was screaming inside him, the Jones woman had touched him. She had reached over and laid her hand on his.

And the pain was gone. A peace such as he'd never known had settled over him.

It had been a brief peace, because he'd quickly pulled away from her soft touch. Yet still, he recalled it. And couldn't help cherishing the sweetness of it in memory—not to mention being a little astounded that tonight he could write out a whole verse of that song without any agony at all. All he felt was a tender sadness, that Carolyn was gone.

Hardly knowing he would do it, Erik wrote a certain name:

Evie

Then he wrote the whole name:

Evie Jones

And then he wondered at what "Evie" might stand for. Evelyn or simply Eve. But he didn't think so.

She was like . . . an angel. Yes, her skin so pale, her eyes brandy colored like her silky hair. Her nose slim, perfectly shaped. And her mouth so soft and pliant and full.

He wrote the name *Evangeline* and knew that it was right.

And then, with great care, Erik capped his fine pen. He swiveled on his stool so that he could look out the window at the night. His studio was on the second floor, so he could see beyond the backyard to the dry late-summer grasses of Ebert's field, which lay between Pine Street and Gold Rush Way. He could see the final sliver of an old moon, pale and silvery in the starry sky.

Evangeline, his mind whispered. He smiled at the skinny bit of moon.

Funny how, after today, he felt so... warmly toward her. It wasn't like him. Not as he'd been these past years. He hadn't felt warmly toward a woman in the longest damn time. Truth to tell, after all the agony with Carolyn, he had never expected to feel much for any woman ever again—excluding the safe and supportive love he shared with the women in his family, of course. To Erik, for a long time now, the thought of a woman equaled pain, pain that could grab hold of him out of nowhere, pain that could find him in something so sweet and simple as the melody of an old hymn.

But Evangeline had taken the pain away. And she drew him. He had to admit it. He wanted... to get to know her better.

Erik shifted on the stool, thinking. Of course, he realized, he couldn't get to know her *too* well. He could never allow it go beyond friendship. Beyond friendship, what did he have to offer a woman? Responsibility for another woman's three children and a mountain of debt, that was what.

No, she could never be *his* in the most complete way.

But friendship was possible, wasn't it? If she were willing. And if he were totally honest with her right from the first about all of the reasons they could never have more.

In her bed in the apartment over her shop, Evie lay gazing dreamily out the window at the sliver of moon. She grinned to herself.

She was thinking of Erik. Thinking of how... warmly she felt toward him now.

True, she should probably watch out for him. He'd proved twice that she was vulnerable to him, dangerously vulnerable. He could break down the wall.

She should be frightened.

But she simply wasn't frightened. Not one bit.

Since this morning, since what had happened in the shop and afterward, she *trusted* him in a deep and instinctive way. Of course, she knew she could never trust him *too* much. She could never actually give her heart and soul to him, because if she did that, he was bound to find out about her special gifts. And that was never going to happen.

Evie never spoke of her gifts with anyone, not even her sisters.

Nevada and Faith accepted that Evie *knew things,* that she had a *soothing touch.* They'd seen for themselves that when Evie became too agitated, breakable objects nearby could be in danger of destruction—without Evie ever actually bumping them. But it wasn't something they discussed. Evie always refused to talk about it.

And what good could talking do anyway? Nothing that Evie could see. She'd been hiding her gifts ever since she'd turned eighteen and her sisters helped her get away from her father. In fact, hiding her gifts had become so ingrained with her now that she had no idea how to break the chains of secrecy that bound her.

Evie rolled onto her back and frowned at the white lace canopy overhead. What was she thinking? The truth was, she had no *desire* to reveal the truth about her gifts. Not to anyone, and not ever.

She wanted a normal life—or as normal a life as someone like her could ever have.

And that *normal life* would never include love and marriage. She'd accepted that long ago.

But friendship. Now maybe that would be possible. With a certain kind of man. A good man, an understanding man. A man like Erik Riggins, as a matter of fact.

Erik saw Evie on the street the very next day. North Magdalene was such a small town. They were bound to run into each other often.

They met in front of North Magdalene Grocery. He was coming out and she was going in.

"How are you feeling?" he asked, shifting his brown bag full of groceries from one arm to the other, thinking that her eyes were softer, bigger, browner than he'd remembered. And that her hair was the deepest, richest auburn he'd ever seen anywhere. And had there ever been a face like that? A perfect oval, and then there were those eyes, that nose, that mouth. She seemed to glow. As if her skin had been lit from within by the warm soft light of a candle's flame.

As a rule, Erik never painted portraits. When he could get a rare few hours to himself, he painted high snow-capped mountains and Alpine valleys—wild places where no people went, because such work made him feel free. But just this once, with Evie Jones, he'd like to make an exception. He'd like to paint her in her odd little shop, surrounded by all the lace and china figurines—or as the fairy princess in the snow globe, the one he'd seen on the counter by the cash register, which had been shattered a few minutes later, when he so roughly grabbed her and she must have knocked it down trying to pull free.

"I'm feeling wonderful," she was saying. "Just wonderful."

He focused on talking to her, instead of just staring like a fool. "Completely recovered from that big scare I gave you?"

"Yes. Completely. I really am doing great."

He ran out of things to say. But she didn't seem to mind. They stood and smiled at each other, there on the sidewalk in front of the store, each knowing they should make more small talk or move on, yet neither quite doing it. As they stood there, Roger McCleb, a local yahoo in his twenties who'd recently found a job again after a long dry spell, pulled up in his pickup right beside them and climbed out.

Roger slammed his door good and loud, then called out over the roof of the cab, "Hey, Erik. How's it goin'?"

Erik blinked and tore his gaze away from Evie. "Hey, Roger," he called back, then returned to looking in Evie's incredible brown eyes.

"How 'bout a cold brew, Erik?" Roger offered. "I'm workin' now, so it's on me."

Erik wasn't listening. He was thinking about Evie's eyes. They were kind of a *golden* brown, actually. And they shone, the same way her skin did.

"Erik, buddy, you listenin'?"

Erik went on looking at Evie. But he did raise his hand and give Roger a wave. "Thanks, Roger," he said. "Some other time."

Roger looked from Erik to Evie and back again. Then he grunted and turned to stroll across the street, where he disappeared through the double doors of the Hole in the Wall Saloon.

Right about then, Erik actually thought of something to say. "You sell shoes, in that store of yours?"

Evie nodded. "Oh, of course. Lots of shoes."

"I didn't see any yesterday. Not that I was really looking."

"Well, I do have them. Most of them are upstairs, in the storage area. The fall order came in, but I just haven't brought them out yet. In a few weeks, when tourist season's over, I was planning to bring more of them downstairs and to generally move things around a little, in preparation for the winter."

He wasn't following. "Move things around?"

"Yes. In winter, I switch some of my stock around. I put the emphasis on more practical stuff, like shoes, everyday clothing, winter outerwear and school supplies. That way, during the off-season, people who live around here will start thinking of Wishbook as an alternative to some of the stores in Grass Valley and Nevada City." She paused to wave at ancient Alondra Quail, who was toddling by, leaning heavily on her walker for support. Then she turned those brown eyes his way again. "Am I making sense?"

"Perfect sense." Erik really did feel like an idiot—but he could not stop smiling.

"So who needs shoes?" she asked.

"Everyone."

She chuckled. There was actually a dimple on the side of her mouth when she did that. *"Everyone?"*

"Well, all three of the kids. Pete and Jenny. Becca, too. For school. They need school shoes."

"Bring them in. I'll bet I can fit them."

"I will. Probably Saturday."

"Anytime is fine."

"Good, then."

They looked at each other some more. And then they both sighed at the same time and agreed that they'd see each other soon. Evie vanished inside the grocery store and Erik strolled off up the street, whistling, not realizing he was headed in the wrong direction until he was passing the post office. Then, his face feeling hot to the roots of his hair, he shot a quick glance all around to see if anyone had noticed.

When he saw that no one seemed to care that Erik Riggins was going nowhere, he turned around and marched back to where he'd left his truck.

At home, the girls ran to greet him. His sister Tawny, who had looked after the kids today, came from the kitchen to take the groceries from him. The moment his hands were free, he hoisted a giggling Becca up on his shoulders and hooked Jenny, squealing, beneath an arm. Then he carried them both over to the couch where he plunked them down, which was cause for even more giggling and squealing.

When they'd settled down a little, Becca said, "Daddy, I made you a picture."

"And I dusted," Jenny announced with great pride, "the whole house, by myself."

He praised Jenny and then waited while Becca produced her picture, of which he was appropriately admiring and grateful. He suggested, with great gravity, that it should be displayed in the place of honor—on the refrigerator door. Then he asked where Pete was.

"Next door at Marnie Jones's," Jenny told him and stuck out her lower lip. "They wouldn't let me play. Marnie's got cousin Kenny and Mark Drury and Petey, too, all over at her house. They told me 'No girls allowed.' And I said to them, 'Well, Marnie's a girl.' And you know what Petey, my own brother, said to me?" Jenny was too eager to tell the rest to wait for Erik to ask, *No, what?* She rushed on. "Petey said, 'Marnie doesn't count as a girl. She's a true Mountaineer.'"

Erik frowned. "A *Mountaineer?*"

"Oh," Jenny snorted. "It's just some stupid club they have."

"They wouldn't let me play, either," Becca complained.

Jenny looked sideways at her sister. "Well, I can understand it with you. You're too young."

"I am not."

"You are so."

"Am not. Daddy, tell her I'm not."

Erik put up both hands. "Hold it, hold it."

Two obstinate faces looked up at him, waiting, demanding that he solve all their problems, expecting him to have the answers to questions they hadn't even asked yet.

He waited for the feeling of inadequacy that was his constant companion so often now to rise within him.

It didn't come. In his mind, he saw Evie, on the street a little earlier, looking at him with those amber-brown eyes. And he felt calm. He felt that it was all right if he didn't have all the answers, that the world would go on turning even if Erik Riggins didn't know it all.

"Daddy," Jenny whined. "Daddy, tell her. She's too young."

"No, I'm not. Not, not, not..."

Erik only smiled.

After a moment, when their father's face didn't twist up with anguish over the squabble they were having, both girls fell silent.

Becca said to her sister, "I think we're being dumb."

Jenny scratched her arm. "Well. Maybe. But I wanted to play with the Mountaineers."

"Your brother's eleven," Erik pointed out to Jenny. "And you're eight. Maybe both you and Becca are a little young to be tagging along with him all the time. Maybe you ought to find some friends your own age."

"But *who?*" Jenny wailed.

"School starts in a little over a week," Erik said. "You'll meet more kids then."

"What kids? If there were kids my age I didn't know about in this dinky town, they'd have to be kids who never leave their house. Who wants a friend who never leaves the house?"

"Jenny, be patient."

"A *week*," Jenny moaned, as if that were forever and a day.

"You'll live until then," Erik promised.

"I'll die from being bored," Jenny vowed.

And then Tawny appeared from the kitchen and announced that dinner would be ready in half an hour. Erik chucked Becca under the chin and ruffled Jenny's hair and headed upstairs for the long, hot shower that would wash the smell of paint thinners from his skin and his clothes.

Jenny turned to her aunt Tawny when Erik was gone. "Does he seem . . . different to you?"

"What do you mean?" Tawny asked.

Jenny's analytical abilities weren't yet as well developed as her instincts. "I don't know. Just different."

Tawny flipped a hank of pale hair back over her shoulder and shrugged. "Hmm. Maybe. Come on. Set the table for me. Becca, you can put the napkins around."

Becca fell right in step behind her aunt. Jenny lingered for a moment, staring in the direction of the stairs where her father had gone. And then she, too, shrugged and followed after her sister and Tawny.

"Shoes," Evie muttered happily. "Time to start getting ready for school."

She'd just finished cleaning up the dishes after her light supper. Now was as good a time as any to start moving things around a little down in the shop. It was hours before bedtime, and there was nothing she enjoyed so much as setting up a new display.

Humming to herself, Evie strolled across the landing to the storage rooms on the other half of the second floor. Her extra shoe stock was in the back. She got to work, digging out the shoes, trekking up and down the stairs, exchanging floor stock for storage and vice versa. When she had all the shoes downstairs, she cleared an area near the front door and set up a shoe display, complete with a big sign that read:

Back-To-School Sale—20% Off Ticketed Price

That done, she brushed off her hands, feeling very satisfied with herself. And then she started thinking that maybe she ought to go ahead right now and rearrange the stationery section to put the emphasis on school supplies. She'd had an order come in just a few days ago—rulers and binders and the like. They were waiting upstairs for her to unpack them.

Yes, she might as well get a head start on that now. Still humming, she started for the stairs again.

It was well past midnight when her head finally hit the pillow. She went to sleep smiling and woke the next day feeling absolutely great.

Though Erik was working that Saturday, he knocked off a little early. Then he went home and cleaned up and got the kids together and walked them over to Main Street to buy them some shoes from Evie Jones.

Pete complained through most of the short stroll to Evie's shop. He'd been having fun over at Marnie's and everyone was going over to Mark's, because Mark had a new computer game called Space Death.

"Mark and Marnie and Kenny are all over at the Drurys' house now, playing Space Death," Pete said pointedly. "They'll be getting really good at it, and then when *I* finally get there—if I *ever*, get there—they'll just be able to wipe me out."

"And who cares about dumb shoes anyway?" Pete kicked a rock off the sidewalk and into the street. "We can get dumb shoes anytime, but Space Death is brand-new. And all's I want you to realize, Dad, is I'm missing out on something really important to me, to go over and buy some stupid school shoes...."

Erik let him moan. He'd been a kid once himself, after all.

They had to stop twice to wait for Becca, who was always getting sidetracked. She'd see a cat sitting on a front porch and she'd have to stop and call to it. Or she'd spot a ladybug on the trunk of a tree and have to study it, up close and personal, her eyes almost crossing as she peered at it from a fraction of an inch away.

Erik didn't mind waiting for Becca. Not today, anyway. Nothing could really bother him today. He was on his way to buy shoes he probably couldn't afford from the most beautiful woman in the whole damn world. And he felt wonderful.

When they reached the shop, Evie hurried to greet them, her pale cheeks pinkening, her smile wide and bright.

"Oh. You came," she said, and then she laughed a little.

Erik grinned like a fool. "Gotta have those shoes."

"Yes," she said. And then they were quiet, just looking at each other, both wearing wide, silly smiles.

Pete broke that up. He groaned. "Can we get this over with? Please?"

"Pete." Erik turned and leveled a warning look at his son.

Pete rolled his eyes and groaned once more. "Gee, Dad. I explained to you, I've got things to do, you know?"

"The shoes are over here," Evie said, pointing the way.

Erik saw the display she'd set up then, shoes of all types and sizes with a big sale sign looming over it.

He knew immediately that she'd set the thing up for his sake—and probably marked the prices down for him, too. He didn't like it.

A few minutes ago, he'd been positive that nothing could bother him today. But he'd been wrong. His pride jabbed him at the thought that she'd go and lower her prices because of him.

"Dad, are we buyin' these things or not?" Pete moaned.

The day didn't seem so damn bright anymore. Erik realized that he probably shouldn't have gotten himself into this. But what could he do at this point? To back out now would only make things worse.

"Sure." He looked at Evie again. She was still smiling, but he knew that *she* knew something had gone wrong.

Still, she gamely suggested, "Why don't you decide what you'd like to try on? And then I'll get to work measuring some feet."

Evie was quick and helpful. She treated him and the kids like they were her only customers, all the while managing to be polite and welcoming to other shoppers who came in while she was waiting on them. Twenty minutes after he'd entered the shop, Erik was standing at the cash register writing out a check while Evie bagged up a pair of shoes for each of his kids.

Then Jenny, who'd been surprisingly quiet through the whole process, suddenly asked Evie, "Where's the snow globe that was here before? The one with the fairy princess. Did you sell it already?"

"No, I didn't sell it."

Erik could feel Evie's eyes on him. He met her gaze. The memory of that other day rose, a memory that was magical to him—though he couldn't exactly say why.

"Well, where is it, then?" Jenny wanted to know.

Evie took the check from Erik and put it in the cash register. "I'm afraid it's been broken."

"Oh, no. How?"

"It fell. From the counter."

"And you threw it away?"

"Well, yes. Most of it, anyway."

Jenny's eyes grew brighter with hope. "You kept the princess. That's what you mean, isn't it?"

"Yes."

"Where is she? Could I see her?"

"She's upstairs. In my bedroom, on my dresser."

"Dad..." Pete was rolling his eyes and groaning again. "Can we get going, *puhleeze?*"

Erik started to reprimand him, then changed his mind. "We're done here," he said. "Head on home if you want to."

"Great. See ya." Pete was at the door in a flash. He stopped just before he went out. "Oh. If you need me, I'm at Mark's."

"I figured," Erik said, but he doubted Pete heard him, since the boy was already gone.

"I really would like to see that princess." Jenny was looking up at Evie with beseeching eyes.

"All right, follow me," Evie said, then she handed Erik his receipt and the big bag with the shoes in it. "Would you keep an eye on things down here, just for a minute?"

"Sure." He watched them go, Jenny following Evie, and then he looked around for Becca, who had suddenly disappeared.

His younger daughter hadn't gone far. He found her in a corner, sitting on a miniature bed amid a mountain of stuffed animals and dolls. She saw her father looking at her, and shyly held out what looked like a stuffed chipmunk.

"I like this one. It's my fav'rit." She gave him the same beseeching look Jenny had just given Evie.

There had been a time when he would have bought the toy for Becca without thinking twice about it. It was small, after all, and probably wouldn't cost much more than a few dollars.

But now, every dollar really did count. A few days ago, he'd spent more than a week's grocery money on a pen and pencil set. And these shoes he'd just bought, even with twenty percent taken off, were more expensive than the shoes he would have otherwise picked up at a discount store in Grass Valley, had he not been looking for a way to hang around Evie Jones again.

Hell. He *was* a fool. An outright idiot. This wasn't going to work, this thing with Evie. He couldn't *afford* it. He couldn't afford jack diddly right now. He had to keep his mind on his children, on paying the rent and getting on his feet again.

This... *friendship* he was hoping for with Evie would only get in the way, distract him. Like today. He could have put in another couple of hours before he knocked off. He could have finished up that job over at the Tibbitses' place. But instead he'd come here. And now the job was still waiting. He'd have to go over there Monday and wrap up before he could start on the Daylin place out at the end of Bullfinch Lane.

"Daddy?" Becca said, still begging him with those sweet blue eyes of hers.

"Put it down, Bec. Get off the bed."

"But, Daddy—"

"I said, put it down."

Tears welled up, but Becca did as her father instructed.

A moment later, when Jenny came bouncing down the stairs with Evie behind her, Erik and Becca were waiting for her at the door.

"Look, Dad." Jenny held up the tiny figurine that had once been inside the snow globe. "She said I could keep it."

Beside him, he heard his younger daughter suck in an indignant breath. He knew what would be coming out of her mouth next: *If Jenny gets that, why can't I have the chipmunk?* And he just wasn't going to let it get started.

"Jenny, you can't keep that. Give it back," he told his older daughter.

Jenny's face, glowing a moment ago, now flushed a dull red. "But, Dad . . ."

Erik felt like a total jerk. But what else could he do? If he let Jenny have the princess, then Becca would be slighted. Unless he bought her the damn stuffed animal. Which he simply wasn't going to do. "Give it back. Now."

"Erik, it's only—" Evie began.

"Please don't," he told her quietly.

She bit her lip and said no more. Slowly Jenny turned and handed back the princess from the broken snow globe.

Erik opened the door. "Come on," he said. "Let's go home now." The afternoon light outside was blindingly bright. The day was warm.

But Erik didn't feel the warmth anymore and the beauty of the late-summer day was wasted on him now. He grimly put one foot in front of the other and took his silent daughters home.

Evie felt terrible all the rest of that day and through the night. She hardly slept, she was so disgusted with herself.

What could she have been thinking? she kept asking herself, as she tossed and turned in her bed.

She knew about Erik's pride where money was concerned. But still, she'd discounted her shoes and not given a thought to how he might feel about that, after he'd told her expressly that he'd be coming in to purchase three pair.

And then the princess. Evie wasn't quite sure what had gone wrong concerning the tiny figurine. It had all happened so fast.

But in hindsight, she knew she should have at least asked Erik before she'd told Jenny she could have the figurine. Unfortunately it had been just like the pen set. Evie had seen Jenny's pleasure when the girl looked at the little fairy princess with the bent wing. And she'd thought, *Why not give it to her?*

After all, the figurine, unlike the pen set, was worth nothing in terms of dollars and cents. In reality, it was a piece of a broken snow globe and nothing more. Evie had only kept it because... well, because it represented that strange and wonderful moment when she and Erik had truly touched.

It had seemed fitting, perfect, that she should give it to the man's daughter when the girl admired it so.

But Erik hadn't understood. He'd made Jenny give the princess back and then walked right out the door.

Oh, she'd made a mess of the whole thing. She really had. If she wanted to be Erik's friend, she was going to have to do better than this.

She was going to have to find out more about him, so she wouldn't make such dreadful mistakes in the future.

The forbidden thought rose in her mind: *Let down the wall. Who knows what you'll pick up?*

Evie groaned and sat straight up in bed, deeply ashamed of herself. She had made a solemn vow, fifteen years ago, that she would never go seeking the secrets of another in that particular way again.

So that meant she was going to have to ask somebody, someone she could trust. Someone who might be likely to know about Erik and what he'd been through in his life.

Several people came to mind. North Magdalene was a small town, after all. Regina Jones, her cousin Patrick's wife, might know. And certainly Amy, Erik's sister and Cousin Brendan's wife.

But there was an even better choice, Evie knew. There was someone who knew everything about everyone in North Magdalene.

She would call her uncle Oggie after church tomorrow, and ask him over for lunch coffee.

Evie lay back down again and snuggled up with her feather pillow. She felt better already, just knowing what she was going to do next.

Before she drifted off to sleep, she remembered she was out of sugar. That wouldn't do at all. She sighed and closed her eyes and made a mental note to stop in at the grocery store on her way home from church.

Chapter Five

Evie watched with great fondness as her uncle Oggie spooned sugar into his coffee. When he'd ladled in enough to put a diabetic into a coma, he gave the coffee one quick swipe with his spoon, lifted the mug to his mouth and drank long and deep.

"Ah," he said, when he lowered the cup. "That's heaven. Believe it. Gives the old ticker a real kick start, if you know what I mean."

Evie, who was drinking lemonade herself, granted her uncle an indulgent smile and took a nice, refreshing sip.

Oggie plunked his mug on the table and pushed his plate away. "That was one fine lunch, gal." He stretched a little, and ran his thumbs under his frayed red suspenders. "Now. Down to business."

Evie sent him a sharp glance. When she'd invited him over, he'd said nothing about any *business* that she could recall.

"I got a sense you got something on your mind," he said, as if in reply to a remark she hadn't actually made. "Am I right?"

Instead of answering, Evie pushed her own plate away and rubbed at a watermark on the table. Now that the moment had come to talk about Erik, Evie found she had no idea how to begin. She felt foolish and awkward and much younger than her years.

Oggie reached across and put his wrinkled hand over hers. "Come on. What is it? You still worried about Gideon?"

Evie pulled away and folded her hands in her lap. She'd hardly thought of her father in the past couple of days. Her whole world had centered down to Erik and all these wonderful new feelings she had for him.

Oggie was still watching her, his beetled brows drawn together. "Did something happen, then? Have you gotten somethin' suspicious in the mail? 'Cause I ain't heard nothin' else beyond that postcard I showed you."

Evie shook her head. "No. Nothing. Nothing at all."

"Well, then. What is it?"

Evie looked away.

Oggie refused to give up. "You can tell me. Come on. Look at me, gal. Tell me what's going on in that mind of yours."

Evie made herself face him. She gazed into his beady little eyes and knew that he was right. She *could* tell him.

"I've...made a friend." The words were out of her mouth before she really knew she would say them. They sounded urgent and breathless. And they made her feel ridiculous—someone so backward and socially inept that she fell all over herself, just confessing she had a friend.

Oggie inquired, "And who is this friend?"

"Oh, Uncle Oggie..."

"Come on. Who?"

"Well, he's not *really* a friend. Not yet."

Oggie picked up on the operative word. "It's a he."

"Yes. And I do feel that we *could* be friends. But I don't really know him that well. That is, I *feel* as if I know him. And I'd like to *really* know him."

"Who is he?"

Evie cast her uncle a pleading glance. "This is so hard."

"You're doin' fine."

"I... oh, how can I explain? I feel this natural... closeness to him. Just in a *friendly* way, of course. Because we'll never be more than that."

"More than what?"

"Friends."

Oggie emitted a snorting kind of noise. "Look, Evie. Just tell me his name, okay?"

"Oh, Uncle Oggie..."

"Come on. Say it."

Evie gulped.

"Say it. Who is this guy?"

Somehow, she managed to murmur, "Erik."

"Eh? Speak up."

"Erik."

"You said Erik."

"Yes."

"Erik who?"

"Riggins."

Oggie had been leaning across the table. Now he sat back in his chair and folded his hands over his slight paunch. "Ah," he said.

Evie wasn't sure she liked the way he said that. "What does that mean, *ah?*"

"Nothin', gal. It's just an expression. Ah. Like in *I see.* Like in *I understand.*"

"Oh. Well. All right."

"And what do you mean, you'll never be more than friends with him?"

"Well, he told me."

"Told you what?"

"That he has his kids to raise and he doesn't have any time for women right now."

Oggie pondered that information, then he asked, "And what about you?"

"Me?"

"Ain't no one else here, gal. Just you and me. How do you feel about just bein' *friends?*"

"Well, I feel as he does. Friendship is all I'm looking for. I'll never become...romantically involved with anyone."

Nothing ever offended Oggie Jones, but he looked offended now. "You mean not *ever?* Not in your entire life?"

"Yes. That's what I mean."

He slapped a hand on the table and snorted in disgust, "Why the hell not?"

Evie didn't answer. She was not going to explain that. Not even to Oggie. To explain that, she'd have to talk about her gifts, which she would never do.

She wanted to *forget* her gifts and go on with this nice, normal life she'd found in North Magdalene. That was all she wanted, really. A normal life.

A normal life and one thing more, a soft voice whispered inside her head, *to have Erik Riggins for a friend...*

"Well? I'm still waitin' for an answer here," Oggie prompted.

Evie picked up her lemonade glass, looked into it and set it back down. "I'm just not ever going to fall in love. That's all. It's...something I've always known."

"But why?"

"It's just the way I am, Uncle Oggie. Please. Let it go."

"But lovin' between a man and a woman is God's greatest gift. If you've had true love, you've had it all. A man can live through hell on earth, if he's known real love with a good woman. And for a woman, it's the same."

All unexpected, Evie felt tears at the back of her throat. Could that be true? Could love—lasting, committed love—between two people really make all the difference in life?

She brought herself up short. What did it matter if it *was* true? She was never going to know love like that with a man. And getting all misty-eyed about it was self-indulgence, plain and simple.

Evie gulped down the useless tears. "I understand, Uncle Oggie," she said quietly. "But some people never have what you're talking about. And they get by. I'm one of those people. I know it. So please. Just let the subject go."

Oggie looked at her sideways across the table. Then he let out a long sigh. He lifted his empty mug. "How 'bout another cup?"

Evie pushed herself to her feet and gave him more coffee, which he loaded up with sugar just as before. After he'd taken a good, long drink and she'd returned to her chair, Oggie spoke again.

"All right. So you just want to be *friends* with Erik Riggins."

"Yes. I do."

"Good enough. And how can I help you to make that happen?"

Evie felt a smile bloom on her face. "I love you, Uncle Oggie."

Oggie shifted around in his chair. "Don't get sappy on me, gal. I'm an old man. I can't take too much affection comin' at me at one time. What can I do? Come on, I'm here to help."

"Well, I was hoping you might tell me..."

"What?"

"A little about him. About his life, I mean. And his family. And about the woman he was married to. Things like that. So I could get to understand him better. It's important, I think, to understand your friends."

"You want a little history lesson, is that it? You want the history of Erik Riggins?"

"Yes," Evie said. "That's exactly what I want."

"That could take a while."

"It's Sunday. My shop is closed. I have all day."

A crafty look came into the little black eyes. "I'm gonna need a good cigar, to tell it all. Mind if I smoke?"

"Uncle Oggie, you're impossible."

"No argument." He pulled out a cigar. "Can I smoke?"

Evie rose and opened both of the kitchen windows, then found an ashtray at the back of a cupboard. She set it before him.

He cackled and beamed up at her. "You're a jewel, Evie Jones. A queen among women."

She sat down opposite him. "Just tell me about Erik."

And he did, smoke curling up from his cigar, his chair tipped back and his eyes full of memories of the way things once were.

"Erik is a Riggins. That's the first thing you gotta understand," Oggie told Evie. "And you gotta understand that there've been Rigginses in North Magdalene even before there were Rileys—the Rileys bein' my sainted Bathsheba's people, in case you don't recall my tellin' you before. The Rigginses are good people. Salt of the earth. Workin' people, if you get my drift."

"Yes."

"Tradespeople and laborers," Oggie elaborated. "And some of them are just a little wild and crazy. Erik's older brother, Jacob, comes to mind when I say wild. But not *that* wild. Probably not as wild as my own boys have been in their time.''

Evie made a sound of understanding. Since she'd moved to North Magdalene, she'd heard no end of tales about the wild Jones boys.

"But my boys are another story," Oggie said. "This story's about Erik. And how he came from workin'-class people. And he had this talent."

"Talent?" Evie put her elbows on the table and leaned closer to her uncle, eager to hear every word.

"Yeah. For paintin' pictures and stuff. Very un-Rigginslike, if you know what I mean. The Rigginses are not artsy types. They don't paint pictures and they don't send their kids to college. They get jobs after high school and settle down as close to home as they can manage."

"So Erik grew up unhappy, because he wanted to paint pictures and go to college and—"

"Whoa, gal. Give me time. Let me tell it."

"Okay. I'm sorry."

Oggie puffed on his cigar a few times. Then he continued, "No. As far as I recall, Erik Riggins was not an unhappy kid. Everyone just thought of him as a little bit odd, that's all. Because of the picture paintin', I mean. But he started workin' with his uncle Dewey, paintin' houses, on weekends and during school breaks when he was in his early teens. It was obvious he was goin' to do what all Rigginses do. Learn his trade and marry a nice girl and settle down in North Magdalene—and only paint those pictures of his on the side."

"But then?"

Oggie flicked his cigar in the ashtray Evie had provided. "Then he fell in love with Carolyn Anderson."

"Anderson?" Evie whispered to herself, remembering the vision of Nellie, when Erik had grabbed her arm down in the shop four days before.

"If you go with him, I have no daughter," Nellie had said.

Oggie confirmed Evie's suspicions. "Yeah, Anderson. Carolyn was Nellie Anderson's one and only baby girl."

Evie shook her head. It was hard to believe. "Does this mean Nellie was actually married once?"

"She was married, all right. Delbert Anderson's long gone, now, though. He was long gone fifteen years ago, when Carolyn and Erik fell in love. Died of a massive coronary when Carolyn was barely in school. You ask me, I don't know how he lasted even that long. Bein' married to Nellie Anderson would have to be damn hard on any man."

Evie was nodding. "Nellie hated the idea of her daughter and Erik together, am I right?"

"Bingo. Nellie Anderson always thought of herself as high-class. She wasn't havin' her precious little darlin' takin' up with any *laborer,* for all he was a hardworkin' kid with a heart as big as the Sierras and a good head on his shoulders, too." Oggie lowered his voice a little, to a conspiratorial level. "Between you and me, I don't think anyone would have been good enough for Carolyn, so far as Nellie was concerned. Not any mortal man, anyways. Nellie ain't got much use for mortal man, if you get my drift."

"So what happened?"

"*Love* happened, between Erik and Carolyn. And even Nellie Anderson couldn't make it go away. As soon as they graduated high school, Erik an..! Carolyn were married, right here in the community churc¹. Nellie refused to come to the wedding."

"She turned her back on her own daughter." It was a statement. Evie knew the truth. She'd *seen* the truth, four days ago.

"Yes, she did. Erik and Carolyn moved to Sacramento, for a fresh start. See, Carolyn loved her mama, even though she loved Erik more. And she was a sensitive kind of girl. She couldn't stand to stay here and be snubbed by her own mother every time they passed on the street."

"And how did it work out for them—for Erik and Carolyn?"

"Word was, they were happy. For a while. Erik built up a solid business painting houses and Carolyn worked for a year or two, then stayed at home to raise the kids. Everything was goin' great guns. But then, sometime after the youngest was born—"

"Becca."

"Becca, right. Sometime after she had Becca, Carolyn went into some kind of depression. She was in and out of medical and psychiatric hospitals for three or four years. It broke Erik, financially."

Evie saw again the vision of the blue-eyed woman, stepping unknowingly in front of the advancing truck. "And then Carolyn was hit by that delivery van," she murmured, more to herself than to Oggie.

Oggie peered at her through the smoke and clucked his tongue. "So. You've heard some of the story already, haven't you?"

Evie shrugged, a gesture that might have meant just about anything. "And now he's come back home. To start over."

"That's about the size of it. From what I understand, he was too damn proud to get any assistance from the government, or to work out some kind of debt reorganization. He sold the house in Sacramento to pay off a big chunk of the bills. And now he's rented the house our Regina grew up in, the one next door to where she and Patrick live."

"Has he made up with Nellie?" Evie asked the question even though she was reasonably sure she already knew the answer.

"No," her uncle confirmed her suspicion. "They avoid each other as much as possible, from the way I hear it."

"But the children are her *grandchildren*. At least she spends some time with them, doesn't she?"

"Nope. She disowned her daughter when Carolyn ran off with Erik. And now she's nothin' more than a stranger to those three kids."

"Oh, Uncle Oggie. That's so sad."

Oggie sighed. "I never claimed to understand what goes on in Nellie Anderson's head."

Another question came to her. "And what *about* the children, then? Who takes care of them while Erik's working?"

"He's got Tawny, his younger sister, to help him with the kids. His mom helps out, too, from what I've heard." Oggie smashed the stub of his cigar in the ashtray Evie had provided. "Anythin' else you need to know right now, gal?"

Evie rose, went to her uncle and placed a kiss on the crown of his sweet, balding head. "That'll do, Uncle Oggie. Thank you so much."

Oggie grunted. "You got any whiskey around here? I got a thirst that coffee won't quench, if you know what I mean."

Evie went to the cupboard to get the shot glass and the lone bottle she kept there for occasions like this. She carried them over and set them before Oggie, who poured himself a shot, knocked it back and then grimaced.

"Ah. That takes the edge off the day, for a surety. Now." He handed her the bottle and the glass. "Put this away.

Whiskey's one of my many weaknesses. And one shot is more than I need."

Evie put the bottle away and rinsed out the glass.

"So what are you gonna do now?" Oggie asked her, when she returned to the table.

Evie hadn't the faintest idea.

And Oggie knew it. "Maybe you ought to just make yourself... available. Can you do that?"

"Available for what?"

"Family get-togethers. Social events."

"But I don't understand how that will—"

Oggie pulled out a second cigar. "It's a small town. And Rigginses and Joneses do a fair amount of... interactin'. You just go when you're invited somewhere. And maybe that new *friend* of yours will be there, too."

Chapter Six

The Tuesday after Evie spoke with her uncle, she saw Erik on Main Street again. He nodded politely and walked on by.

Her heart sank.

But then she reminded herself that they were bound to meet again. She shouldn't try to rush things. A friendship, after all, would take time to build.

That Saturday, Regina and Patrick Jones gave a barbecue in their backyard. Erik and Evie were both there. Evie felt all nervous and fluttery at the sight of him.

But then for the first hour or so, he seemed to go out of his way to avoid her. Evie's spirits drooped. She actually considered pleading a headache and going on home.

Jenny and Becca saved her from running away like that. Jenny approached shyly, with Becca right behind her.

"'Lo, Evie."

"Jenny. How are you?"

"Okay. How's the princess?"

"She's fine. Still on the dresser in my bedroom."

"Honest?"

"Oh, yes."

"I thought maybe, since she wasn't in her snow globe anymore and nobody would buy her, that you might have just thrown her away."

"Oh, no," Evie assured the child. "I would never do that."

Jenny beamed. It was clear she still hoped that her father might someday relent and allow her to claim the broken prize.

Becca hoisted herself into the vacant folding chair on Evie's left side. She put her soft little hand on Evie's arm. "And how about Chippy? How's he doing?"

Puzzled, Evie turned to the younger girl. "Chippy?"

"The chipmunk. The stuffed one. On the bed in your store. I named him Chippy. You didn't...sell him, did you?"

There were a lot of stuffed animals on that bed. Evie wasn't exactly sure she remembered "Chippy," yet she had no memory of selling a stuffed chipmunk recently. "I'm sure he's fine. Still right where you left him."

"Well, that's good," Becca said with obvious relief.

After that, Evie asked the girls if they were all ready for school to start. Jenny said she was ready, all right, and hoped to find a best friend there. Becca announced she was starting first grade and would be able to read her favorite story, *Corduroy,* all by herself by the end of the year. *Corduroy,* Jenny explained, was the story of a stuffed bear who lived in a department store and wanted nothing so much as for a child to come and take him home.

As she talked with the girls, Evie was very much aware that Erik was watching them. And when it came time to eat, somehow he ended up sitting beside her. They didn't say much to each other. But when he passed her the butter, his finger grazed hers.

Evie felt the slight touch right down to her soul and for one brief luminous moment, she understood that she wanted much more than friendship from the big man with the rough hands. But she swiftly put such a scary thought right out of her mind.

There was a street dance the next night, in honor of Labor Day. Evie attended, though she usually eschewed such activities. Erik was there, too. They ended up standing beside each other. And then he turned to her.

"Maybe you would . . . like to dance?"

She said she most definitely would. He held out his arm, she hooked hers through it. He led her out into the open space in the middle of the street. They danced, by the light of the paper lanterns that she'd helped the Ladies Auxiliary string from streetlight to streetlight that very afternoon.

They talked of everyday things. Erik said that next year, the Labor Day Dance would be held in the new town hall, which was visible a hundred yards away, across the street from Lily's Café. The hall was nearly completed, and being built with money donated by the wealthy writer, Lucas Drury, who was Mark Drury's father.

Erik smiled down at Evie, his hand riding lightly on the small of her back as the band played a slow country song. "My own boy, Pete, seems to have formed some kind of club with Mark Drury and Marnie Jones and my brother's boy, Kenny. They call themselves the Mountaineers."

"Very imaginative," Evie whispered a little breathlessly. It felt to her as if her body burned all along the front of her, where it was lightly touching Erik's.

The following Tuesday, they happened to drop by the post office at the same time. In North Magdalene, since there was no house-to-house delivery, most people visited the post office daily to check the boxes they rented. When Erik walked in, Evie was sorting through her mail, standing at the little counter that ran along the side wall.

He came through the glass door, caught sight of her—and his face changed. He smiled, but it was more than a smile. It was a look of...gladness. She knew without a doubt that he was thrilled to see her. She felt exactly the same.

He approached and they stood right there talking, beneath a bulletin board that was covered with pictures of America's Most Wanted. Evie felt flushed and excited through the whole conversation.

When they parted, she realized she had no memory at all of what they had talked about. All she knew was that she loved talking to him, watching him smile and tip his head to the side. She loved the way he listened, as if he really wanted to hear what she was telling him. So many people only waited for their turn to talk. They didn't take the act of listening seriously. But Erik did. He truly listened and he was thoughtful, always stopping to carefully consider his words before venturing an opinion.

On Wednesday, after school was out, Becca and Jenny came into Wishbook.

Evie was dusting a display case when they appeared. Jenny declared that she wanted to own a shop just like Wishbook when she grew up. Then she asked to be allowed to help. Evie gave her a dust cloth. The two of them carefully polished several shelves of china and knickknacks while Becca sat on the bed among the stuffed animals, conversing with Chippy.

When the girls left, Evie put Chippy away on a storage shelf beneath one of the display cases. Even if Erik would never allow Evie to give his daughter the toy, no one else was ever going to own it, and that was that.

That night, at a little after nine, Evie's phone rang.

"I think we should talk," Erik said without preamble.

Evie's throat, which had felt perfectly normal just a moment before, was suddenly like sandpaper, while her palms had gone clammy with sweat. "I . . . all right."

"I'll come over there."

"Umm, right now?"

"Yeah."

Evie's legs went wobbly. Slowly, she sank to a nearby chair. "But . . . the children. Who'll watch them?"

"My mom said she would."

"Oh."

"Evie?"

"Yes?"

"Is there some problem with my coming over now?"

"No. Certainly not. Just come up the back stairs to the door there. It opens onto the hall that leads to my apartment. You remember my apartment, don't you?"

He made a noise in his throat, which she took for a *yes*. Then he muttered, "Ten minutes," and hung up.

He was there in eight and a half minutes. Evie had counted the seconds, so she knew precisely how long it took him.

Once inside, he seemed to fill up her small living room, as he did most enclosed spaces. He was wearing tan corduroy jeans and a forest green, slightly threadbare T-shirt and he was the handsomest man she'd ever seen in her life.

"Sit down." She gestured at a chair.

He dropped into it. She made herself perch on the end of the couch.

Then she sprang to her feet again. "Oh. Can I get you something? Lemonade?" She thought of the bottle she kept for her uncle. "Whiskey?"

"No. I just want to talk."

She made herself sit on the couch again. "All right." Surreptitiously, she rubbed her hands together. They were clammy again. Her mouth felt like cotton. "What do you want to talk about?" she managed to ask, then swallowed quickly so she wouldn't have to cough the dryness away.

"You and me."

Oh, my Lord, she thought as she managed to murmur, "I see."

He said, "Evie, I like you. A lot."

"Me, too," she replied, ridiculously eager. She made herself take a deep breath, then said, with more dignity, "I mean, I like you, too."

He was leaning forward in the chair, his elbows on his slightly spread knees, his hands clasped between his legs. He rubbed his hands together, thinking. Then he spoke again. "I thought that we might become friends."

Her eyes widened. She felt a big smile break across her face. She opened her mouth to say she'd thought the same thing.

However, he spoke again before she could get the words out. "But then, I thought about it some more. And I knew even friendship wasn't going to work."

Evie felt the smile melt from her lips. Her shoulders drooped.

He went on, "But it looks as if friendship is happening anyway, no matter what I thought."

She sat up straight again. This wasn't so bad, after all.

"As I said, I really do... like you. And so do my girls. They told me they came to the shop today."

She licked her dry lips. "Yes. They were here. I love having them here."

"Well, I guess that's good. Because it would break their hearts if I told them not to come here. They... they seem to have sort of fastened on you and your shop as something just a little bit magical. And they've had a rough time, losing their mother. You know, don't you, about their mother?"

Evie nodded.

Erik looked down at his shoes. "I suppose you know the story. About Carolyn's illness."

"Well, I—"

He met her eyes again and waved a big hand. "Don't feel bad. It's okay. Around here, everybody knows everything. That's just how it is."

"Yes, I've, umm, noticed that." Another rather wavery smile lifted the corners of her mouth.

Erik stared at her; he looked slightly stunned. "Lord," he said in a near whisper. "You're so damn beautiful." Then he looked down at his shoes again. "Sorry."

Evie blinked. "What for? I don't...I don't understand. All you said was—"

His head shot up. His gray gaze burned right through her. "It can only be friendship, Evie. That's all."

She realized she wasn't breathing, and it took her a moment to get air into her lungs. "Well," she said, when the oxygen had found its way to her brain once more. "That's fine. Friendship is fine. It's exactly what I want, too."

Now he was the one blinking. "It *is?*"

"Yes." She cleared her throat. "The truth is, I'm a very...independent woman. I have never married—and I never will."

"You won't?"

"No. I like my life just as it is. But I can always use a friend. Someone to talk to, to laugh with. To spend time with now and then."

"Yeah," Erik said. "Yeah, I'm with you. Me, too."

"Then," she said happily, "we have no problem, do we?"

"No." He shook his head. Evie thought he looked like a man who'd just won the lottery. There was a dreamy, half-disbelieving grin on his face. "No, I guess we don't."

He stayed for a while after that and even said yes to a can of orange soda. They talked of how her shop was doing and how his business was quite brisk. She told him about the shop in Santa Fe and how much she'd loved it.

"But I love Wishbook more, because I love North Magdalene so much. After all, my family's here."

Erik said he knew just what she meant. He was glad to be home again himself, to tell the truth.

After she walked him to the door, Evie floated back into the living room and dropped to the couch. Life was wonderful, it really was, when one had a special friend.

The next day, the girls came to the shop again after school. Evie produced Chippy for Becca. The little one carried the toy around the store with her as Jenny pitched in on the book display Evie was putting together in a back corner.

A half an hour after the girls came in, another child around Jenny's age appeared. Jenny introduced the newcomer as Peg Clark and said they'd made friends in school just today. Peg quickly became involved with the display, too, helping to arrange the low bookshelves to form a reading nook, setting the books out to look inviting, positioning a stool and an old rocking chair just so, to tempt any browsers to sit for a while.

Not long after Peg's appearance, Peg's mother, Tondalaya Clark, came in looking for her daughter. When she saw the girls were having fun, she said that Peg could stay awhile. Before she left, she bought four children's books that Peg had pointed out she'd like to read.

A few minutes after Mrs. Clark left, the bell over the door rang again. It was Amy Riggins Jones. Amy's little daughter, Bathsheba, toddled along at her side.

"Hi, Aunt Amy," Jenny called from the corner where she and Peg were still at work.

Amy allowed Bathsheba to join the other children, once they'd solemnly promised to keep a close eye on the three-year-old. As soon as her daughter was off with the others, Amy explained to Evie that she was looking for a new dress. Then she ruefully patted her round belly. "Do you think you can fit me?" She was seven months pregnant with her second child.

Evie promised to give it her best shot.

However, since Evie didn't sell maternity clothes per se, finding the right dress did present something of a challenge. There was much laughter and happy chatter as the children kept busy in the corner and the two women plowed through Evie's racks of dresses, looking for something that might work. At last, Evie pulled out a jumper with a high Empire waist and a tie back. Amy tried it on and loved it.

Evie was ringing up the sale when the entry bell chimed once more. Evie looked up, her professional smile of greeting freezing on her face as Nellie Anderson marched in the door.

"Hello, Evie," Nellie said, clutching her ubiquitous clipboard to her bony chest. "I've come to firm up your commitment to Septemberfest."

Evie looked at Amy, who wore the same grim expression Evie knew was on her own face.

"Good afternoon, Amy," Nellie said stiffly.

Amy inclined her head. "Miz Anderson."

Nellie turned to Evie again. "Is this a bad time?"

It was, of course. A *very* bad time. The granddaughters Nellie pretended didn't exist were over in the corner, giggling and whispering as they went about their task.

Evie almost told Nellie that another time would be better. But then she held her tongue. The children lived in the same town with the woman. They were going to meet up with her every now and then.

And just maybe, the more often they met up, the more likely that Nellie Anderson would come to understand just what wonderful kids she was turning her back on.

"No," Evie said. "Now would be fine."

Amy said, "I think I'll look around a little more."

"Go right ahead," Evie replied, understanding Amy's intention completely. If there was going to be any unpleasantness, Aunt Amy would be there to protect her own.

Nellie approached the counter, apparently still oblivious to the fact that the childish voices in the back belonged to her own grandchildren. She coughed officiously and slid a typed sheet of phone numbers from under the clip on her clipboard. "Now. What I'd like you to do is to call these people tonight—tomorrow at the latest. Remind them that we must have those donations of clothing and baked goods delivered to the church by eight in the morning Saturday." Nellie gave a small, put-upon sigh. "People just don't seem to remember their long-range commitments like they used to. They need to be reminded, or they don't deliver as promised. It's unfortunate, but these are troubled times."

Evie took the sheet. "I'll be glad to make the calls, Nellie."

"Good. And I have you down for a personal donation of—"

"Two cakes and ten dozen cookies, I think it was."

"Right. Exactly." She looked up and her lips twitched in what was probably intended as a smile. "So. It's all settled. You know what you have to do?"

"Oh, yes. I know."

"Well, then, I'll be on my—"

Right then, from back in the corner, Amy called, "Becca, no! Come back. Evie's busy right now . . ."

But it was too late. Becca was there, clutching Chippy to her heart, and staring up, openmouthed, at the thin woman who gaped back at her in white-faced disbelief.

Chapter Seven

There was a long, awful pause. Nellie gripped her clipboard so tightly, Evie feared it might crack in two.

And then Becca asked in a puzzled voice, "Are you my grandma? My brother, Petey, says you are."

Nellie went on staring at the child. For a moment, Evie thought the older woman wouldn't be able to speak. But then she whispered, with great difficulty, "I . . . yes, I am."

"Oh." Becca held out her chipmunk. "This is Chippy."

Amy, who'd run to Becca's rescue and was now standing a few feet behind the child, made a small, bewildered sound. She opened her mouth—and then closed it without speaking when she saw Nellie Anderson solemnly shake the stuffed animal's paw.

"How d'you do, Chippy?" Nellie asked with absolute seriousness.

"He's fine," Becca answered for the toy.

"Well, that's good. Very good," Nellie told the child. Then she looked up at Evie and spoke in a voice so brittle it was painful to hear. "I really do have to be going now." She held up the clipboard. "So much to do." She actually giggled, a frantic sound. "So little time."

Evie wanted to reach out and soothe the older woman with a touch. Instead, she remained scrupulously nonchalant. "Of course. But come back anytime."

"Yeah," Becca said. "Me and Jenny are here lots. We like it here."

"I . . . maybe I will return sometime soon. Maybe I just will." Nellie backed toward the door. She opened it without turning and slid out still facing the inside of the shop.

As soon as the door was shut, Amy put her hand on her big stomach, as if to soothe the tiny one within. She shook her head. "Did that really happen?"

Evie had no chance to answer, because Becca had stepped up and wrapped her fingers around Evie's thumb. "Come on, Evie. Come see. The book place is all done."

Erik called that night at a little after ten.

"The kids are in bed and my sister Tawny's here. I really need to talk, Evie."

"Then come on over. That's what friends are for."

He was there in seven minutes and forty-three seconds. She gave him an orange soda and they sat at the kitchen table.

He said, "Amy told me. About Nellie coming in today, while the girls were here."

His big hand rested on the table. Evie longed to cover it with her own, but she didn't quite dare.

He was watching her. "You said you knew, about Carolyn's illness and about how she died. Did you also know that Carolyn was Nellie's daughter?"

"Yes."

"You know that Carolyn and I moved away because Nellie disowned her, when she married me?"

"Yes."

Erik focused on the middle distance, somewhere over Evie's shoulder. She wondered if he could see the past there. "Carolyn never really forgave me for that, for costing her Nellie's love."

"Did Carolyn say that?"

"No. She would never admit it. But sometimes, even in the good years, I'd come home from work and her eyes would be all red and puffy. She'd be smiling, but I'd know that she'd been crying, missing Nellie. I'd ask her what was wrong, but she'd insist there was nothing." He sighed. "She was real close to her mom."

"Oh, Erik . . ."

The big hand that was lying on the table clenched into a fist. "Over the years, I've tried to be careful, with the kids, not to say bad things about Nellie, not to turn them against her. You know what I mean?"

"Um-hmm."

"I want . . . I want my kids to have *both* of their grand-mothers, can you understand that?"

"Oh, yes."

"It's one of the reasons I came home—not the main rea-son, but one of them. To make my peace with Nellie." He drank from his can of soda, then set it down and stared at it as if something important might be written on the side. "Carolyn and I tried several times over the years to work things out with Nellie. But the woman is just too damn stiff-necked. She wouldn't come around. When Carolyn started having her troubles, I called Nellie. Nellie told me it was all my fault, and then hung up on me."

"Erik, I'm so sorry. . . ."

He looked up from the soda can and forced a smile. "Hey. That's how it goes sometimes. There are people who just never let go of old hurts."

Evie hastened to reassure him. "I'm not sure Nellie's that bad. I really think she wants to get to know those girls."

He nodded. "I agree. I think that Carolyn's death has changed her, just a little."

"How so?"

"I think she's softened. Not much, but some. Last November, when Carolyn died, I called Nellie and told her. She said 'Thank you' in this tiny voice, and hung up the phone. I called her a day later and told her that the funeral would be here, in North Magdalene, at the Community Church. She thanked me again, very civil and low."

"Did she go to the funeral?"

"Yeah. She didn't speak to me or anything. She stood off to the side, her face even more pinched looking than usual. But just the fact that she was there meant something."

"Yes. Yes, I can see how it would."

"And since we've been home, I've... I don't know, I've tried to think of a way to approach her again. I've felt like she might be willing now."

"I think you're right. I really do."

Now his smile was genuine. "From what Amy told me about what happened today, so do I." His gaze moved over her face. "And it's all thanks to you."

She waved her hand, dismissing her own part in what had occurred. "Thanks to Becca, you mean."

He lifted a big shoulder in a shrug. "Well, maybe Becca deserves a little of the credit, too." He stood then and carried his empty can to the sink. She watched him move, thinking that her little kitchen, like most rooms, was too small for him.

He set the can on the counter, then turned and leaned against the cabinets, crossing his arms over his chest. "It's good to talk about this. Especially now, when it's beginning to look like things just might work out with Nellie after all."

"I know what you mean. Family's important."

"Yeah," he agreed. "Yeah, it is."

And then he fell silent. He was watching her again, standing there against her counter. His eyes were soft.

Evie gazed back at him, feeling warm all over. She really did like just looking at him. He was so big and...solid.

She remembered how good it had felt, that day down in the shop, when he'd scooped her up in his strong arms and held her against his chest. She'd felt safe then, safer than she'd ever felt in her life. She'd known with absolute certainty that anything could have happened, and he could have handled it. He was a man to count on. If she needed him, he would be there.

Behind Erik, she could hear water dripping in the sink. The faucet was tricky if you didn't turn it off firmly, it always dripped.

It occurred to Evie, as she listened to her leaky faucet, that the seconds were continuing to tick by. And neither of them was talking. Maybe she ought to say something.

Yes, she definitely should say something....

But she didn't, and neither did he. The moment was just too lovely to ruin with words. It felt so good, simply to look at him and have him look back at her.

Her body, she realized, felt heavy, suddenly. It was a languorous heaviness. As if she'd fallen asleep in the sun on a summer afternoon. Even the dripping of the water in the sink had taken on a seductive quality. And she could feel each slow breath as the air filled her lungs, expanded her rib cage and made her breasts rise high and proud.

But then Erik seemed to shake himself. He straightened from his relaxed posture against the counter. "I . . . should go."

"Yes," she heard herself answering. "Of course. I understand."

She stood and saw him to the door.

Erik stopped in at the shop on the day of Septemberfest. He was carrying a slightly lopsided chocolate cake on a plastic platter and several cookies on a paper plate.

"I heard a rumor you baked these."

"Oh, really? From who?"

"Linda Lou Beardsly. She's the one behind the counter at the church bake sale booth. Was she straight with me? Did I get what I paid for?"

Evie cast a rueful glance at the cake. "I don't know if I should admit I made *that*."

He held it up and studied it. "What do you mean? This is a hell of a cake. I know. I'm a cake expert."

"Oh, are you?"

"You bet." He hefted the lopsided confection. "Nice and heavy, too."

If he'd been a little closer, she would have punched him on the arm. "Oh, you . . ."

"Come on, Evie. Confess. You made this cake."

She faked a glare. "All right, all right. I did."

"Good." He looked inordinately pleased with himself. "So come on over to the house tonight. About six. My mom will cook us dinner—and this fabulous cake will be our dessert."

Erik's mother, Darla, was there in the kitchen when Evie arrived at Erik's house. A large, sturdy woman with a lined face, Darla said she was glad to meet Erik's new friend. She reached for a towel, then held out her hand. Evie took it. Darla's grip was firm, her smile sincere.

Right then, Becca and Jenny came bouncing in.

"Evie, come with us," Becca said. She grabbed one of Evie's hands and Jenny grabbed the other and they towed her from the room.

They took her upstairs, where she admired their bedrooms and was personally introduced to Becca's ten stuffed animals and seven dolls.

After she'd seen both of the girl's rooms, they showed her Pete's room, complete with a painting of some kind of space module circling the earth dominating one wall, a scale model of the USS *Enterprise* hanging from the ceiling, erector set pieces scattered everywhere and an unmade bed.

Jenny remarked rather sadly, "Petey's a slob."

"He's a boy," Becca said, as if that explained it all. She tugged on Evie's hand again and led her to the next bedroom. "That's our dad's room. He has his own bathroom. The kids have to share."

Evie peeked in at the plain room with the nice bow window, the king-size bed and the two rather battered maple bureaus. Over the bed there was a painting of a secluded forest glen, with a pond in the center. A willow drooped into the pond, making ripples as if from a slight breeze.

Jenny saw the direction of Evie's gaze. "My dad painted that."

"Very nice," Evie said inanely. Actually she thought the painting was much more than merely "nice." There was great peace in it—and also a breath-held, expectant kind of feeling.

Evie's gaze dropped to the bed below the painting. And her cheeks were suddenly warming at the thought that this was the room where Erik slept.

Wanting to take her mind away from thoughts it shouldn't be pondering, she quickly pointed to the next door, which was shut. "Is that the guest room?"

Becca's eyes widened. "Oh, no. That's Dad's *special* room."

"She means his studio," Jenny explained. "We're not allowed in there. It's Dad's private space. He does his paintings in there." Jenny's reverent tone said it all. Evie longed to see the room. She felt that she could learn much about Erik, just by seeing the work he did in there.

"Hey, everyone." The man in question appeared at the top of the stairs. "Your grandmother could use a little help with the table." He smiled just for Evie. "And I'd like to get a little time with Evie, too, you know."

"We're coming right now," Becca said and started pulling on Evie's hand again.

Evie tossed one last wistful glance at the closed door, then followed Becca to where Erik waited for them.

Downstairs, the girls set the table in the dining room while Erik and Evie sat in the kitchen talking to Darla. Pete showed up just before they sat down to eat. He greeted Evie rather warily and said little during the meal.

The dinner was plain and good. When dessert was served, everyone agreed that the cake was delicious.

"You can't even tell it was crooked when you're eating it," Becca declared.

Pete ate his cake as quickly as he had devoured his meal, then asked to be excused to return to Marnie's house next door.

"Back by nine," Erik called as he left.

Pete waved in answer.

After that, everyone pitched in on the dishes and then Erik, Evie and the girls played Go Fish and Old Maid. The evening passed quickly. Too soon, it was nine o'clock and

Pete was trudging in the back door, on time but grudgingly so.

Darla volunteered to put the kids to bed so that Erik could walk Evie home.

"Did you paint the scene over your bed—of the pond and the willow?" Evie asked when they were strolling down the sidewalk toward Main Street.

"Yeah."

"And the one of the space module, in Pete's room?"

"Guilty, again." He was smiling. "And the twin fawns in Becca's room as well as the Mad Hatter's Tea Party scene in Jenny's room."

"My uncle Oggie said you were talented."

"Oh, did he?"

"Yes. And he was right."

They strolled a few steps in silence. Then Erik said, "Sam Fletcher dropped by my house the other day." Sam Fletcher was the husband of Evie's cousin, Delilah. He owned Fletcher Gold Sales, several doors up from Evie's shop on Main Street. Sam's store sold mining and camping equipment along with gold nuggets and jewelry and fine wooden sculptures which Sam carved himself.

"And what did Sam Fletcher have to say?"

"He wants me to bring some of my paintings into his store. To sell on consignment. What do you think of that?"

"I think it's an absolutely terrific idea."

They paused then, right there on Pine Street, and grinned at each other. Then, of one accord, they started walking again.

Evie said, "I like your house. It has such nice, big rooms. It seems just right for your family."

Erik nodded. "I've been lucky. Regina's renting it to me for next to nothing. I'm going to do a few improvements for her—including painting the whole place inside and out. And then maybe, eventually . . ." He let his voice trail off.

"Eventually what?"

He looked up at the blanket of stars overhead. It was a mild night, an Indian Summer night. The moon was a silver disk above the mountains. "Hell. I can't say what will happen. Not at this point."

"What, Erik? Come on."

He cast her a glance, then looked at the sidewalk in front of them again. "Regina said she wouldn't mind selling the place to me. So maybe, if I ever get back on top again, I'll buy that house someday. That's all I was going to say." They were at the corner of Pine and Main. Across the street was the grocery store and a hundred yards away to the right was Wishbook and Evie's apartment above it.

Reluctant to turn the corner, Evie hung back. "Why was that so hard to say?"

Erik stopped, too, a few steps after she did. He turned back to her. She could seen the reflection of the moon in his eyes.

"Sometimes it's hard," he said, "to learn to dream again."

Evie said nothing. She knew exactly what he meant. She took the few steps to catch up to him.

Then, side by side once more, they started up Main Street. When they reached Wishbook, Erik accompanied her up the stairs in back, where they lingered for a moment in mutual silence, listening to the crickets and the croaking of a lone frog somewhere in the little field between Main Street and Rambling Lane.

"Dinner was wonderful," she said at last.

A devilish glint came into his eyes. "And that cake. Unbelievable."

She did punch him then, very lightly, on the arm. "Don't push it, Riggins."

He chuckled, but said no more.

She asked, hesitantly, "Would you like to...come in?"

He shook his head. "I should get back."

She watched him run down the steps. Before he rounded the corner of the building he turned and waved. Her heart seemed to hover high in her chest, as light as a moonbeam, as she waved in return.

Each day, as the leaves turned to red and gold on the trees, the friendship between Erik and Evie deepened and grew stronger.

The girls came into the store several times a week. And more than once, Nellie appeared at the same time as the children were there. It was rocky going in the beginning, as Nellie tried to get to know her grandchildren without actually admitting what she was doing. The first few times she appeared, she backed out the door only minutes after she'd entered.

Evie continued to treat the whole process very offhandedly. She'd wave as Nellie was scurrying out and call, "Bye, Nellie. See you soon."

By the time September came to an end, though, things were improving. Nellie had begun reading stories to Becca, who would sit in her lap in the "book nook" in back. And one day at the beginning of October, Nellie even challenged Jenny and Peg to a game of jacks. She was thoroughly appalled when neither girl had even heard of the game.

"It's another sad sign of our times," Nellie intoned bleakly. "Two perfectly bright eight-year-old girls, and they've never heard of jacks."

And with that, Nellie marched out the door. She returned five minutes later, having paid a visit to Santino's

Barber, Beauty and Variety up the street. In her hand she clutched a paper sack and in the sack was a ball and several small, uniformly star-shaped metal objects—the "jacks" in question.

"May we use a small section of your floor, Evie?" Nellie inquired.

"Anywhere you can find the room," Evie said.

Nellie, Jenny and Peg settled on an area near the wrapping table. There—with Becca and Chippy included, of course—they sat in a circle and Nellie began teaching the girls how to play.

Soon after, Tondalaya Clark came in looking for Peg. Evie had to suppress a chuckle at the look on Tondalaya's face when she saw Nellie Anderson down on the floor bouncing a red rubber ball and scooping up the jacks in her swift, skinny hands.

"Will wonders never cease?" Tondalaya asked.

"I certainly hope not," Evie replied.

Erik came over that night, as he had been doing once or twice a week since the night of Septemberfest.

They sat in Evie's kitchen. Erik drank one of the orange sodas she always kept in the refrigerator for him as Evie told him all about how things were going between his former mother-in-law and his daughters.

"You're a miracle worker," he said, after she'd described the game of jacks. "That's what you are."

"No. I'm not. I'm just...a woman. Just an ordinary woman."

"No. No, you're not."

"Yes. Yes, I am."

And then they laughed together. Erik reached across the table and snared her hand.

And everything went absolutely still.

Evie gasped, for a split second fearing they were in for another episode like the one that had occurred down in the shop all those weeks ago.

But then she breathed easier. Because no "episode" happened.

Nothing at all happened, really. Except for the fact that Evie had found heaven.

Heaven in the touch of Erik's hand on hers.

They both remained very still.

"I don't want to let go," he said into the quiet.

"Good. Then don't," she whispered in return.

"But we said we'd only be friends," he reminded her, his voice rough and as warm as the clasp of his hand.

"I know what we said."

His hand closed tighter over hers. "Evie..."

Evie waited, her heart pounding loud in her ears. It was impossible. She'd always known it. She could never take the chance of...

But the thought wouldn't form completely. Her old fears seemed groundless now. He was Erik. Through these magical recent days, it had begun to seem as if he'd been born to be a part of her life. As if she'd waited through all the lonely years for him.

Only for him.

He spoke again. "I thought I wouldn't let you become too important to me. But it didn't work. I look at you and I know you aren't mine. So then why is it I also know I couldn't stand it if I lost you, if you left?"

Her silly eyes were filling. Evie swiped at them, impatiently, with the hand that wasn't clutched tightly in his.

"I'm not going anywhere. Honest," she promised.

"Lord. I hope that's true."

"It is. I swear it. I've...I've spent my life leaving. One place after another. But not anymore, Erik. This is my home. Here. In this town." *With you,* her heart added, though she didn't say those words aloud.

He murmured her name again.

She whispered his.

And then he said, "This has to stop. Now." He let go of her hand.

"No. Erik..."

But he was already up and headed for the door.

"Erik. Stop."

He froze.

"Erik, please. Wait. Don't go."

He turned back. His eyes met hers. His face was set, determined. But within seconds, he was softening, giving in to the power of what lay between them.

Evie stood, a slow movement. The action brought with it a sharp awareness of her body. How heavy and weak it felt—but it was a fluid kind of weakness, very seductive, as if she floated in warm water, every movement deliciously hindered by liquid resistance.

"Ah, Evie..." Erik whispered. It was a plea. And a kind of surrender, as well.

She felt like a sleepwalker, a very willing sleepwalker, as she took the few steps that would bring her to stand before him.

He drew himself up as she approached—in wariness or preparation, she couldn't tell which.

She kept looking in his eyes, *willing* him not to turn away. When she reached him, she lifted her right hand and laid it on his chest.

He groaned.

"Shh," she said. "Don't...pull away. Don't move at all. Please."

He held himself perfectly still, but his heart galloped beneath her hand.

Evie thought that she liked how he smelled. For a moment she got lost in that, in the soap-and-man scent of him. Then she recollected herself enough to go on, "I want you to know..."

"Yeah?"

"That I trust you, Erik."

A beat, then he said, "Maybe you shouldn't." The words were rough, but tender, too.

She felt the corners of her mouth lifting in a knowing smile. "Oh, yes. I should. You're a man worth trusting."

"God. Evie." He was looking at her mouth. She knew in her woman's soul that he wanted to kiss her. And she *wanted* to be kissed by him.

She spoke the truth to him, boldly. "I know nothing of men, Erik. Do you... know what I'm saying?"

"I think so."

"Men have asked me out, a few times. And once or twice, I went. But I was always careful. Never to let them get too close. I didn't want to know them, not in any way that really mattered. I guess I've been afraid, deep down, that all men are like—" She cut herself off, appalled. What was she thinking of? She'd almost mentioned Gideon.

He prompted, "Like who?"

There was not much choice but to tell him. "My father."

"What was wrong with your father?"

She was trapped now; she had to say *something*. She tried stalling. "Oh, it's such a long story. He... he wasn't a very good father. Someday, maybe, I'll tell you all about him."

Erik closed his eyes, as if gathering his forces. "Evie, I *have* been wondering." He opened his eyes and looked at her probingly. "About your past. You never say much about it. I'd like to know, about all those places you say you *left*. And about what your life was like growing up."

Evie had no idea what to say then. Half of her wanted to tell him everything. Yet some things could never be told, not even to him.

"Evie?" Beneath her hand, Erik's heart beat more slowly now, a deep and insistent rhythm. He was waiting for her reply.

She hedged, "I can't tell it all in one night."

He wouldn't be put off. "You could make a start of it."

She bit the inside of her lip. "What do you want to know?"

He had the first question ready. "What about your mother? What was she like?"

It was a question that required no evasions. She relaxed a little and searched her memory for what she could recall of the woman who had given her life.

"My mother died when I was five. I hardly remember her. I have... an impression of gentleness, when I think of her. And of singing. I think she used to sing to me. And I know she either had a little money from somewhere or held a steady job. While she was alive, we had a house to live in and food on the table."

"But not after she died?"

"No."

"Why not? Couldn't your father take care of you?"

Evie was careful to keep looking right at him. Every word was a risk. Hesitantly she explained, "My father was... a gambler, a con artist, really. He lived on the road. After my mother died, he took us with him."

"Us?"

"I have two older sisters, Nevada and Faith. After my mother died, I grew up with them and my father... on the road, as I said. My father, he, umm, could never really afford to take care of us very well. But he wouldn't let go of us. He'd been in foster homes a lot, as a child. And he'd been abused in them, I think. So even though he couldn't really provide for us, he always swore no welfare people were going to get their hands on his girls.''

Erik's eyes were full of understanding. ''It was rough for you, wasn't it?''

''Yes.''

He asked one of the questions she'd been dreading. ''Is your father gone now, too?''

She knew what he meant: was Gideon dead? But she chose to take the question in the more general sense. She answered, ''Yes. He is. Gone.''

''I'm sorry.''

''Don't be. Not for me, anyway. As I said, he wasn't a good father. When we lost our mother and our home, we lost everything.'' She felt a smile play on her lips then. ''And you know what?''

''What?''

''In all those years, I've never felt I had a home till now. Here. In North Magdalene.''

''Yeah,'' he said, his smile answering hers. ''I know the feeling. North Magdalene has always been home to me, too. I missed it, all those years I lived away.''

Evie's hand still rested against his heart. She became aware of his heartbeat again.

Warm, she thought, he was so warm beneath her hand. She let her hand slide upward, over the hard bulge of his shoulder. She touched his tan neck with her thumb.

His eyes changed; they turned smoky and hot. ''Don't go too far, Evie,'' he warned. ''Be careful.''

But Evie was not feeling very careful inside. A giddiness swept through her. She had just navigated a conversational mine field, and had come out all in one piece. She'd managed to tell him something of her father and her childhood, without revealing anything about her strange gifts or her years as her father's pawn.

Now she felt bold; she felt she could handle anything. She could risk it all—and win.

She brushed her thumb against his neck and took the plunge. "It's more than...friendship between us, Erik. Isn't it?"

He closed his eyes again, as her thumb lightly moved on the side of his neck, back and forth, in a caress that was shamelessly intended to beguile.

"Isn't it, Erik?"

He breathed the word, "Yes."

Her heart jumped. It knocked against her ribs. Suddenly she didn't feel so bold. She whispered, "I'm afraid."

"So am I."

And then she sighed. "But I don't think...I can stop it. I don't think I *want* to stop it. Not deep in my heart, anyway."

His eyes were still closed. "You *should* stop it."

"No. Don't say that."

"I have to say it."

"No—"

"I have nothing, Evie. Nothing to give you."

Her fingers slid up, over his jaw to his wonderful mouth, which was so soft, in counterpoint to the rest of him that was so unyielding and strong. "Shh." She covered his lips with her fingertips. "You have everything. Everything that matters. Never, never say that you don't."

He captured her hand again then, his big fingers encompassing hers in strength and heat. And his eyes were open again, probing hers. "I don't understand this. I never thought I'd want to...trust anyone again in this way. It seems impossible, that this is happening. But then lately, since I met you, *nothing* is impossible."

He wrapped his free arm around her, unable to resist bringing her closer anymore. He pulled her to his body. She went, eagerly, hungering for just that, to be closer, to be touching him in one long caress.

A small sigh of pleasure escaped her. It was wonderful, to be pressed against him. She'd only been this close to him two other times—the day he carried her up the stairs, and Labor Day night, when they'd danced together under the stars. She looked up at him, waiting, yearning.

He said what she was thinking. "I want to kiss you, Evie."

"Yes," she said. "Oh, yes."

"But it will be stepping over the line completely, when I kiss you."

"Listen," she whispered. "Listen to what you just said. You said *when*, Erik—*when*, not *if*."

"*If* would be lying." His mouth was right above hers. She could feel the sweet warmth of his breath on her face.

"Yes. *If* would be lying," she solemnly repeated his words. "Let's not lie to each other, Erik. Not ever." She felt a twinge of guilt. She lied by omission. He didn't know all her secrets.

And he never would.

"No lies. Ever. It's a deal," he said.

She pushed the guilt away, down into the deepest part of her and she dared to ask, "Now, will you kiss me?"

"If I kiss you—"

"Shh," she chided. "No lies, remember? Not if. *When*."

"You're so beautiful."

"I'm glad you think so."

"You are. Almost...too beautiful to be real. Are you real, Evie?"

"I am. Oh, Erik. I am."

"I couldn't bear it, if you weren't. Sometimes I fear that. I think this is all a dream, that *you're* a dream. And I'll wake up. You won't be there."

"No, that will never happen. I'm in your arms, Erik. I'm here. And I'm real, so real—"

"I don't..."

"A kiss."

"We shouldn't—"

"Just kiss me," she pleaded, not caring if she sounded too bold.

His eyes seemed to burn down into the center of her, seeking something there—she wasn't sure exactly what. And then he muttered a low oath.

His arms tightened around her and at last—at last—his mouth met hers.

Chapter Eight

With a tender cry of pure exultation, Evie wrapped both arms around Erik's neck. She pulled him closer, tighter, as she surged up on tiptoe and pressed her mouth to his.

There was heat, heat passing between them, like a current through a wire. Evie sighed and the sound seemed to echo in her head. His lips moved on hers, coaxing.

Her mouth parted slightly and he touched her, beyond her lips, with his tongue.

Evie gasped, startled and aroused by such an intimate caress. His tongue went farther, tasting the moist inner surface of her mouth, while his arms tightened around her. Every inch of her body seemed to ache and yearn. Her skin felt hot, her breasts hard and full. His hand moved at the curve of her back as he molded her body to his. Evie knew enough about male physiology to comprehend that it was the evidence of a man's desire she could feel, pressing at her belly.

The sheer reality of that shocked her a little.

She stiffened.

Erik moaned. And then he went still.

His hard arms relaxed; they cradled her instead of crushing her close. He lifted his head and looked down at her.

And then he smiled.

Evie managed a dazed little grin in return.

He stepped back from her and dropped his hands away. "Take some time. Think about this."

She stared. He had to be kidding. How would she think of anything else?

"Take a few days. The rest of the week," he was saying. "I'll call you on Friday. You'll come to my house, for dinner. And then later, after the kids are in bed, we'll decide where we're going with this."

Evie managed a numb little nod before he turned on his heel, strode through the arch that led to her living room and let himself out the door.

Evie moved through the rest of the week in alternating states of bliss and apprehension.

On the one hand, she just knew that everything was going to work out fine. She and Erik had found each other at last. They would say as much to each other on Friday. And after that, they would never be parted. They would share the kind of love that her uncle had talked about—the true, lasting, committed kind. Evie would know what Oggie had called "God's greatest gift."

Yet at the same time, Evie was absolutely positive she and Erik were headed for disaster. Since she'd been twenty-two, and she and her sisters had gone their separate ways, Evie had lived alone. There was a good reason for that. She was not like other women. And she'd always feared what might happen, should she try to get too close to other people—or to become intimate with a man.

When she let down her guard, strange things occurred. Like they had that day, down in the shop.

And yet, since that day, everything had been normal. No visions. No objects flying off counters and crashing to the floor.

Evie couldn't help it. She was human, after all. She couldn't stop herself from hoping that she and Erik might share what she'd never dared to dream of before. That she might have the kind of life other women enjoyed: a family of her own and a good man to stand at her side.

"Evie, are you sick or something?" Becca asked on Thursday, when the girls came in for one of their after-school visits.

"No, honey. I'm fine."

"You don't seem so fine."

Jenny jumped in. "Becca's right. Lately you seem like something's bothering you."

"I have . . . a lot on my mind."

Becca and Jenny exchanged a glance, then Jenny said, "Dad told us you're coming over tomorrow night for dinner."

Evie's stomach tightened at the mention of the fateful day and time. She took a breath and let it out slowly. "Yes. Yes, I am."

"Dad's going to cook," Jenny said in a grim tone.

Evie looked from one child to the other. Had they figured out what was going on between their father and herself? She answered blandly, "Well, that will be great."

Becca wrinkled her button nose. "You never ate what our dad cooked, did you, Evie?"

"No, I haven't, not that I recall."

"I didn't think so."

The girls glanced at each other again.

"Is something the matter?" Evie delicately inquired.

Two angelic faces gazed up at her. "Uh-uh," they said in perfect unison.

Then Jenny announced that she was going to go over and straighten out the stationery section. "People are always putting the cards back in the wrong places," she said.

"I'll help," Becca volunteered.

Evie let them go, shaking her head, still unsure whether or not the girls sensed that something momentous was going on.

But then she shrugged. She was probably better off not knowing what the girls sensed at this point. She had enough on her mind without worrying about how the girls were going to take it all. There would be plenty of time to deal with the children later—if things worked out the way she prayed that they might.

The girls stayed until five, when Tawny called and asked Evie to send them on home. After they left, Evie closed up and mounted the stairs to her apartment.

The phone, which was the same number both in the shop and in the apartment, had started ringing just as she opened the door. Evie hurried to the kitchen extension and caught it on the second ring, "Wishbook. How may I help you?"

There was silence.

"Hello?" she said, a little more carefully than before.

Another beat, then at last the caller spoke.

"Hey there, Evangeline."

Evie knew the voice. It was the voice of her childhood, of her nightmares.

"Found you again," her father said.

A mug on the counter by the sink slid off and crashed to the floor. Evie shuddered at the sound.

"I'll always find you," her father went on. "But this time was a piece of cake, since you left Santa Fe with my own brother and he's lived in the same town for about a century."

A numbness seemed to claim her. It took her vocal chords first. She opened her mouth, then shut it, since it was clear to her that no sound would be coming out.

Her father didn't seem to be bothered by her silence. A low, dry chuckle came over the line. "I've known where you are for months now, and that's the truth of it. I've been bidin' my time, that's all. Givin' you an opportunity to really settle in before I called and let you know you haven't shaken your dear old dad yet." The chuckle came again. "'Course, I did drop my big brother a line a couple a months ago. Just a hint, you might say. Did he happen to mention that?"

Evie thought of the postcard with the poker-playing dogs on it as her knees started shaking. Slowly she sank to the straight chair against the wall by the phone.

"Evangeline?"

"Leave me alone." Evie didn't know where she'd found her voice. But she had *found* it. And it was surprisingly firm. "Leave me alone. Stay out of my life."

She heard a sigh on the other end.

She went on. "I'm not running away this time, Father. I'm through running. Do you understand?"

There was a beat, then he said, "Sure, I understand. And I think it's damn gutsy of you. Yes, indeed."

"I'm staying put. Here, in North Magdalene."

"Well, certainly." The voice dripped sarcasm. "Of course you are. How terrific. And convenient for me, too. I won't have to go wanderin' the western states tryin' to find out where you're off to now."

"Just leave me alone," she said once more.

"Now, now. You know I can't do that. Someday you're gonna wise up and change your mind. And then—"

"I haven't changed my mind in fifteen years, Father. You might as well accept the fact that I'm not *going* to change it. Ever."

"Now, now. Don't steal an old man's hope away."

"Give it up. I am serious."

"My, my, don't you sound determined?"

"I *am* determined. And if you call me again, I'll—"

"No need to make threats. I won't call you. We know where we stand now. Good night, Evangeline."

The line went dead. Evie sat for several seconds, unmoving, until the dial tone turned to an irritating beep. Then she reached up and hooked the headset on the cradle.

She remembered the shattered mug. Moving slowly, like a very old woman, she slid from the chair and knelt on the floor to gather up the larger pieces. Once she'd thrown those into the trash, she got out the broom and the dustpan and took care of the rest.

After the broken mug was completely disposed of, she had no idea what to do next. Her mind wasn't working too well, actually.

She dropped into the chair by the phone again and spent several minutes staring blindly at the floor.

Maybe she should call Oggie, tell him what had happened.

But what could her uncle do? Absolutely nothing. This was her problem. In the end, she'd have to be the one to deal with it.

And really, she didn't feel like calling anyone right now anyway. All she felt like was lying down.

Yes. She needed to lie down, that was what. To lie down and rest and think all this through.

With a weary sigh, Evie dragged herself to her feet and trudged to her bedroom where she stretched out, fully clothed, on the bed. She folded her hands on her stomach and closed her eyes.

Two hours later, when full dark had descended, Evie had come to two parallel conclusions.

One, she really wasn't going to run away this time. She would remain in North Magdalene, for better or for worse. And two, tomorrow night, if Erik made her dreams come true, if he said he wanted to share more with her than friendship, she was going to tell him about her past.

Oh, not everything, of course. Not the parts that no one would ever believe anyway. Just the facts. About Evangeline, who'd been only a girl, but who'd been known far and wide as a very special girl—a girl with certain unexplainable abilities. A girl who could find lost loved ones when no one else could. A girl who could soothe the most tormented of hearts—all for a price. A price set by her father, Gideon Jones.

She'd saved all the old newspaper clippings, even though she'd been tempted more than once just to toss them out. They were yellowed with age now, stored in a manila folder in a file cabinet downstairs. She'd take them with her tomorrow. Then, when she and Erik were alone—and *if* he said the things she kept praying he might say—she'd show them to him.

And after that, if he still wanted her, she'd say yes with all her heart.

They all sat down to eat not long after Evie arrived at Erik's the next evening. Evie looked from Becca to Jenny to Pete and wondered why they all looked so glum. Did they know that she and Erik planned to talk of the future tonight—a future that, of course, would have a major effect on all their lives? Were they unhappy about the possibility of having Evie and their father get together? Were they starting to resent her, fearing that she'd try to take their mother's place?

But then the food was passed and Evie understood.

It was awful. The roast was stringy and the peas had been boiled until they were a truly unappetizing shade of gray. The gravy resembled brown tapioca and the mashed potatoes had the consistency of large-curd cottage cheese. Becca, Jenny and Pete made faces with each bite they took. Evie realized that all the grim glances had been in anticipation of their father's cooking, that was all.

Twice, Evie opened her mouth to say how delicious it all was, but then she'd catch Becca staring at her as if daring her to say something good about the stuff. Evie said nothing. She simply couldn't tell that big a lie in front of an impressionable child.

For dessert, there was a cobbler that Erik was careful to announce Grandma Darla had made. Everyone had seconds on that.

Once the meal was through, Pete disappeared. Erik, Evie and the girls began to clear the table. Soon enough, Pete reappeared in the doorway to the kitchen with a toothbrush in one hand and a roll of clothing under the opposite arm.

"See you tomorrow," he said breezily, already turning for the front door.

"Back by noon," Erik called.

"You bet."

"Where's he going?" Jenny asked, when the front door had shut behind him.

"A sleep-over," Erik said. "At Mark's."

"Does Marnie get to go?"

"From what I understand, no," Erik said. "And I don't think she's very happy about it."

"'Cause she's a girl," Jenny said, with some satisfaction. "And girls don't get to have sleep-overs with boys."

"Something like that," Erik muttered. "Now clear off the rest of the stuff from the table please, so Evie and I can finish loading the dishwasher."

Jenny went eagerly to the task, a smug little smile on her freckled face.

When the dishes were taken care of, they all retired to the living room to watch *The Secret Garden,* which Erik had rented. The movie held both Becca and Jenny in thrall. It was about an orphaned girl who brought a dead garden to glorious flower, taught her tortured uncle how to love, showed her sickly cousin how to live—and learned to cry. Even Evie, who's mind was on other things, found herself caught up in the beauty and wonder of the tale after a while.

"That was a good story," Becca decreed once it was done.

And then Darla appeared at the front door. "All right. Special night. I want to take two little girls home with me."

Jenny's eyes lit up. "A sleep-over at your house, Grandma?"

"Yes."

Ten minutes later, Erik and Evie stood facing each other—alone—in the living room.

"They're gone," Erik said. "Lord, I love them. But it sure is heaven. This quiet. And you..."

"You planned this, didn't you?" she tenderly accused.

"What? That horrible dinner? The movie? Getting rid of the kids?"

"All of it."

"I did." He held out his hand. "Come with me. I want to show you something."

She thought of the large, sealed clasp envelope in which she'd put the yellowed clippings to carry them over here. It was under her purse on a table in the dining room, where she'd left it when she first entered the house.

"Evie?"

She put her hand in his, reveling as always in the absolute rightness of his touch. The envelope, she decided, could wait a little while.

Erik pulled her into the hallway and up the stairs, past the girls' rooms and Pete's room and even his own, to the closed door of the room that Becca had called his *special* room.

"This is my studio," he said, pausing with his hand on the knob.

"I know. The girls told me."

"They're not allowed in. A man needs one place to call just his own."

"I understand."

His eyes, always so warm and open to her of late, were suddenly impossible to read. He muttered "I hope you do," in a prayerful tone.

"Erik?" she whispered, unsure.

But he had already pushed the door open, reached in to flip on a light, and stepped back out of her way.

Evie blinked. It was the room of her vision—the room where she and Erik had been making love. But in her vision, it had been daytime. Light had flooded in through the windows. Now, after eight at night, those windows were dark.

"Please. Go in," Erik suggested, oddly formal now.

Evie moved across the threshold, aware of the easels, the paintings of woodland scenes and snow-capped peaks, of the worktable laden with paints and brushes and cleaning supplies. Even of the small couch beneath the windows—the couch of her vision, on which she and Erik had been making love.

It took her a moment to pick out the real reason Erik had brought her in here. But at last she saw it. A portrait on an easel in the corner to her right.

She approached it slowly, vaguely aware that Erik had followed her into the room.

"God," Erik murmured prayerfully behind her. "Don't hate it."

Evie glanced back at him, briefly—and that was when she saw all the sketches that were tacked to the drawing board beside her. Sketches of her own face. As the portrait was of her.

She looked at the painting again.

Behind her, Erik put his hands on her shoulders. She closed her eyes briefly, enjoying his touch. But then, once again, she was looking at herself—at herself as Erik saw her. Someone luminous, with shining eyes and a faint, barely there Mona Lisa smile.

"Say something." He squeezed her shoulders gently. "Please."

Evie smiled, and couldn't help wondering if her real smile was anywhere near as mysterious as the one on the glowing face in the painting. "You've made me much too beautiful."

Though he was behind her, she could feel the tension drain from him. "You don't hate it."

"No. I don't hate it."

His hands moved on her shoulders, massaging a little. "I *haven't* made you too beautiful. I've made you as I see you."

She dared to lean back just a fraction, enough that her head touched his chest. "Well, then, you're blind. And I'm flattered."

His body tightened again he gripped her shoulders and held her a little away. "I didn't intend it as flattery." His tone was gruff.

She turned in his arms and slid her hands around his neck. Oh, it was so wonderful. To be able to touch him so casually, as if he belonged to her. As if *she* were *his*.

His face was stern. "It's the way I see you, Evie. It's honest, to me."

"Erik. I was teasing you. I shouldn't have. I'm sorry. I love it."

"You do?" He searched her face.

She nodded, then tried to explain herself. "I . . . I'm just a little stunned, that you see me like that. But stunned in a good way, honestly. I didn't know what to say, so I tried to cover up my own awkwardness by teasing, that was all."

"Good. That's good." He searched her face some more, then explained, "I painted it this week. While I was making myself stay away from you."

"Oh, Erik..." She had no idea what she meant to say, so she let her voice fade off.

He didn't seem to mind that she couldn't complete her sentence. He sighed, then just stared at her. "I can't believe it. That you're here. That we're alone. That I don't have to leave—and neither do you."

She nodded, feeling exactly as he did.

He pulled her toward the couch beneath the dark windows. "Come here. Sit down. I have so much to say."

He pushed her down gently by the shoulders, then sat beside her and gathered both of her hands in his.

"Have you thought about this?" he asked. "About us?"

She swallowed and nodded. "It seems like I haven't thought about anything else."

"Me, too. It's been on my mind all the time, since Monday night when I left you. I know it's impossible, the two of us."

She didn't like the sound of that. "No, I—"

"Wait. Let me get through this. Then it'll be your turn, okay?"

She took in a breath. "Yes. Yes, all right. Go on."

"All right. Listen." He paused, looking toward the dark windows, collecting his thoughts. Then he met her eyes. "I've told myself all along that I've got to stay real with this. Besides having three kids to raise, I'm not out of the woods yet trying to pay off Carolyn's hospital bills. A woman like you shouldn't even be giving the time of day to a guy like me."

Evie wasn't going to sit there and let him run himself down. "That is not true."

He held her hands tighter. "Evie, wait. Don't get mad. I know you couldn't care less that I'm in the red up to my eyeballs."

"You'll pay your debts. I know you, Erik. That's the way you are."

"Fine." A rueful smile flitted across his features. "Go ahead. Believe in me."

"I do."

"I know. And I also know that I've been lying to you—and to myself—from the first."

She gulped. "You have?"

"Yeah."

"But what about?"

"About that stupid friendship thing."

She understood. "Oh. That friendship thing..."

"It was always a lie."

"Oh, Erik. It's all right. It was *my* lie as well."

"I've wanted more from the first."

"I know. Me, too."

"From that day at the end of August, when I first came to your store, everything's changed for me. Can you understand that?"

"Yes. Yes, I—"

"It's crazy. There's no logic to it. Carolyn's barely been gone a year and I've been . . . a mess, emotionally, after all that happened with her. She was mentally ill. I know that. In my mind, I do understand. But in my heart, I think I've always felt that she'd abandoned me. Left me alone with three kids to care for and a mountain of unpaid bills. I was sure it would take decades, till the kids were all grown, till I was an old man—hell, I guess, to be dead honest, I never thought I'd want to really *be* with a woman again.

"But then, there was you. And it was like some kind of miracle happened between us, that day in your shop. And nothing's been the same since then. Now, anything—*anything* seems possible to me, do you know that? My girls are smiling and the days are brighter. And I can't stop believing that together, we can make it all work out." He lifted the two hands held in his and kissed her knuckles, one by one.

"I want more than friendship." He looked right in her eyes again. "So much more. Even though I know damn well I shouldn't even dare to hope that there *could* be more. So just tell me. Tell me straight. Could you ever love a man like me?"

His lips were so close to hers, saying all the things she'd prayed he might say. Evie thought, fleetingly, of the envelope down in the dining room, of the secrets it contained that he had every right to know before this went one step farther.

"*Could* you, Evie?"

She couldn't stop herself; she nodded.

He exhaled then, as if he'd been holding his breath waiting for her answer. "Evie." His voice was a caress in itself. "I want you so." His eyes seemed to have the moon in them, as they had that night he walked her home after the first time she came here, when he told her how hard it was, to learn to dream again. "I want...to take you to my bedroom. To lay you down on the bed. Will you do that? Will you go with me?"

The envelope, a faraway voice in the back of her mind tried once more. She really should get the envelope....

"Evie. I'll go crazy if you don't answer. Tell me. Say you will."

"Erik, I..."

"Just yes or no. That's all you need to say."

"I..."

"Yes or no?"

For a moment more, she hovered there, poised on an invisible line between the truth he deserved and the passion in his eyes.

"Evie?"

The passion in his eyes won out.

"Yes," she said softly. "Yes, Erik. I'll go."

Chapter Nine

Apprehension laid claim to Evie within seconds after she murmured, "Yes." Yet she allowed herself to be pulled along when Erik took her by the hand and led her to the bedroom next door.

Once inside the room, he pulled her over to the bow window and left her there. The blinds were open. She tried to distract herself from the sudden hollow feeling in her stomach by staring out over the backyard and an open field. Off in the distance, silvered in moonglow, she could see the spire of the Community Church.

Behind her, Evie heard a small click, after which the room was just a little lighter. She turned and saw that Erik had flicked on a ginger jar lamp in a far corner, on one of the old maple bureaus.

She watched, her heart loud in her ears, as he came back to her. He cupped her face in his hands.

Their lips met.

The kiss was chaste. His tongue did not broach the soft barrier of her lips. Evie stood on tiptoe, pressing her mouth to his, wondering what in the world she was getting herself into, wondering if she could go through with this after all.

Oh, for a little of the self-possession that had been hers a few nights ago at her place. Then, she'd boldly strolled right up to him and begged for a kiss. She'd told him frankly that she knew nothing of men. And when he'd kissed her at last, she'd known real pleasure. Sensual pleasure. The kind they wrote about in books.

But the other night, they hadn't been standing in Erik's bedroom, not ten feet from his giant-size bed...

Erik lifted his head enough to look down at her. She saw the questions in his eyes. But instead of asking them, he gathered her close. Cupping her head with exquisite tenderness, he pressed her close to his heart.

After a moment, he whispered, "Is this too soon for you?"

She shook her head against his chest, not quite able to speak right then. She *did* want to do this. She truly did.

He stroked her hair. "You said you've never..."

She nodded tightly. "Yes. I don't...I mean I haven't..."

He pulled her closer. "Should I give you a few minutes? Would that help?"

Relief made her knees weak. Yes, that was just what she needed—escape, however fleeting. Time to regain a little composure. Her nerves felt like glass, so fragile, and on the brink of shattering into a thousand shards from outright panic. "Yes. A few minutes. That would be good."

He guided her chin up. It wasn't easy, but she made herself look right at him, she made herself smile.

"Have you changed your mind? You can tell me. It's okay."

She bit her lip and shook her head. "No. I want to," she managed to croak.

He put his hands on her shoulders and stepped back. "All right. A few minutes, then."

"Yes. Good. Thanks."

She shut her eyes, felt his hands fall away, heard the soft thud of his shoes retreating across the floor. The door to the bathroom closed with a snicking sound.

And Evie was alone.

She was also more frightened than before. In fact, she was absolutely terrified.

Maybe asking him to leave her alone hadn't been the right thing to do, after all. Maybe she should have forged on with it, flung herself forward, not allowed herself a moment, like this, to start thinking...

With a low groan, Evie dropped her head back, not opening her eyes. She wanted to whirl on her heel and run out of the room—down the stairs and right out the front door.

She was thirty-three years old, for heaven's sake. Much too old, as far as she was concerned, to be doing something like this for the very first time. Most women of thirty-three went into a bedroom with a man and knew what to expect. They didn't worry about things like how much it was going to hurt. And when and how to undress. Usually a woman her age had at least an *idea* of what they were in for.

Evie hadn't a clue.

And then there were the other things. The things even another thirty-three-year-old virgin wouldn't be worrying about. Like whether that ginger jar lamp over there was going to lift itself into the air and throw itself to the floor out of nowhere.

Or if she would *see* things. Things that had happened in the past. Or things that hadn't happened yet. Things no normal woman had any business seeing.

Because she wasn't a normal woman. And it was very, very likely that, before this night was through, Erik was going to find out just how normal she *wasn't*.

In the bathroom, Erik had turned on the water. She could hear it running.

He wasn't going to stay in there forever. She had to get a grip on herself. She had to either turn and run, as she longed to do.

Or...

Evie looked at the bed. Erik's bed.

And it was Erik in the bathroom. Erik. Not some stranger. Erik, who she trusted. Erik, who she...

The word came: loved.

Yes, she did. She loved him.

And that was the thing to remember. Her love. Whenever something—like what they were about to do together—seemed totally impossible, then she had to remember love. And that miracles were possible. Love was...more than a miracle, just in itself. And she loved Erik. And this thing they were about to do, this terrifying thing, well, it just had to be done, or she and Erik could go no farther.

In the bathroom, the water had stopped running.

Evie sucked in a deep breath and let it out slowly. Then, as quickly as she could, she began taking off her clothes.

It was no easy task. Her fingers felt like ten thumbs. She tried to get them to unbutton her blouse, but they wouldn't do it. So she yanked it from the waistband of her skirt and pulled it off over her head.

There was a padded seat in the bow window. She threw her blouse there. Then she shimmied out of her skirt and tossed it on top of the blouse. She got rid of her slip. When she couldn't work the clasp on her bra, she pulled it over her head as she'd done the blouse. Then all that was left were her panty hose, her panties and her spectator pumps. She tore the panty hose getting out of them, but the panties and pumps got away unscathed.

At last, there she was, standing in Erik's bedroom, as naked as a newborn. She ran for the bed, jerked back the covers and slid in. The sheets were cool. Shivering a little, she pulled the covers up beneath her chin and peered over the rim of the blankets.

For a moment, there was quiet—except for her own torn-sounding breathing, of course. She could see the light beneath the door in the bathroom. But Erik wasn't moving around in there. She wondered what he could be doing.

And then, with a sigh, she let her head drop back on the pillow and she looked at the high, molded ceiling overhead.

The door to the bathroom opened. Evie bit back an involuntary cry and lifted her head once more to peer, wide-eyed, over the hem of the blankets.

Erik stood silhouetted in the doorway to the bathroom. He'd taken off his shirt, socks and shoes, though he still wore his slacks. She could clearly see the bunching of his muscles where his shoulders met his neck, the powerful shape of his arms and the way his broad chest tapered down to his waist.

He turned off the bathroom light. Evie, who'd been staring wide-eyed, was blinded by the afterimage of his body, there, in the doorway. She blinked and knew he was walking across the room—she could hear the whisper of his footfalls—but all she could see were shifting, popping flashes of him in the doorway. He went to the bureau in the corner and turned off the ginger jar lamp. The fading afterimage of him leapt into brighter relief for a moment, now the room itself was darker.

She heard him coming toward her as he approached the bed.

"Evie. Sweetheart."

Sweetheart, she thought, bemused within her terror. He'd never called her *sweetheart* before.

He was standing by the bed now, on the other side.

She turned her head and blinked several times, trying to clear her sight.

"Evie, are you *sure?*"

She simply was not going to back out now. She reminded herself again that she loved this man. That love was a miracle and a miracle was going to happen here. Tonight.

She pressed her eyes closed and nodded.

Erik sighed. It was a resigned sort of sound.

Oh, this wasn't going well at all. And it had all begun so beautifully, too, back there in his studio. But then they'd come in here. And she'd frozen up. And now it seemed as if Erik might be just as unsure of the wisdom of this undertaking as she was. Evie turned her head away and looked out the window at the almost-full moon.

On the other side of the bed, she heard the rustle of clothing. And then there was a slight draft, as Erik lifted his side of the blankets. The bed gave beneath his weight. He stretched out, settled the covers around him.

And then there was stillness. Evie rolled onto her back and lay looking up at the molded ceiling once more as the last of the afterimages finally faded away. She could feel Erik, a foot or two away, though not touching her. She just couldn't make herself turn her head and look at him.

Gradually his body heat came creeping to her, banishing the coolness from when he'd pulled the covers back.

"Evie, do you know—" his voice, so calm and mild and out of nowhere, startled her a little "—that two people could sleep in this bed all night and never have to touch each other once?"

Was he being sarcastic? She shot him a quick glance. He wasn't looking at her. He was lying on his back, as she was, and he had one big arm thrown across his eyes.

His tone, she decided, really had been offhand. If the comment had been intended to point out her distance from him, he didn't seem to be all that bothered about it.

She said, "It's a very big bed," knowing how silly and self-evident the remark was, but not really caring. The important thing right now was to relax, to share a little conversation, no matter how utterly inane.

He seemed to think so, too. Or at least, he played along. "Yeah. When I was a kid, that was a major fantasy of mine."

She knew what to say next. "What?"

"To have a bed like this."

"Really?"

"Uh-huh." He sighed and shifted his legs, settling in.

Evie realized it was her turn to talk again. She asked, "You mean because you were such a big kid?"

"Yep. From the time I was about twelve and I hit five-ten or so, my feet were always hanging off the end of the single bed that my parents had bought for me after I outgrew my crib. I felt like I was sleeping on a postage stamp. But my folks never had a lot of money. And there were three other kids besides me—four, including Tawny, who came along when I was fifteen. There was no way I was going to get a king-size bed while I was living at home. Even if they could have afforded it, there wasn't *room* for one. You know what I'm saying?"

"Yes," Evie replied. He certainly did sound relaxed as he chatted about his love of large beds. She darted another swift glance his way. He was still facing the ceiling and his left arm still covered his eyes.

He continued, "I didn't get a king-size bed until I was married. This is the second one I've bought. I gave up a lot of things, to try to pay all the bills. But not this bed."

There was a silence. Evie realized it was once again her turn to contribute to the conversation. "Well. It's a very nice bed."

"Thank you."

"You're welcome."

The topic of large beds appeared to have exhausted itself. Evie cast about for something new to say.

But then she felt movement, between them, in the middle of the bed, down near her left hip. She realized his free hand was down there, under the covers. She stayed very still, longing for him to touch her at the same time as she *feared* that he would.

But he didn't touch her.

The seconds ticked by.

And then carefully, she reached out. She found his hand.

Erik remained, as before, absolutely still. Evie inched her fingers over his palm and entwined them with his. He gave her a squeeze.

She realized she did feel better; she *was* more relaxed. She rolled her head to look at him and didn't look away this time, "Erik?"

Slowly, he brought his arm down. He turned his head toward her and smiled. "Umm?"

The moonlight from the window behind her silvered his face. He looked so...very much a man. And good. A good man. His eyes were the gentlest eyes.

"Maybe," she dared to whisper, "*you've* changed *your* mind. About this."

Down under the covers, his hand squeezed hers once more. "Never in a thousand years."

"Oh." She looked away, then back. "I'm glad."

He was quiet for a moment, looking at her, perhaps seeking something in her face, which he couldn't possibly see too well with the window behind her as it was.

At last, he asked, "Which side do you sleep on?"

"Huh?"

"Do you sleep on your left side or your right? Or on your back? Your stomach?"

She pictured herself as she usually slept, turned on her side in her own bed. "Umm. My right side."

He pulled his hand from her grasp. "Okay, then. Turn over. On your right side."

"But..."

"Go on."

"But I thought you—"

"Evie." He actually chuckled. "Give it time. What's supposed to happen will happen. Have a little faith, for heaven's sake."

"You... you want me to go to sleep. Here? Now?"

He nodded. "Exactly. Here and now."

"But I—"

"You said the other night that you trust me."

Eager for him to understand, she rolled onto her left side, facing him. "I do. Oh, I do."

"Then turn over and go to sleep and we'll leave the rest for another time."

She levered up a little, not really realizing that she was losing her self-consciousness until the covers fell away and she had to catch them from sliding too low and revealing her bare breasts. "Oh!" She clutched the covers to her chest.

"There." She looked at Erik once more and told him tartly, "I think we should get it over with first, before we try to sleep, I really do."

He laughed aloud then, tossing his big head on the white pillow. "Get it *over* with?"

She found she was irritated with him, very irritated indeed. She scooted right up against him and glared down into his eyes. "This is no laughing matter, Erik Riggins."

And then she remembered the situation here—they were both completely naked. And right at this moment, her soft breasts were pressed against his bare chest.

Her fear surged to the forefront again. She froze. "I...umm..."

He closed his eyes and let out a sort of strangled groan. "Don't worry, Evie. I'm not laughing now."

She started to retreat to her side of the bed. But then she didn't do that after all. Because she realized that it felt...rather good, actually, to be lying across him this way. She felt...very soft. And he felt very hard. There was hair on his chest, silky hair, she could feel that, against her breasts. Her nipples were responding, tightening into firm little buds.

She cleared her throat. "As I was saying..."

"Right." His voice came out rough, and growly sounding. "You think we should get this over with."

"Yes, I do. I'm never going to be able to sleep, until it's all behind us." She moved, just a little, creating a lovely friction.

A look of mild agony flitted over his face. And then he relaxed. He breathed in and out. She bobbed up and down on his chest like a rowboat on a wind-stirred pond.

"Okay." Now he was actually smiling—a smile that was far too smug, as far as Evie was concerned. "Convince me."

"Convince you?"

"Yeah."

"How am I supposed to do that?"

He shrugged, one sculpted shoulder lifting against the sheet. "You could start with a kiss, I suppose."

She realized then what was going on, so she narrowed her eyes at him and tried to sound stern. "Am I being seduced?"

He shrugged once more. "Could be. Am *I*?"

And then everything was serious again. But in a wonderful way.

"Oh, Erik."

"Come on, Evie. Kiss me."

Her fear was still with her, but it no longer controlled her. She had all her clothes off, so the undressing part was behind her. And if the lamp in the corner was going to fling itself to the floor a few minutes from now, well, she'd deal with that when the time came.

Erik whispered, "Concentrate on the way it feels, Evie. On you and me. Touching."

It was great advice. All her thoughts focused on the wonderful way her body felt, resting on top of his, she lowered her mouth.

Their lips touched, and parted. She felt his tongue, seeking, tasting. Shyly she allowed her tongue to touch his. It felt wonderful. His tongue teased hers. And she teased back.

Evie sighed, and settled herself more comfortably on Erik's chest as the kiss stretched out for the most delightfully long time.

At last, when she felt she knew his mouth almost as well as she knew her own, she raised her head. They shared a smile.

He laid a hand against her cheek. "It's been a long time for me, Evie. I'm probably not going to be able to go slow after a certain point." His fingers slid back a little, into her hair. He touched her ear, rubbing it lightly between his thumb and forefinger, making something deep inside her seem to open and yearn. "What I'm saying is, if you want to stop this, let's stop it now, all right?"

She swallowed. "I don't want to stop."

His hand moved a little, downward, over her throat. It felt rough against her soft skin, rough and warm and good.

"Like something impossible, the feel of you." His voice had gone all husky. "Like silk and water at the same time..." The words were so low, she would never have heard them had her lips and his not been mere inches apart.

His hand moved lower, he pushed at the blankets. "Let me see you, Evie. In the moonlight, all silvery and smooth. Let me look at you."

The fear resurfaced—a bitterness at the back of her throat. "I..."

But his eyes were so tender, so full of the moon.

"All right," she heard herself whisper. She retreated to her side of the bed and stretched out, beside him. For a moment they lay there, side by side.

And then he rolled closer and levered up on an elbow, so he could lean over her. He took the blanket in his hand and slowly pulled it back.

Evie closed her eyes.

Erik sighed. "Beautiful."

She shivered.

"Are you cold?"

With her eyes still closed, she murmured shyly, "You could make me warm." She held up her arms.

But instead of going into them, he spoke. "Open your eyes. Please look at me."

Evie let her arms fall back to the bed and did as he asked. He smiled. Tremulously she smiled back.

He reached across her body and touched the center of her palm. Her fingers tensed, closing around his finger briefly, but then she ordered them to relax.

For a moment, his finger lingered there, tracing a circle in the heart of her hand. Then slowly, his touch trailed up, over the fleshy pad at the base of her thumb, skimming the pulse at her wrist, the pale inside of her arm and the blue veins of her inner elbow. He rubbed her shoulder, a tender massage, then traced the shape of her collarbone.

And then his hand, rough and tender, moved downward again. He touched her nipple. She gasped.

He cupped her breast.

Evie stiffened, then relaxed. His hand held her breast so lightly. And actually, she realized, she wouldn't mind if he held it tighter.

She lifted herself, into his touch. He made a low noise in his throat and picked up her cue, leaning closer to her as he cupped and molded her breast, which seemed to have grown so firm and full of want in his hand. He lowered his head and kissed her other breast, taking the nipple into his mouth.

Evie cried out as he suckled her. She pulled him close and cradled his head and felt the way her own body responded—as if a tiny thread trailed down from the nipple he sucked into the very core of her.

And then his hand was gliding downward once more, over her ribs and the tender flesh of her quivering belly.

Evie stiffened again, as he found her most secret place. He combed through the silky hair with questing fingers and parted her.

Lightly, gently, he stroked her. And soon her body had gone all pliant and hungry again. It was lifting, opening, offering itself.

She felt her own wetness, there, where he did such forbidden and wonderful things to her. And something was gathering inside her, readying her for something—an explosion, a completion—something that she didn't quite know how to find.

His mouth left her breast. She moaned and writhed. He moved down her body.

And he put his mouth there. Where his hand had been. She was so shocked at first that she let out a startled, frightened cry. She froze absolutely still.

But then he made a sound, a hungry, pleading sound. And she was liquid again, open to him. She was . . . part of him. So that she could hardly tell where he stopped and she began.

Her body went with him, where he was begging her with his lips and his tongue to go.

She cried out, and the whole world was quivering, shimmering, breaking apart. And through it all, though she bucked and writhed and pushed at him, Erik kept kissing her there, urging her on.

At last, the wonder faded. Evie lay limp upon the sheets.

Erik moved quickly then, rising and getting something out of the drawer by the bed, putting it on himself.

She looked at him, dazed.

He said, "My eyes, Evie. Just look in my eyes for now."

At that moment, she would have gladly followed him over a cliff. She did as he told her. She looked in his eyes. And he came down upon her.

Even as moist and open as she was, it was a shock to her body, to take him in. But she followed his urging, she kept her eyes locked with his. And she did take him, all of him.

He had braced himself above her on his arms and he muttered her name, low and hungrily. He was shaking, trying to hold back, trying not to hurt her.

But then it was too much for him. His own need claimed him. His eyes rolled back and he groaned deep in his throat. She clutched him, pulling him down, opening herself around him as far as her inexperienced body would allow.

He moved faster then, lost in an ecstasy all his own. And Evie surrendered to it, let herself relax completely. She found it felt better then. It felt fine. It felt... rather delicious, actually. She moaned and wrapped her legs around him, her body taking its cues from him now.

But he was far gone, lost in his own need. He let out a long final groan and stiffened in completion before she could find her own way to fulfillment again. But it didn't matter, not really. The next time, she had no doubt, they would find heaven as one.

His body went limp on top of her. Evie cradled him close. They were both panting and wet with sweat.

Evie lay there, crushed beneath his considerable weight and not minding at all. So sated and dazed was she that it took a few moments for the truth to really sink in.

She had done it.

After all these years, she'd finally made love.

And all that had happened was what was *supposed* to happen. None of her worst fears had come to pass.

Evie turned her head to peer into the shadows across the room. She could make out the rounded base of the ginger jar lamp, on the bureau in exactly the spot it had occupied before. As far as she could tell, no object in the room had so much as shifted—let alone flung itself to the floor.

She hadn't seen a single vision—beyond the welcome sight of Erik, rising above her, telling her to look into his eyes.

It had been all right.

Much more than all right, actually.

It had been beautiful.

Erik rolled to the side, taking her with him, so their bodies didn't part. He stroked her hip, idly, possessively, while the arm that was beneath her pillowed her head.

Evie heard a purring sound of womanly satisfaction and realized it was coming from her own throat. She let her hand trail over the powerful bulge of his shoulder and reveled once more in the feel of him.

There simply were not enough superlatives to describe how she felt. It was... a revelation to her, this earthbound magic that was somehow all the more incredible because it was magic meant for two.

And beyond that, she had a sneaking suspicion that in the future, as they grew more comfortable with each other, more *accustomed* to pleasing each other, it would get even better.

Everything, Evie realized as she went on caressing him, would be all right now. Her doubts were dust. With Erik, all things were possible.

Oh, in all her lonely life she'd never felt this way before. Something was rising inside her, as effervescent as fine champagne, and yet as warm and comfortable as an old pair of slippers.

It was joy.

And a hardy kind of joy, too. A joy that could survive anything.

Nothing could kill a joy like this. Not her father. Not the old, ugly truths that she had yet to share with Erik. None of that could touch what she was feeling right now.

Yes, it was all right. She *could* have it all.

And soon, very soon, she would tell Erik of the past.

She should have done it earlier, of course. But that hadn't worked out. And it didn't matter, not really. Because she would take care of it soon.

Not right now, though. No. Right now was simply too perfect a moment to ruin with unpleasant truths.

Erik stroked her sweat-damp hair away from her temple. "Evie."

"Hmm?"

"Evie, listen."

She felt . . . liberated. She felt fully, completely free. She nuzzled his chin, and even dared to taste it with the tip of her tongue.

"Evie. Don't distract me."

She nipped at his Adam's apple. "Umm. You taste so good."

"Listen. I mean it."

"I am listening. Honest. Go ahead."

"Evie, I love you."

Now, *that* was exquisite to hear. She kissed the pulse at the base of his neck. "I love you, too."

"Evie, this is important."

Against her lips, his skin was so warm. She could feel that pulse, beating, tender and vulnerable, like the wings of a moth. It excited her, to think that his lifeblood flowed there, rich and red, carrying nourishment to every part of his big, powerful body.

He gripped her shoulders. "Will you marry me?"

She purred again, deep in her throat, as she went on nuzzling his neck.

"Evie." He pulled back then, and their bodies parted.

A little whine of disappointment escaped her. And then she looked down and saw a few drops of blood on the sheet. She also saw that most private part of him. Right now, it didn't look quite so large as it had felt a short while ago. It was sheathed in what she knew must be a condom.

She remembered him, opening the bedside drawer, pulling the thing on—and commanding her to look in his eyes.

She was moved at how carefully he must have planned all this—and how understanding and patient he'd been throughout.

"Oh, Erik..."

"What?" That gruffness was there in his voice once more.

"You... protected me."

He caught her chin and made her look at him. Then he brushed a strand of hair back from where it had been caught in the corner of her mouth. "I went to Grass Valley yesterday and bought the damn things when I bought the groceries for tonight. Just in case my dream came true." The brushing touch had turned to a caress. He rubbed his rough thumb against the curve of her cheek and then lower, across her lips.

She caught his wrist in her hand, so that she could kiss the thumb that teased her lips. He groaned.

She whispered, "And did your dream come true?"

"Almost."

The joy was bubbling up inside her again. She just felt so wonderful. She couldn't resist teasing him. "Almost? What's missing?"

"You haven't said you'll marry me. It's what I want Evie, more than I've ever wanted anything else in my life. Maybe I don't have any right to want it. But I do."

"I'm glad."

"Then answer me. Will you marry me?"

Evie knew she should answer then, that it would be cruel to string this out one second longer. But she wanted to touch him. She let go of his wrist and hooked her hand around his nape, bringing her mouth right up to his. "I want to kiss you. I want to kiss you all over..."

He grabbed her shoulder, holding her still, so their lips couldn't meet until she gave him the answer he sought.

"Answer me, Evie. I can't take any more teasing. Will you marry me or not?"

Evie sighed—and then she smiled. "Of course I'll marry you. Name the day."

They talked half the night, of when they'd marry and when they'd tell the children and how they'd combine their two households into one. They decided the ceremony would be in this very house in two weeks' time and they'd tell the children tomorrow night, after a dinner that Evie would cook for them all.

Then, to celebrate, they reached for each other once more. This time, as Evie had known they would, they reached fulfillment together. Then they drifted off to dreamland, wrapped tightly in each other's arms.

When daylight came, Evie was eager to be gone before the children returned and started asking uncomfortable questions about why Evie was still here.

She could just see Jenny in her mind's eye. "Evie," Jenny would scold, "you know that girls don't get to have sleepovers with boys..."

But Erik only laughed when she said she had to get out of there.

"Relax, sweetheart. The kids aren't due home until noon at the earliest."

"Are you sure?"

"Trust me. It's handled."

So they made love again, showered shamelessly together and then shared a simple breakfast that Evie prepared from what Erik had on hand. And then, since ten o'clock was approaching and Evie had to open the shop, it was time for her to go.

But of course, since they were lovers, the goodbyes just never seemed to end. At quarter of ten, they were still standing at the front door, whispering of all the things they needed to remember to do, and kissing in between the words.

Evie held her purse and the unopened envelope of clippings in one hand and, in the midst of a kiss, the envelope happened to brush against Erik's leg.

"What's that?" he asked tenderly.

Her stomach knotted. A while ago, with Erik standing right beside her, she'd scooped up her purse and the envelope from the side table in the dining room. Then they'd walked, side by side, to the door, without him saying a word about it. She'd actually started to believe he hadn't even noticed she had it in her hand.

But no such luck.

She stalled for time, keeping her expression relaxed and planting another in a long string of kisses on his chin. "Umm? What?"

He tapped the envelope with a finger. "That." He kissed her nose.

Tell him, tell him right now, her conscience prodded.

But then Erik *really* kissed her—a long, knee-melting, heart-bonging kiss. When he pulled back, she was glad she had her free hand on the doorknob to steady herself.

He was grinning. "So? What is it?"

"What?"

"Are we talking in circles here?"

"You mean this envelope?"

"Yes. That envelope."

"It's..." The moment of indecision lasted for less than a heartbeat. And then she lied, "...Only some mail I picked up on the way over last night."

Since Erik trusted her, it never occurred to him not to believe her. "Ah," he said, and kissed her again. This time, she let go of the door handle and held on to him.

And then, dazed with desire, she was out the door, on her way back to the shop. The kiss had been so consuming, that she didn't start feeling guilty about her lie until she was turning the Open sign around twenty minutes later.

Guilt dogged her all through that day.

And for the next few days after that, she kept planning how she'd tell him everything. But there were a thousand things to do—helping the kids to adjust to the idea of having Evie for a stepmother, putting the small wedding together, beginning to plan the kind of life she and Erik would share. And whenever they were together, there was so much to talk about, things like getting blood tests and the license. They even spoke of contraception. They decided that they'd wait awhile before they had more children and that Evie would go on the pill.

And somehow, as the days went by, it began to seem wiser to her to just let the past go. She truly was Evie Jones now. And soon she would be Evie Riggins. Evangeline was no more.

Sometime in the future, of course, she'd tell Erik the whole sad story. But every time she allowed herself to think about exactly *when* she'd tell him, that time seemed to move a little further away.

On the day before her wedding, when Uncle Oggie dropped by for a visit, she told him of how she'd tried and failed to tell Erik about her past. Then she gave Oggie the envelope with all the old clippings in it.

"For safekeeping," she said. "Until the day I get up the nerve to explain it all to him."

Oggie tried to tell her she ought to trust her heart—and her love—enough to tell Erik now. But she waved away his advice.

"Just keep it for me, Uncle Oggie, won't you please?"

Shaking his head, he agreed to do as she asked.

Chapter Ten

On the third Saturday in October, Evie stood before the mirror that hung on the closet door in Erik's bedroom. She was dressed all in white.

Her sisters flanked her on either side. Faith had arrived a few hours before from Sausalito. Nevada, who'd flown from Phoenix to Sacramento and rented a car to drive the rest of the way, had just walked in the door.

The ceremony was minutes away. Downstairs in Erik's living room, a small group of guests sipped champagne and anticipated the appearance of the bride. Evie could hear Regina's piano, wheeled over from next door for the occasion. Regina was playing "Chances Are."

"You are the beauty of the family, no doubt about it," Nevada declared as she admired the simple sheath of floor-length silk that Evie had chosen for this special day.

"Yes," Faith's softer voice chimed in. She made a tiny adjustment to the Juliet cap of satin and pearls that adorned

Evie's sleekly pinned-up hair, then stood back a little to admire the effect. "You look...like a bride."

The sisters laughed at that, then fell silent as a gust of wind flung a sheet of rain against the panes of the bow window behind them.

Nevada turned briefly toward the window and remarked with some irony, "Beautiful day for a wedding."

"Sorry." Evie pretended to look rueful. "I put in an order for sunshine. But God must have thought we needed rain more."

Faith suggested in that soothing voice of hers, "Does it matter, really?"

Evie slowly smiled. "Uh-uh. It doesn't. Not one teeny bit."

Nevada was grinning, too—and shaking her curly head, the thin gold hoops in her ears swinging and glinting with the movement. "I don't believe it's really happening. One of us is getting hitched."

Faith made a gentle noise of agreement. "Yes. If one of *us* can marry, I suppose anything is possible."

They were silent again. Evie knew her sisters' thoughts echoed her own. Each remembered their self-absorbed, heedlessly cruel father, who had never once put his daughters' needs before his own.

Evie shook herself. Today of all days, she refused to dwell on old hurts. She looked at her wrist, wondering if it was time to go down, and saw only the silk point of her sleeve since she'd taken off her watch when she put on her wedding gown.

Faith read her movements and glanced at her own watch. "One thirty-two. Almost a half an hour to go."

"Can you sit in that dress?" Nevada wanted to know.

"Sure."

The three sisters went together to the side of the big bed nearest the bow window—the side that Evie had already come to think of as hers, though she hadn't actually slept in it since that fateful night two weeks before. They sat down in a row, with Evie in the center.

Once comfortable, they looked out the window at the blustery, wet day. Down in Ebert's Field, a few saplings, bare of leaves now, bowed to the force of the wind.

"I met your...fiancé—" Nevada stumbled over the word just a little, "—before I came upstairs. A total hunk. In a blue-collar sort of way."

Evie wrinkled up her nose. "Thanks. I think."

Nevada gave her youngest sister a teasing nudge with her elbow. "Is this like...true love?"

Evie turned from the storm outside to face her sister. She knew that her expression said it all. "Yes. It is."

Nevada studied Evie's face. After a moment, she murmured, "Wow. I believe you."

"Of course you do. Because I'm telling the truth. This is real love, true love, the *best* love anyone has ever known."

Nevada put up a hand and the thin gold bangles on her wrist tinkled like tiny chimes. "I said I believe you." A teasing light came into her big brown eyes. "But what about this town? Do you still adore the place?"

"To me, it's the home we always used to dream of in the rough times, back when we were kids."

"Ahh," Nevada said. There was no need to say more. Evie read Nevada's look, then glanced at Faith and knew that they all three shared the same thoughts.

For a suspended moment, they were thrown back in time to the earliest years, when they used to wander from town to town. When there never seemed to be enough to eat and at bedtime they all slept piled up together in the back seat of a decade-old Buick—or, if it was a lucky night, in some run-down motel.

Evie caught herself. She was letting her thoughts get away from her again.

She turned her mind to a brighter subject. "Have you met Uncle Oggie?"

Faith spoke. "I have. He's quite a character. He looks a lot like Father, only with mischief in his eyes instead of meanness." As soon as the words were out, Faith seemed to regret them. She looked down at her pale, slim hands, which were folded in her lap.

But Nevada was squaring her shoulders. "Wait a minute. Don't be glum. It's no crime to mention dear old Dad. He's behind us forever, right?"

Now Evie was the one looking down at her hands. Today was the most wonderful day of her life. She really didn't want to think of their father, and she certainly didn't want to talk about him. "Actually, I would prefer just to forget about Gideon for today."

"Of course," Faith agreed, raising a slim arm to smooth back her tidy brown hair. "Whatever you say. It's your wedding day."

But Nevada wasn't so easily silenced. "Evie. He *is* behind us all, isn't he? You've been safe from him, since you moved here. Right?" When Evie didn't look up, Nevada groaned. "Something's happened. Tell us."

"No. Please." Evie's voice was very small. She despised the weak sound of it. "I'm getting married today. I don't want to talk about all that."

"What happened? Tell. Let us help."

Evie looked from Nevada to Faith, hoping to get some support from the younger of her two sisters. "There's really nothing you can do about it."

Faith frowned. "About what?"

Evie knew she was outnumbered now. She sighed.

Nevada gripped her arm. "*What* happened? Tell us."

Evie looked out the window once more, at the driving rain and the dark, heavy clouds. She admitted, "All right. Father sent Uncle Oggie a postcard a few months ago."

"What did it say?"

"Nothing and everything. It was vague. He didn't even mention me. It was just kind of a 'hello, how've you been all these years?' type of thing. But the intent was obvious. To let me know that *he* knew where I was."

Nevada looked doubtful. "And that's all?"

"No."

"Come on, Evie. What else?"

"A couple of weeks ago..."

"Yes?"

"He called me."

"He *what?*"

"He called me."

"You mean, he called you at *home?*"

"Yes."

"You're saying that he knows for sure that you live here?"

"Yes."

Nevada let out a cry, then grabbed Evie by the shoulders and pulled her close, heedless of the delicate wedding gown. "Oh, honey. I love you."

Behind Evie, Faith made a sound of agreement and patted Evie's back.

Then Nevada straightened her arms and looked into Evie's eyes. "I can't believe it. This is terrific."

Evie frowned at her sister. "It doesn't seem very terrific to me."

"Come on, honey. Think about it. He *called* you. There's no doubt that he knows where you are. And yet you stayed put. You didn't pack up and run. This is progress. This is one giant step forward for Evie Jones.''

Evie felt herself blushing. She *had* made progress and she knew that she had. And it was nice to hear her sister's praise. ''You think so?''

''Absolutely. I'll bet it's that fella of yours. I'll bet that with him in your corner, ready to back you up if there's ever any trouble, you feel safe at last.''

Guilt washed over Evie at those words. Nevada was right, Evie did feel safer than she'd ever felt before. And perhaps she even subconsciously trusted Erik to come to her aid no matter what. However, the secrets of her past still lay untold between them.

Nervously Evie smoothed the folds of her gown over her knees.

Faith immediately sensed her distress and ascertained the cause of it. ''He doesn't know about Father. That's it, isn't it? Erik doesn't know.''

Evie smoothed her gown some more, then muttered, ''That's right. And he's not going to know. Not for a while, at least, not until we've... had some time together, not until I can be sure he'll understand.''

''But, honey—'' Nevada began.

Evie didn't want to hear. ''No. Don't lecture me. It's my decision. I don't want him to have to know right yet.''

Even gentle Faith had to disagree. ''But what if he found out somehow, and you hadn't told him first?''

Evie's stomach lurched at that thought. It was one she'd been doing her best to avoid pondering. She drew her shoulders up. ''No one's going to tell him. Uncle Oggie's the only one in town who knows, and he's sworn never to say a word. And as I said, I *will* tell Erik. Just not right away, that's all.''

"What if some reporter shows up asking questions again?" Nevada asked.

"I'll deal with it if it happens."

Faith had another point to make. "What if...Father shows up?"

"He won't," Evie said through clenched teeth, willing her words to be true. "He said on the phone that he wouldn't call me anymore."

"Since when has Gideon Jones ever done what he said he'd do?" Nevada demanded. As if nature itself agreed with her, another powerful gust of wind beat at the house, and rain sluiced against the windowpanes.

"I am not telling Erik all those shameful old stories right now," Evie said, when the wind had faded to a low, sad whine. "Erik and I need time now, with each other and the children, time to make a family together, time to settle into our life as a couple."

Nevada groaned. "But, Evie. You can't just bury your head in the sand about this. Gideon is..." She groped for the word and when she couldn't quite find it, settled on, "...A problem. He's gone downhill over the years. You know that. And the way he's stayed so obsessed with you, it's not good."

Evie put up a hand. "Look. He's never really done anything, not in all these years. Once I was grown-up, he had no real power over me, I've realized that at last. For a long time, instead of staying put and dealing with him, I ran every time he found out where I was. Well, I'm not running again. I'm a grown woman and I've made my own life. And if Father ever dares to show up here in North Magdalene—"

Nevada stopped her. "Exactly. That's the point. If he shows up here, what in the world will you do?"

Evie gulped. "I'll... I'll tell Erik about him then. And we'll take it from there."

"This isn't wise, Evie."

But Evie wouldn't listen to that. She sat tall and looked from one sister to the other. "I love you both. And I know that you saved my life all those years ago."

"Oh, stop it," Nevada scoffed. "*You* saved *us*, before that. You saved us from a living hell. And we know it. We were vagrants, that's what we were, until Dad discovered your... talents and started making use of them. After that, because of you, none of us ever went to bed hungry again."

Evie patiently waited until Nevada was through, then she picked up where she'd left off. "It was all a scam. It was dishonest in the worst kind of way, to make a living off of people's heartbreak like that."

"No." Faith was adamant. "Sometimes you did help people, we all know that you did."

"Only if it was profitable." Evie shot back the words, and then realized that if she went any farther, she'd have to go into the part they never talked about, the things Evie sometimes knew that no normal person could know, the way she could sometimes touch a person and seem to soothe all their ills. She returned to the relative safety of her original point. "Look. What I'm saying is, when the time finally came that I couldn't go on with it anymore, you two took me away. And you loved me and protected me and showed me how to live in the world on my own. I owe you my life."

Nevada tried to interrupt. "No, you—"

Evie cut in, reiterating, "I owe you my life. And now, well, I'm going to ask for even more."

"Evie..."

"Wait. Let me finish. I want one more thing from each of you."

Nevada looked grim, but still she said, "Name it."

"I want your word that you won't tell anyone in North Magdalene who I used to be. I want you to promise me you'll say nothing about Evangeline."

"Oh, Evie..." Faith murmured sadly.

Nevada just shook her head, the gold hoops in her ears gently swinging.

"Please," Evie whispered.

After a moment, Nevada spoke for both of them. "It's your life. We know that. It'll be the way you want it to be."

Evie breathed deeply then. Gratitude and fierce love seemed to wash over her in one giant wave. She groped blindly with both hands, and found her sisters' hands, one on each side. "Thank you. I love you. Thank you so much...."

There was a discreet knock at the door.

Evie squeezed both of the hands she held. "Come in."

The door swung inward. Amy, hugely pregnant and glowing with excitement, stood on the threshold. "Evie. It's time."

"All right."

The three sisters stood as one, hands still linked.

"We'll go on down," Faith said.

One more squeeze and Evie's hands were empty. Her sisters moved toward Amy at the door.

"I've saved you a couple of chairs," Amy told them.

Nevada murmured, "Thanks."

Amy ushered the other two out, then turned back to Evie at the last minute. "I just have to tell you. Do you know who's out there?"

"Uh-uh. Who?"

"Nellie."

"No kidding?" Evie had made it a point to invite Nellie, but she hadn't ever imagined she'd come.

Amy went on. "She walked in five minutes ago. Stunned everyone. If the wind hadn't been howling so loud outside, you could have heard a pin drop. I thought you'd want to know."

"Yes. I'm glad to hear it. Thanks."

"And now I'll get out of here. Shall I close the door?"

"If you would. I'd like a moment."

"By the way, you look beautiful."

"Thanks," Evie said again.

Amy tiptoed out. And then Evie was alone. She breathed deeply, seeking inner peace and true composure, putting away all the old fears, calling up her joy.

Once her mind was entirely focused on what really mattered, Evie went to the bureau in the corner to collect the bouquet of white roses waiting there. Then she left the room and approached the stairs, the sweet music from Regina's piano growing louder in her ears. Evie smiled as she recognized the melody; it was the country and western ballad the band had been playing on Labor Day, when she and Erik had shared their first dance.

As she descended the stairs, Evie made herself walk slowly. She didn't want to rush. This moment and the ones soon to follow were each and every one a miracle to her. They were moments to be savored.

She was marrying Erik. The impossible had come to pass. She was becoming what she'd never dared to dream she might be: a wife. And a stepmother. A woman with a family, a woman with . . . responsibilities for others whom she loved. A *normal* woman, one who truly *belonged* in the most important of ways.

Her joyful thoughts filling every corner of her mind, Evie traversed the hall that led to the dining room. And then, before she knew it, she stood in the wide arch that framed the living room.

Her eyes took in every aspect of the gathering before her. For today, the living room furniture had been moved out of the house, stored in the trailer of Brendan Jones's big rig. Folding chairs, arranged in rows, took up most of the space. Every chair was occupied. An aisle had been left down the middle. It led through the room on a diagonal to the far corner, where Erik and Reverend Johnson stood waiting. Pete—the combination best man and ring bearer—stood on the far side of Erik.

A quick glance at Pete's face showed Evie nothing new. His hazel eyes gave nothing away and he wore no anticipatory smile. Unlike Becca and Jenny, Pete was less than thrilled at the prospect of having Evie as his stepmom. But he was dealing with it well enough. Over time, Evie was certain, she'd win his love as she had his sisters'.

Reverend Johnson, as always, looked terribly intense and serious. Sometimes Evie wondered if the poor man ever cracked a smile.

Evie was careful not to look at Erik yet. As soon as she met his eyes, she knew very well she would see nothing *but* him—and she wanted to see everything else first, to absorb each smallest detail, in order to save it all in her heart.

"Evie? Now?" The childish whisper came from a few feet to her right. It was Jenny, holding her own bouquet of pink roses, wearing a creation of ivory satin and English cotton tulle with a wide powder-blue bow at her waist. Becca, standing beside Jenny and dressed identically to her big sister, carried a basket of rose petals.

"Yes, *now*," Evie whispered back, her love for the two of them creating a warm ache in her chest.

"Give me your arm then, gal." Uncle Oggie stepped up from behind her, dressed in a suit that smelled faintly of mothballs, leaning lightly on a fine new cane, one with a handle of hammered silver and an ebony staff. Evie took the free arm he offered.

At the piano, which was against the far wall to Evie's right, Regina seized the moment and launched into the wedding march. The guests stood and turned as one to better view the small procession.

At a slight nudge from Jenny, Becca started up the aisle, strewing petals as she went. Jenny soon followed, marching with great dignity, both hands on her bouquet. When they reached the top of the aisle, the two girls moved to the side.

And then it was Evie and Oggie's turn. In deference to Oggie's bad foot, they progressed even more slowly than the girls had done, Oggie's cane tapping the hardwood floor with each step they took.

Though it wasn't really possible, Evie did her very best to make eye contact with every person there. She traded warm looks with her sisters and Amy. And she saved a special smile for Nellie, who stood so stiff and proud near the front, her very presence at this gathering a minor miracle that spoke more clearly of love and forgiveness than words ever could.

When they reached the top of the short aisle, Reverend Johnson took over. The guests sat once more. Oggie stepped aside and then Erik was there, enfolding her hand in his.

Evie turned, looked into tender gray eyes and knew that after years of wandering, she had truly found the home she sought.

Outside, the wind howled and the rain poured down. Evie hardly heard it. Nothing could touch her or harm her now. The long years of guilt and loneliness were behind her at last and the future was a shining thing, as clean and new as the first day of spring.

Chapter Eleven

That night, Evie slept with her new husband in his giant-size bed. Since money was tight, they'd decided to forego a honeymoon until some later date when finances allowed. But neither of them really cared about the missed wedding trip. They were newlyweds in the truest sense. Just being together was a fabulous vacation in a beautiful place for each of them.

The first few days of their married life were heaven. But then, reality did set in to a degree. They discovered a few elements of their lives that could stand improvement.

For one thing, Pete remained standoffish toward Evie. He rarely looked directly at her, and he always ducked away anytime she tried to show him affection. Erik wanted to confront the boy about his attitude. But Evie held him back. Things had happened so fast, really. Pete deserved a little leeway to deal with it all at his own pace.

To help him accept her more easily, Evie made it a point to show Pete she was there for him. Pete played soccer; Evie learned the rules and attended every match, hiring Tawny to cover for her part-time at the store.

And cheering at soccer matches wasn't all Evie did to try to get closer to Pete. Pete was a good student; she made sure to praise him for the way he always took care of his schoolwork with no need for reminders. She packed his lunch daily and watched for which foods he ate with gusto, so she could make sure they appeared frequently when dinner was served.

Her efforts garnered no immediate results. But she told herself to be patient. Such things took time.

Also, Nellie's relationship with her grandchildren remained touch and go. True, Nellie had taken a big step when she came to the wedding. And she continued to visit the girls at Wishbook.

But she made no attempt at all to get to know Pete. Evie suspected that was because the boy never came into the shop. To see him, Nellie would have had to seek him out at home. There, she would be too likely to run into Erik.

Erik said that Nellie was still avoiding any situation where she might actually have to share a few words with him. Evie agreed with her new husband. Even at the wedding, Nellie hadn't gone so far as to actually speak with her former son-in-law.

In those first halcyon days after she and Erik were married, when Evie was sure she could resolve anything, she dared to approach Nellie about the problem. Nellie blinked and said she really had to be going. She flew out of the shop and didn't return for five days, during which time Becca continually asked for her. After that, Evie decided she'd leave it alone for a while.

And then there was money. Erik was so sensitive about it. And as far as Evie was concerned, his hang-ups on the subject were an obstacle to their future. Evie had some financial plans, sound ones. But she couldn't carry them out until Erik gave the ōkay.

The most important step right now, the way Evie saw it, was for her to cash in a few certificates of deposit that she'd stashed away. Then they could pay off the rest of Erik's debts and get rid of the whopping interest charges that kept accruing. But Erik flatly refused when she suggested as much. He insisted that the debts must be paid from money he himself had earned.

The first couple of times he brushed off her suggestions about dealing with the debts, Evie let him do it. But she didn't give up. She kept coming back about it.

Finally, exactly two weeks after the day they exchanged wedding vows, they traded their first harsh words as husband and wife.

It was right before bedtime and they were in the bathroom, standing at the sink together as they brushed their teeth. Erik, dressed as he usually did for bed in a pair of briefs, was already scrubbing away.

Evie, wearing a pajama top she'd stolen from him and a pair of heavy socks, carefully squeezed a line of toothpaste onto her brush. Then, with the brush poised halfway to her mouth, she met Erik's eyes in the mirror.

Though nothing had been said yet, he could read her look as if they'd been married for a century rather than just fourteen days. He knew that she was about to say something that he wasn't going to like.

"What?" he muttered around a mouthful of minty foam.

"I keep thinking about those certificates of deposit I mentioned before," she told him in a tone so offhand that it sounded suspicious even to her.

He glared at her in the mirror, his mouth still full of toothpaste. "Don't start."

"Well, now just hear me out."

He continued to glare.

So she went ahead. "Listen, I really do want to cash them in and pay off those two outstanding hospital loans you've got left. Then, we're going to be in a great position to approach Regina about—"

Erik spat into the sink. "Drop it. I've told you. I pay my own bills."

Evie stayed reasonable—with just a touch of placation thrown in. "Erik, please. You've done a terrific job. Really. You've accomplished the impossible, single-handedly. But now you have me. And together, we can—"

Erik turned on the tap and stuck a glass beneath the faucet. "I mean it, Evie. It's not open for discussion." He lifted the glass and took a mouthful of water, then sloshed it around in his mouth.

Evie's reasonableness began to fray at the edges. "This is ridiculous. We're married now. What's mine is also yours."

Erik spat the rinse water in the sink with more force than was necessary, then he reached for his hand towel and dried his mouth. "Right. We're married now. And I'm the husband here." He shoved the towel back on its hook. "We'll buy this house when I can afford to. Save your money for yourself. Providing for you and the kids is my responsibility."

That did it. The delicate approach was getting her nowhere. She demanded, "Where did you live before you came home to North Magdalene—a cave?"

"What is that supposed to mean?"

"It means that men don't club women over the head anymore and drag them off to a hole in the side of a mountain when they want to romance them. It means that times change. You, apparently, haven't noticed that I have been taking care of myself for a lot of years. In fact, I've become quite good at taking care of myself, considering I started with nothing and now I run a business of my own. Actually I'd venture to say that I'm ready to go further. I'm ready to extend myself a little and help to take care of *us*, too. I don't think that's unreasonable. But you seem to think a person has to have hair on their chest to be able to help pay the bills.''

Their eyes were locked on each other in the mirror. Erik muttered, ''That was quite a mouthful, sweetheart.'' The endearment didn't sound nearly as tender as usual.

Evie set her toothbrush, still wearing its neat line of paste, on the edge of the sink. ''This money thing is a problem, Erik. And I think it's *your* problem. Get over it.''

His eyes were like twin slabs of slate. ''I *am* over it.''

''Good, so we can—''

He didn't let her finish. ''No, not *we*. You. You can keep your damn money. The subject is closed.''

Evie wanted to punch him. But she didn't. She asked, very quietly, ''Did you treat Carolyn this way?''

He blinked. ''What way?''

''Like a second-class citizen. Like someone not quite capable of doing her part?''

It seemed he couldn't stand still then. He stepped around her and went out into the bedroom. She followed right behind. ''Well, did you?''

He stalked to his side of the bed, flung the covers back and got in.

''Erik?''

He stretched out on his side and pulled the covers up to his chin.

Evie marched around the end of the bed and stood right in front of him. ''I asked you a question, Erik. You haven't answered it.''

He stared at her for a moment. Then he seemed to realize she wasn't going to go away. He rolled to his back and sat up. "What are you getting at? Until she got sick, Carolyn did her part. She took care of the house and the kids and that's no easy job, in case you don't know."

"I *do* know." Her voice was gentle now.

"I took care of Carolyn." In his eyes, there was hurt.

Evie spoke even more gently still. "I know you did. But it's important, Erik, for a woman to know she's contributing in every way that she can. To know she's an equal with the man she loves."

He looked away. "Carolyn and I were equals."

Evie perched on the edge of the bed and tugged on his arm. "Are you sure?"

He met her eyes then. "What are you trying to tell me?"

Evie let her hand stray up, until she was stroking his shoulder. "I don't know. I started out just to tell you that I'm going to cash those CDs."

"Well, now you know what I think about that."

"Let's leave the CDs for now."

"Yeah, leave them right where they are. For good. Because I'm not going to change my mind."

"You are a stubborn man." She went on stroking his shoulder.

"So I've been told." His voice was gruff, but he turned enough that she could rub the back of his neck, which often tightened up with the kind of work he did. He sighed and closed his eyes. She pulled and rubbed, easing the powerful, knotted muscles, ordering warmth into her hands, focusing on drawing all the tightness away.

After a moment, when she felt him begin to relax, she suggested in a whisper, "I think I hit a nerve about Carolyn."

When he said nothing, she scrambled up on her knees right behind him and nipped his ear. "Did I?"

He let his head drop toward his chest, stretching the neck muscles a little more. "Rub farther down. Maybe."

She fisted both hands and pressed the knuckles on either side of his spine, then slowly began working her way down his broad back. He grunted in pleasure.

She instructed, "So talk. Tell me what I said that got to you. And why."

"Hell. It's just . . ."

"Yes?" She'd reached the base of his spine with her massage and she wanted to be closer to him. So she slid her arms around his hard waist and leaned her chin on his shoulder, pressing her body against his back. Since she was wearing only the thin pajama top, she knew he could feel the softness of her breasts. She reveled in the way his breath hitched, before she prodded again, "Come on."

He turned his head enough to kiss her cheek, then he confessed, "Yeah, maybe you did hit a nerve."

"When?"

"What you said reminded me of what Carolyn's doctors told me."

"And that was?"

"Hell. More than one of them said that Carolyn felt as if she'd made no—" he sought the right words and found them "— *important contribution* to our lives together. That Carolyn's life had been run by Nellie and then by me. And that she felt a sort of *worthlessness,* they said. That she never really believed she could take care of herself."

"Did they say that was the cause of her illness?"

"Uh-uh, they didn't go that far. They only said that Carolyn's feelings of worthlessness had *exacerbated* her *condition.*" He stressed the big words with some irony, then went on, "But unfortunately, they never really could figure out what caused her condition, let alone what the hell her condition actually was. At first, since it was after Becca was born that it really started, they called it *postpartum depression*. And then, when they couldn't get rid of it, they said it was *Chronic Fatigue Syndrome*. Later, they started calling it just 'her' condition' and 'her case,' as if they'd run out of ways to explain what was wrong with her.''

''So you feel partly responsible for Carolyn's illness, is that what you're getting at?''

He spoke after a pause. ''Well, I guess, now I think about it, that maybe I did keep her from really being self-sufficient. Carolyn was so... fragile. She was like some delicate flower. When I fell in love with her, I wanted to take care of her. And I did. Maybe too well.''

With a sigh, Evie turned her head, so her cheek rested on his shoulder.

He had more to say. ''There were witnesses, the day that she died. They said she just... wasn't looking. That she walked into the street and the driver of that truck didn't see her and she was hit. But I'll always wonder what was in her mind, what she could have been thinking at that moment. She had come home from the hospital just a few days before she was killed. We all thought she was ready. But I can't help thinking that maybe she wasn't ready. Maybe she *wanted* to die...''

In her mind's eye, Evie saw again the vision of the red bird in the blue sky, of Carolyn, watching the bird and stepping in front of the white van. She pressed herself closer to Erik. ''No. You mustn't think that. I don't believe that she wanted to die.''

He chuckled then, but it was a sad sound. ''Evie. There's no way to know.''

''No. No, there isn't. There's only... what you choose to believe. And if I were you, I'd believe she saw something beautiful—or at least something that distracted her. And then, just the way the witnesses said, she forgot to pay attention and there was an accident.''

He shook his head. "I wish I could believe that.''

Though she never did such things anymore, Evie pressed her hands against his hard belly. She closed her eyes and sent the belief into him. It was only a small thing, after all, and something he needed so very much.

She felt the easiness come over him, the way his body went loose and limber under her hands. He sighed. "Yeah. It's a good way to think of it.''

She lifted her head enough to place a kiss on the hard, smooth bulge of his shoulder. "I love you.''

He turned, then, and gathered her into his arms so that she lay across his lap. They shared a kiss, and when they came up for air, his eyes shone with a teasing light. "But come on. Be straight. Admit I'm no caveman.''

"The heck you're not.''

He contrived to look noble. "I let you buy the girls' dresses and the champagne for the wedding. And throw out half my beat-up furniture to move in all that fancy stuff of yours. And when you drive off to Grass Valley and come back with a van full of groceries that I know I didn't pay for, I don't say a word.''

"But when the rent came due, you wouldn't let me pay half, which I can certainly afford since I'm going to be subletting the apartment over the store as soon as I can find the right tenant.'' Evie didn't actually own the building that housed her store; she leased it, very cheaply, from a friend of Oggie's.

"I pay for the roof over our heads,'' Erik said in a *drop-it* tone of voice.

She just couldn't let it go yet. "But if you don't let me help with the rent, I'll actually be making a *profit* on moving in with you. How do you think that makes me feel?"

Erik groaned. "Please. Give it up."

"Never."

He put on a pitiful expression. "It's not easy for a macho dude like me. I have to take this liberation stuff in stages."

She rubbed her thumb and forefinger together. "Know what this is?"

"No. What?"

"The smallest violin in the world playing 'My Heart Bleeds for You.'"

"Now you're in trouble." He tickled her.

She yelped and tried to squirm away, but he held on tight. Finally, when she lay still in his arms again, he suggested, "I'll tell you what."

"What?"

"If you kiss me again like you did a moment ago, I just might forgive you for trying to wear the pants around here."

She pretended to have to think about that, then pointed out, "But if I kiss you again, I'll never get back to the bathroom to brush my teeth."

He held her closer. "Too bad. You should have stuck that toothbrush in your mouth when you had the chance—instead of trying to impress me with all that talk about your damn CDs."

"Erik—"

"Shh." His mouth covered hers and she knew she wouldn't get back to her toothbrush until a lot more than kissing had taken place.

Later, after the lights were out, Evie lay on her side with Erik wrapped around her back and marveled at how very much she loved her life.

It wasn't a perfect life by any means. But it was certainly everything and more than she'd ever dared to hope it might be. She slipped off to sleep with a smile on her face. And woke in a cold sweat several hours later.

Chapter Twelve

"No!"

Evie's own cry woke her. She opened her eyes to find she'd jerked bolt upright in bed.

"Evie?" Erik's sleepy voice came to her through the dark. "Evie, what is it?"

He sat up beside her.

"Nothing."

"You're shivering." She felt his big hands gripping her arms. "And you're sweating, too." He felt for her forehead, then turned her around so she could rest against his chest. "Are you sick?"

She sagged against him, grateful for his warmth, his strength and the familiar clean scent of him. "I'm okay. It was just a bad dream." Already, her frantic heartbeat was slowing.

He rubbed her arms, taking the last of the chill away. "A bad dream about what?"

Bleak images crowded close.

A room with black walls—the same room, she was almost certain, as she had seen in the vision that day in her shop, when Erik grabbed her arm.

In the dark room, her father bent over her.

And she was weak in the dream.

There was a feeling of utter hopelessness.

Of soul-draining despair...

"Sweetheart?"

She burrowed against him. "I don't remember anything about it," she lied. "Only that it was...bad. A bad dream."

He rocked her a little and stroked her hair. His touch was so tender, so soothing.

"Evie..."

"Umm?"

"Sometimes..."

"Yes?"

"I think you keep secrets from me."

"No..." She whispered the word, since it was another lie and she hated the lies. But she just didn't know how to get out the hard truths. She and Erik had so much together. And if she told him anything, she knew she'd end up telling it all. All the things she'd never told another soul.

And how would he, a good and simple man who painted houses for a living, believe what she told him?

And, worse, if he *did* believe, how could he continue to love her when he learned of the ways she'd once allowed herself and her strange abilities to be used?

It just all went in a circle, when she let herself think about it. A circle going nowhere...

"Evie."

She raised her head and sought his mouth. He tasted of salt and sleep. Of goodness. And of love.

He stiffened for a moment, still wanting to talk. But then her kiss beguiled him. With a hungry groan, he gathered her closer and his tongue met hers.

She kissed him shamelessly, teasing and taunting, seeking to excite him, to bring him pleasure—and to make him forget his questions about the secrets she so feared to reveal.

Her passionate subterfuge worked. His breathing quickened. Urgently he pulled at the pajama top she'd stolen from him, seeking her body beneath. Soon enough, he was shoving the thing off her shoulders, pushing it down her arms and away. He made a low sound of masculine satisfaction when he touched her bare skin. He stroked her shoulders and her arms, as if claiming them all over again for his own.

Then his hand closed, hot and possessive, over her breast. Evie moaned and thrust herself up to him as the kiss they shared went on and on, as she became every bit as lost in it as Erik was.

She left all thoughts of distracting him behind. There was only herself and Erik and this white-hot thing called desire.

Eagerly Evie returned the caresses he lavished on her. As comfortable with his body now as she was with her own, she reached down between them. His belly tensed as she slid her hand under the elastic of his briefs and found him. He gasped. She went on kissing him, loving him, as she wrapped her hand around him, stroking.

He groaned into her mouth. And then, shameless and hungry for him as it seemed she always was and forever would be, she raised both hands to his shoulders and pushed him down, onto his back.

Little ardent noises escaped her as she straddled him, worked off the briefs and tossed them away. Then she took him, hard and ready, into her mouth.

Erik moaned her name and lifted himself eagerly, urging her to have her way with him. Evie didn't need the urging. She loved him, loved all of him, and she showed him just how much.

When she knew he wouldn't last much longer, she slid up his body and took him into her. She settled onto him slowly, wanting every sensation to last a lifetime and more.

At last, the moment came when he was deep within her. She stilled. He looked up at her, his eyes smoky and hot and questioning through the dark. She met his gaze and began to move, slowly at first and then with more speed. He took the cues her body gave him, never hesitating, never holding back.

Their eyes held, through the whole of it—until the final shattering moments, when they cried out as one and she fell, quivering, against his chest.

Gradually, as she lay there boneless and limp upon him, her strength returned to her. Her breath came evenly, in and out. But she didn't pull away and he didn't move. She remained there, pressed close to him, resting on his chest.

His hand was in her hair. She moved her head, a silent plea that he would stroke her. But instead of caressing her, he tangled his fingers in the long skeins and pulled her head up, so she had to look at him.

His fingers, knotted so tightly against her scalp, hurt a little. "Erik?"

He neither loosened his grip nor spoke. Starlight from beyond the window bathed his face. Her breath froze in her chest at the sight.

He looked different than she'd ever seen him. The tenderness that she'd always thought so much a part of him seemed wiped away. His expression was hard, his jaw set. His eyes probed hers, hungry, insistent, giving nothing back.

"Keep your secrets if you have to." His voice was rough. "Just swear to me..."

She whimpered a little, not from pain, but from distress. She'd almost succeeded in forgetting her own deceit. But he hadn't. She'd thought to distract him and ended up only fooling herself.

"Promise," he said.

She had no urge at all to argue. "Yes. Anything. You know that. Anything..."

"Never leave me." The words were harsh. A command. Yet some of the coldness had left his eyes. She saw that the command was also a plea.

"No. I won't. I swear it, Erik. I'll never leave you. I would rather die..."

His hand gentled in her hair. He guided her head back down. After a moment, he gave her the tender caresses she'd been yearning for.

In the weeks that followed, Evie had the same nightmare several times: the nightmare of her father leering down at her in the dark, cold place. Sometimes, she woke from it without disturbing Erik. When that happened, she waited quietly in the dark for her heartbeat to slow and her terror to fade, grateful that at least Erik didn't have to know and worry about her.

Other times, when her tossing and turning woke him, it was always the same. He would hold her and urge her to confide in him. And she would tell more lies of how it was nothing, just a bad dream, she was fine.

And she *was* fine, really—aside from the nightmares, which she was sure were symptoms of nothing more than a guilty conscience. She knew the way to get rid of them: tell Erik the truth about everything.

But the thought of doing that frightened her ten times more than facing a bad dream every other night. The possibility existed that if she told Erik everything, she could lose him. She didn't *think* she would. Yet she couldn't be completely sure.

And having once known his love, she couldn't bear the thought of returning to her lonely single life.

So she said nothing. She put up with the nightmares. And if she cried out in her sleep and disturbed Erik, she told him tender lies.

And she didn't regret the lies, not really. The lies bought her time with her new family.

Every day she rose smiling and made breakfast for Erik and the kids, then saw them off to work and to school. In the afternoon, the girls came into the shop. They often brought their friends and there was laughter and fun.

Two or three times a week, Nellie dropped by and read stories and played jacks. In fact, Wishbook had started to become a community gathering place. Much as the Hole in the Wall across the street tended to cater to the men of the town, Wishbook was becoming a place for the children to play and the women to sit and visit.

Often now, the mothers of Becca's and Jenny's friends would drop by to chat. Amy would show up pushing Bathsheba in a stroller and carrying her tiny new daughter, Eliza, against her chest in a baby sling. Nellie's closest friend, Linda Lou Beardsly, started dropping in, too. So did Evie's cousin, Delilah, and Oggie's three daughters-in-law, Regina, Eden and Olivia.

Evie began serving light refreshments, to promote the atmosphere of a home away from home. Business, though not as brisk as during tourist season, was steady at least. And Evie knew that folks in town were starting to think of her store as a definite option when they needed something nice to wear or an interesting birthday gift.

Things were going well with the girls, too. They seemed to feel completely comfortable discussing just about anything with their new stepmother. Evie had even spoken with both of them about Carolyn. They'd told her how they missed their mother—and were a little mad at her, too. And Evie reminded them that Carolyn *had* come home to them before she was killed. And that she knew Carolyn would have been with them still, were it not for the accident that had taken her life. The girls looked up at her and nodded and said they were so glad she'd married their dad.

But if the girls adored her, Pete remained unimpressed. He continued his practice of avoiding the store and answered in monosyllables whenever his new stepmother asked him anything.

Evie refused to be daunted. Loving Erik had changed her so much. From someone who lived in the shadow of her past, ready to pick up and move the moment it caught up with her, she'd become a decisive woman who faced a challenge squarely.

She determined what she had to work with in winning Pete's trust. The boy loved soccer, his Mountaineer buddies, and computer games.

Evie had done what she could with the soccer; she continued to attend every single match. However, Pete hardly seemed to notice her unfailing presence on the sidelines. She was sure her being there would mean something to him in the long run. But how long *was* the long run, anyway? She was hungry for results right now.

Evie schemed some more. She had Mountaineers and computer games left to work with.

A brilliant idea occurred to her. She'd get a computer. A home computer. A nice big one with a giant-size color screen.

So that Erik wouldn't argue about the expense, she'd claim she needed it to make her bookkeeping chores easier. And she *would* use it for bookkeeping. But she'd also make sure it was the kind of computer on which Pete could play all those games he loved so much.

And really, the more she thought about it, a computer was an important addition to their household. She read all the time now that this was the "information age" and that more and more colleges expected incoming students to bring their PCs with them when they checked in at the dorm. She wanted her stepchildren to grow up with every advantage she could offer them.

From what Pete had let drop around the house, she'd learned that twelve-year-old Mark Drury was the next thing to a computer genius. If she got Mark involved in the purchase of the computer, Marnie and Kenny would probably come along for the ride. Evie would get the advice she really did need—and she'd have the Mountaineers in her corner as well.

Evie called Mark, who turned out to be a thoroughly charming and articulate boy. He was eager to help her with her purchase and, after conferring briefly with his father to get permission, agreed to accompany her to Sacramento on a shopping expedition the next Saturday.

The minute Evie hung up the phone, she went up to Pete's room, where she knocked on his closed door.

"Yeah?"

Evie pushed the door inward and found Pete sitting at his small desk beneath the mural of the space module, a schoolbook open before him. He turned and hooked an arm over the back of his chair.

"What?"

Her heart went to mush. He looked so much like his father had looked before Evie grew to know him: serious and impatient and a little bit disdainful.

A cold had been plaguing Evie for the past several days. It chose that moment to make itself felt. She coughed, then reached into the pocket of her cardigan sweater for a tissue so that she could blow her nose.

"Maybe you oughtta take something for that," Pete suggested, sounding so mature suddenly that Evie had to hold back a smile. He was at a fascinating age, really. One moment all boy, the next displaying faint signs of the man he'd someday be.

"It's nothing." She gave one more good blow into the tissue and tucked it away.

Pete said, "I got a lot of homework, Evie."

"I know."

"Well, then?" There it was again, that impatience, that guarded disdain.

"I just, umm, spoke with Mark Drury. On the phone."

Pete frowned, not understanding what she was getting at.

She hastened to clue him in. "I've decided to buy a computer. For our use here at home. And I remembered you mentioned that Mark knew a lot about them, so I asked for his help."

Pete said nothing for a moment. Evie knew he was taking in the information, turning it over in his mind, not quite daring to believe what it might mean to him. Times had been so tough since his mother's long illness. Pete had learned not to expect too much in the way of things with big price tags.

"What did he say?" Pete asked.

"Mark?"

"Yeah."

"He said he'd be glad to help me buy a computer. So he'll be driving down with me to Sacramento on Saturday to pick one out."

Pete's hand tightened on the back of the chair. "Saturday? You're gonna buy a *computer* on Saturday?"

"Yes."

"*This* Saturday?"

"Um-hmm."

Pete looked down at the rag rug that covered the floor between his chair and his bed, then up at the ceiling. His excitement was palpable. The room seemed to hum with it.

Evie used another brief fit of coughing to hide her own elation. She saw it all, then, in her mind's eye. Petey at the computer she'd bought for him. Petey patiently showing her how to use the darn thing. Petey trotting off to college with his laptop under his arm...

When Evie had finished coughing and Pete had collected himself, he suggested, "I suppose I'd better come, too."

"You mean Saturday?"

His head bobbed up and down. "Yeah. I'll need to be there. I know a little about computers myself, you know."

Evie stuck yet another rumpled tissue into her pocket. "I was hoping you'd say that. Your dad has to work, and having you there to discuss it all with would really be a big help."

"Yeah. That makes sense. And maybe we could take Marnie and Kenny, too. I mean, if it's all right with you..."

"I was thinking the same thing. We could stop off for lunch at a hamburger stand. Get back home by, maybe, two or three."

"Yeah. That'd be great. That'd be the way to do it."

"Yes. I agree completely."

For a moment, they just looked at each other, the glories of the coming Saturday shining in the air between them.

Evie longed to step beyond the threshold of the room where she hovered, to venture across the rag rug to Pete's side, to wrap her arms around him and tell him what a great kid she thought he was.

But she knew enough not to press her luck. The hugs would come. These things took time.

"Well," she said. "I'll let you get back to work then."

"Uh, yeah. Gotta get my math done."

Evie backed out of the room, gently pulling the door shut as she went.

Saturday, Evie woke feeling lousy. The cold that wouldn't go away seemed to have settled like a lead weight in her chest. She had a low fever that she hadn't been able to shake for three days now. Erik urged her to put off the trip to Sacramento and let Tawny watch the store as planned.

"You can stay home. In bed. On regular doses of night-time, extra-strength cold medicine. What do you say?"

She coughed into her hand, her chest aching as it convulsed, and then put on a grin for him. "No way. Petey and me and the Mountaineers are outta here. At nine as planned."

"You'll come back with a computer *and* pneumonia, if you don't watch out."

But Evie wouldn't be dissuaded. She'd watched the anticipation and excitement building in Pete since Tuesday night when she'd first told him of her plans. She wouldn't disappoint him, even if she ended up staying in bed for a week once the trip had been accomplished. So she took the nondrowsy formula of the medicine Erik had recommended, piled the Mountaineers into her van and headed for Sacramento.

Once there, they spent well over two hours walking the aisles of a computer superstore. Evie felt dizzy with all the talk of memory capacities and CD ROM drives, of Sound Blasters, fax-modems, high resolution monitors and surge protectors. Part of her dizziness, she was sure, could be attributed to the effects of her never-ending cold. But not all of it. Pete was smiling from ear to ear the whole time. The sight did Evie's heart good.

Her euphoria faded a little when it came time to pay for everything and Evie discovered firsthand what a major acquisition a computer could be. As she plunked down her credit card, she realized she was glad she still had those certificates of deposit that Erik wouldn't let her cash in. She was probably going to have to use one of them to cover her credit card bill next month.

But then her heart grew light again. After all, what was a few thousand next to the stars in Petey's eyes? They loaded everything into the back of the van and headed for the nearest taco stand.

They arrived home, where Darla was watching a slightly sulky Jenny and Becca, at a little after two in the afternoon. Erik was still over at the town hall; he'd snared the contract to paint the newly constructed building and he was working on the interior now, planning to save the exterior for next spring when the weather became dependable again.

Evie pulled up in front of the house and left the kids to unload the mountain of hardware and software and user manuals on their own. She went inside and knocked back another dose of cold medicine. That done, she gave permission for Pete and the rest of them to start setting everything up in the living room. She hugged the girls, careful not to breathe on them and pass on her cold, and waved at Darla, who'd generously agreed to stick around at the house for a while longer.

At last, with everyone happy at home, Evie headed over to Wishbook to relieve Tawny and see if she could drum up a little business to help pay for the technological monstrosity she'd just bought.

Outside, the underbellies of storm clouds lay heavy in the sky. There would probably be rain by evening. But Erik had his truck over at the hall. If Evie walked over to Main Street, she could hitch a ride home with him should it get too wet.

However, she really wasn't feeling all that great. She decided not to waste the energy the short walk would demand of her. She slid in behind the wheel of her van and started it up.

Main Street was almost deserted when she got there. It looked like the promise of rain had kept everyone indoors.

Evie pulled into the narrow driveway on the side of the building and parked in the tiny lot in back. When she got out of the van, she had to pause with her head against the cool metal of the driver's door frame while a slight bout of dizziness rolled over her and faded away.

Maybe she really should go on home and go to bed....

But after a moment, she felt a little better. She'd jumped down from the van too fast, that was all. And tomorrow was Sunday. If she could just get through today, she could skip church for once and keep to her bed. Why, if she could only last another couple of hours, she could go home and hit the pillow right away. Let Erik handle dinner. That might not thrill the kids too much, but the man needed practice cooking—and Evie needed the rest.

Something rustled to her left. The sound set off a flash of memory inside of her. She heard her father's voice, from a month and a half ago, when he'd called her on the phone to taunt her with his knowledge of her whereabouts.

Don't steal an old man's hope away....

Evie pushed the memory from her mind and looked toward the sound. It seemed to have come from somewhere out in the small, scrubby field between the parking lot and Rambling Lane, to the east.

But when she looked that way, she saw nothing out of the ordinary. Just a tangle of nearly leafless willow clumps, some dying blackberry brambles and a lone crabapple tree. The tree was a sad sight, much of its wasted fruit already fallen, its branches gnarled and twisted, drooping toward the ground.

With a tired shrug, Evie concluded that the sound must have been some small animal—a jackrabbit or a squirrel— startled as it foraged around in the underbrush. Why it had made her think of her father, she had no idea at all.

Evie pulled open the door she'd been leaning against, grabbed her shoulder purse and hooked it over her arm. She let herself in the back way. In the store, she found Tawny standing by a front window, staring out at the street.

Tawny turned when she heard Evie's footsteps. The smile of greeting that lit up her pretty face faded when Evie moved closer. "You look awful."

"Thanks." Evie went behind the counter to stash her purse in the cabinet under the register. "How's it been?"

"Not bad in the morning. Olive Devon came in and bought a tunic and leggings. And then Betty Brown brought her mother in. They each bought a dress and shoes. And there were even some tourists. I sold that milk glass sugar-and-creamer set."

"Great."

"But I haven't had two customers since noon. Look. Why don't you just close up for the day and go home to bed?"

Evie shook her head. "We're open till five."

"Then let me stay for you," Tawny volunteered. "At a special sister-in-law discount."

"What's that mean?"

"It means I'll work till five for free."

Evie was touched. Tawny was so thoughtful. But she waved away the girl's offer. "Don't be silly. Now get out of here. Go on home."

Once Tawny left, Evie cleaned up the wrapping area and rearranged a few things. But when three o'clock came and went and the bell over the door hadn't tinkled even once, she gave up playing the busy shopkeeper.

With a weary little moan, she dropped into the rocker in the book nook and rested her head on the back rail. She really was letting herself get run-down. Tawny had been right. If she had any sense at all, she'd close early and go on home.

However, now that she was sitting, she just didn't feel like mustering the energy to get up. Maybe she'd just stay here for a bit, rocking in this old chair and letting her mind wander wherever it wanted to go.

Evie closed her eyes and sighed—a shallow sigh, since a deep one would have brought on a bout of coughing. She rocked slowly and imagined what must be happening at home, where the Mountaineers probably had the computer up and running by now and the girls would be watching, wide-eyed and wondering, as Mark and Pete tried to best each other at Space Death.

A furtive sound cut through her thoughts, like a floorboard creaking, near the back of the shop. She sat up straight and looked that way.

But there was nothing. Evie rested her head and closed her eyes again. She was just too tired to last until five. In a moment, she would get up, close the shop and head on home....

Chapter Thirteen

At five-thirty, Erik called it a day.

He took twenty minutes to clean his brushes and rollers and to stack his supplies in the corner of the big downstairs room of the two-story town hall. Then, at ten to six, he threw a paint-spattered tarp over everything and locked up the hall. Outside, it was already dark. The rain that the heavy clouds promised had yet to start falling. The evening air was cool and moist.

Erik grinned to himself as he climbed in his truck. He was anxious to get home. If the trip to Sacramento had gone off as planned, there'd be a new computer on the desk in the living room when he walked in the house. He couldn't wait to see it.

Well, more to the point, he couldn't wait to see the pleasure on his son's face. Or to be the recipient of the smugly innocent looks that Evie was going to be sending his way for the next few days.

Erik knew what his wife was up to. The computer was more for Pete than for herself. But she couldn't have told Erik that because then she was sure he wouldn't allow her to buy it.

Erik's grin turned to a frown. Hell. He *shouldn't* let her buy it. If he had any pride at all he would have nixed the computer idea the minute she started making noises about it. He had a good notion how much something like that cost. She was going to end up cashing in one of those CDs she was so damn proud of to pay for it. And he shouldn't let her do it. He should—

The mental exercise in self-rebuke ended abruptly as Erik saw that the lights were still on inside Wishbook. He hit the brakes just in time to make the turn into the driveway that led to the parking lot in back.

He grunted in disapproval as he pulled into the space beside her van. What could she be up to now, a good half an hour after she should have been home? She didn't think sometimes. That cold she had was nothing to fool with. She shouldn't be working overtime. But she just wouldn't slow down. She loaded up her schedule with the thousand and one things she wanted to do—most of them for everyone else but herself. And then she just wouldn't give anything up.

Erik got out of the truck and went to the back door of the building. He found it unlocked, which neither surprised nor worried him. In other towns, leaving back doors open might be an invitation to robbery. But no one ever robbed anyone else in North Magdalene.

Erik traversed the short hall at the back of the building and entered the main part of the store. A quick scan of the room showed him that it appeared to be empty.

"Evie?"

She didn't answer.

He walked to the register counter, in the center of the room. "Evie?"

Nothing.

He went to the front door. It was locked, the Closed sign facing out.

He realized she was probably up in the storeroom, or perhaps in the vacant apartment up there. He started for the back of the store again. When he reached the stairs, he took them two at a time.

But when he got up there, the storeroom was locked and so was the apartment. For a moment, he was sure she must have gone on home, a thought that sent his heart racing in his chest. Was there something wrong at home then, for her to have left in such a hurry that she forgot to turn off the lights and lock the back door?

But then he remembered her van. If she'd gone home in a hurry, she would have driven the van.

Though he was reasonably sure she wasn't upstairs, Erik knocked on both doors and called her name. As he'd expected, no answer came.

More puzzled by the second, he returned to the lower floor, where he went to the phone behind the register and dialed his own number. His mother answered. He told her he was at the store and couldn't find Evie, then he asked, "Is she there with you?"

"No," Darla said. "As a matter of fact, I've been starting to wonder what could be keeping her."

Erik was standing in front of the ornate antique register. He punched the Sale button. When the drawer slid out, he saw twenties, tens, fives and ones, as well as plenty of change. The extra set of keys to the store and the rooms above was right where it should be, in a spare change compartment. Everything looked undisturbed, it didn't appear that the store had been robbed. He took the keys and stuck them in his pocket, so he could lock up the back dead bolt when he left.

"Erik," his mother said, "is something wrong?"

"No." He pushed the drawer back in. "No, of course not. Look. Could you hang around over there for a little bit longer? I want to make a few calls."

"Certainly. But where is Evie?"

"I don't know, but I'm going to find out."

His mother was speaking again as he hung up.

He bent to look for the phone book Evie always kept near the phone. He found it, in the cabinet beneath the register. Her purse, which he knew she always stowed there, was gone.

A half an hour later, he'd called everyone in town who might possibly have heard from Evie or know where she'd gone. He'd called all of her cousins and all of his own brothers and sisters. When he called Delilah Fletcher's house, he also asked to speak with Oggie Jones, Delilah's father, who lived with her and Sam. Evie thought of Oggie like a second father. If anyone might know where she was, it would be Oggie.

"What's the problem there, boy?" Oggie called every man under the age of eighty either "boy" or "son."

Erik explained that he was looking for Evie and asked the old man if he'd seen her.

"Not in the last couple of days."

Erik thanked him and started to hang up.

"Hold on there, son."

"Yeah?"

"Is everythin' all right?"

"I'm sure there's nothing to worry about," Erik said, trying to convince himself, as much as Evie's uncle.

"You call me. When she gets home."

Erik promised he would and then went on to the next call, trying not to remember how worried Oggie had sounded. The rest of the calls yielded no more than the first ones had. No one had seen Evie all day, except Tawny, who'd left her at the shop at a little after two.

When he finished calling all the relatives, he called home again. Evie still hadn't shown up there. And his mother was getting edgy. She wanted to know what was going on. The kids were starting to ask questions.

"I'll be home soon, Mom. Please. Don't worry them."

"Is there something to worry *about?*"

He didn't know what to say.

"Never mind," Darla said gently. "You do what you have to do. I'll take care of things here."

He thanked her and hung up. Then he stared into space for a moment or two, his nerves humming like high-tension wires. He hadn't the foggiest idea what to do next.

Nellie, he thought.

He hadn't called Nellie. And he should. Nellie came here a few times a week, from what Evie said. She might know something. It was even possible that Evie was with Nellie now.

Erik dialed the number.

Nellie answered after two rings. "Nellie Anderson speaking."

"Hello, Nellie. It's Erik."

There was a deadly pause, then she said, "Yes, what is it?" as if he were some stranger, a salesman trying to sell her something she'd already explained she had no use for.

He tamped down a flash of anger. She was so damn self-righteous. She would never change.

He made himself speak reasonably. "I'm looking for Evie. Have you seen her today?"

"No."

He didn't know whether he felt relief that he could hang up now—or despair that the last person he could think of to call knew no more about where his wife might be than he did.

"I don't understand," Nellie said. "Is she all right?"

He answered more sharply than he should have. "How would I know? No one's seen her since two this afternoon, from what I've found out so far."

"Oh, dear," Nellie said.

"Listen, I have go now."

"Wait."

The urgency in her voice stopped him. "What?"

"I don't know if it matters, but—"

"Tell me."

"Yes. All right. About two hours ago, around four-thirty. I dropped by the shop."

"And?"

"It was closed, that's all. And that surprised me, since Evie never closes until five. Also, when I looked in the window, I couldn't see Evie, but all the lights were on. It seemed odd." Nellie paused, then added, "I suppose it doesn't mean anything, but I just thought you should know."

He turned the information over in his mind. Evie hadn't been in the shop at four-thirty. Wherever she was now, it appeared she'd been gone for at least two hours.

"Erik? Are you still there?"

"Yeah. Listen. Thanks. I have to go."

"Erik."

"What?"

"Will you please call me, when you discover where she's gone? I . . . I will worry. Until then."

"Yes," Erik said, his own voice gentling in response to the hesitancy in hers. "Of course."

"Thank you."

Erik hung up quickly then, trying not to think that Nellie's *Thank you* sounded tiny and lost, exactly the same as the *Thank you* she had uttered a year ago, when he'd called to tell her that Carolyn was dead.

Still trying to figure out if there was anything he hadn't thought of, Erik walked around the shop a little.

Everything seemed to be in order. It all looked just as it should—except for a certain emptiness; a feeling that the heart had gone out of the place.

And it had. Because Evie was the heart. Without her, this store that his daughters thought of as magical was nothing but a jumbled bunch of odds and ends. From the carnival glass collection to the display bed with all the stuffed animals on it, it needed Evie to make it come alive.

Just as *he* needed her...

Erik cut off the self-indulgent thought before it could go farther. There had to be some perfectly logical explanation for this. Evie had gone somewhere in a hurry, that was all—somewhere he simply hadn't thought of yet. And as soon as she got home tonight, all the questions that kept nagging him would be answered.

Once she walked in the door and he'd wrapped his arms around her and hugged her good and hard, they were going to sit right down together and have a long talk. Before that talk was over, he'd get some satisfaction about where she'd disappeared to for half the afternoon.

The minute Erik stepped in the front door, the kids were on him, wanting to know where Evie was. He told them he wasn't sure; they'd have to wait till she got home and she'd tell them all.

Darla had made dinner. They sat down to eat as soon as Erik had cleaned up. Then Darla went home and Erik spent a couple of hours with Pete, trying to learn how to play

Space Death on the new computer. Pete slaughtered him at the game. Pete had all the experience at it, after all—and Erik had a little trouble keeping his mind on the survival of his own personal fleet of intergalactic ships. He kept worrying about Evie, waiting for the sound of the gate opening out front, listening for the tapping of her shoes on the porch steps.

At a little past nine, Erik put the kids to bed, tucking each one of them in, even Pete, who usually considered himself grown beyond tucking in. He noticed, when Becca's turn came, that she cradled the stuffed chipmunk she called Chippy in her plump arms. The toy was one he'd allowed Evie to give her when Evie had said she'd be his wife.

In Jenny's room, he found his older daughter clutching the princess from the snow globe. Jenny had received the princess when Becca got her precious Chippy.

Erik made no remarks to either child about the toys. He knew why they were holding them so tightly. He secretly wished he had some small talisman from Evie to clutch close to his own heart, until she returned to him.

Darla called right after he got the kids to bed.

"Is she home yet?"

"No."

"I'll be right over," Darla said.

Erik didn't argue. He wanted to go back over to Wishbook and look around some more.

When he got to the store again, he turned on some lights and went upstairs. He let himself into the apartment and walked through each room, calling her name, expecting no answer, really. And getting none.

He tried the storeroom next and found it full of things Evie wasn't using downstairs right then, but no sign at all of Evie herself.

Once back downstairs, he went to the old rocker in the corner near the children's books. He sat, leaned his head back on the back rail and wondered for the thousandth time where his wife was—and if she was all right.

He rocked for a moment, the slight creaking sound of the runners on the wood floor vaguely comforting. And then he stopped rocking.

There was no sense in stalling anymore. He knew what he had to do next.

He rose and went to the register counter. He got out the phone book and looked up Jack Roper's number. Jack Roper was Oggie Jones's oldest son, a son Oggie hadn't even known existed until a couple of years ago. Being Oggie's kin made Jack family; he was Evie's cousin and half brother to Amy's husband, Brendan.

Jack was also a deputy over at the sheriff's station.

Jack told Erik to sit tight, he'd meet him right there, at the store.

Jack arrived fifteen minutes after Erik had hung up the phone. He asked a lot of questions. Erik told him everything he knew and explained how he'd called everyone he could think of in town, looking for someone who might know where Evie had gone.

"Erik, was anything bothering her recently?" Jack wanted to know.

"Like what?"

"Did the two of you have some kind of an argument in the past few days?"

"No."

"Is there something going on between you that might have made her want to get away for a while?"

Erik's first reaction to that question was anger. He quelled it. Jack was just trying to find out what was really going on here. "No. I don't think so. She seemed happy today. She's always gotten along great with the girls, but she'd finally found something to get through to Pete."

"What?"

"She bought a computer. She and Pete and Pete's friends drove down to Sacramento today to get it. And Pete was all excited about it. I could hardly pry him away from it to get him to bed tonight."

"So there were no problems, between the two of you?"

"Hell, Jack. Sure, we have problems."

"Like what?"

"We . . . we argue about money sometimes. And I think she pushes herself too hard. Sometimes I get on her about that. She's had a cold she can't shake for two weeks now, and I think it's mostly because she just won't slow down."

"But is there anything that might make her run off out of nowhere?"

Erik answered with conviction. "No. As far as I know, there's nothing like that, I swear it."

"Okay, then," Jack said. He thought for a moment. "She has a couple of sisters, right? They came to your wedding. Nevada and—?"

"Faith." Erik supplied the other name.

"Have you called them about this?"

"Not yet." Erik rubbed his eyes. "I keep thinking she's going to turn up any minute."

"I understand." Jack's voice was gentle. "And she probably will. But it's almost ten now. Eight hours since Tawny left her here for the day. I think it's time you contacted the sisters. Tell them that she's been gone for several hours and ask if they've heard from her, or if they know anything about where she might be."

"All right."

"And what about her mother and father?"

"They're both gone."

"Deceased?"

"Yeah. She never talks about them much."

Jack nodded. His dark eyes, which were such a strange contrast to his white-blond hair, looked sad. "Sometimes there's not much to say. About the past."

Erik gave no response to that. He didn't agree. He'd told Evie everything of his past and he'd wanted to know everything of hers. But she had secrets she insisted on keeping.

Could it be that her disappearance now had something to do with those secrets?

Jack said, "Look. Go on back home. Call Evie's sisters. If you learn anything that sheds any light on this, give me a call at my place. Otherwise, call me in the morning."

"And then?"

"We'll go over to the station and fill out a missing persons report, get her description out to all the law enforcement agencies."

"And that's all?"

Jack sighed. "Erik. There are no signs of a struggle here. Her purse is gone, there's money in the till and you say the store was closed when you discovered she was missing."

"But all the lights were on. The back door was open."

"I know. I hear you. But it still appears as if she walked out of here of her own accord."

"But she left her van. Why would she leave her van?"

"Look. I think you're right. Something's fishy. But to mount any kind of a major search for her, I'm going to have to justify it to a lot of people who don't know her. And they're going to tell me that she's a grown woman who closed up her store and left without telling her husband where she was going. They're going to veto any requests I make about spending taxpayers' dollars looking for her until we have more to go on than we do now."

Erik opened his mouth to keep arguing—and then shut it. What could he say? Jack's reasoning was sound.

So he went back to the house and sent Darla home. Then he called Faith and Nevada.

His conversations with Evie's sisters left him feeling worse than ever. Each sounded worried and acted closemouthed. And when he tried to push them as to what they were hiding from him, each of them insisted she didn't know what he was talking about, then asked that he call as soon as he had any news.

He hung up from both of those conversations feeling misled and unsatisfied. By then, it was nearing eleven. He went upstairs, thinking he might try to get some sleep.

But one glance into the room he usually shared with his wife was enough to put an end to that idea. He'd never fall asleep in their bed tonight without her beside him.

So he went to his studio. There, the portrait he'd painted of her hung on the wall opposite his drawing table. He found himself staring at it, looking into those brandy-colored eyes, a hundred questions chasing themselves around in his head.

Where are you?

Are you all right?

Sweet God, why don't you call?

He remembered what Jack had said, how there was no way they could mount a search for her unless they had some evidence of foul play.

And he remembered the way both Nevada and Faith had seemed to be hiding something.

From the painting, Evie looked down at him, smiling that beautiful, mysterious smile of hers.

He couldn't look at it for one minute more. Though he knew it was childish of him, he marched right up to it, took it down and set it on the floor facing the wall.

Then he went to his worktable and picked up a pallet and a brush. He approached a painting he'd been working on the night before, of a high mountain meadow in summer. The painting was nearly done. When it was, he would take it to Sam Fletcher's store in hopes of a sale. For a few minutes he dabbed at the thing halfheartedly with the brush, trying to finish it up.

But his heart wasn't in it. His mind kept returning to thoughts of Evie.

He couldn't help thinking of the nightmares she'd been having the past couple of weeks, the ones she always insisted she couldn't remember. Every time she'd had one, she'd sworn they meant nothing at all.

He hadn't believed her. But he hadn't pushed her to reveal more than she was willing to. As each moment ticked by now, he felt more and more certain he *should* have pushed her.

Erik set the pallet and brush aside. He dropped to the couch and stared at the painting, not really seeing it.

The questions kept playing themselves, in a loop, through his head.

Where are you?

Are you all right?

Sweet God, why don't you call?

Eventually, with a despairing sigh, he stretched out as best he could on the too-small couch. He stared blindly at the painting and waited for sleep, not really expecting it to come, thinking of all the questions never asked—all the answers never offered....

Chapter Fourteen

Erik woke in a meadow, a high mountain meadow, and found he'd been napping on a bed of bright wildflowers. All around, majestic and grand, rocky peaks reached toward the sky, still capped with the last of winter's white. The sky itself was the pure, sweet blue of Becca's eyes.

It took him an extra moment to realize that the meadow was one he'd created in his own mind, the meadow in the painting he hadn't quite finished yet.

So strange, that he should fall asleep and wake here, in this beautiful place he'd made up himself.

A little *too* strange, really.

Erik shrugged and got to his feet. Best not to examine any of this too closely, he decided.

So he breathed deeply of the fresh, clear air and basked in the feel of the sun shining down, warm and good, on his upturned face.

"Erik?"

Erik's heart bounced into his throat when he heard her voice. He spun around.

She was there, poised on the edge of the meadow, silhouetted against the rugged peaks and the blue, blue sky.

"Erik?" This time the word had a plaintive sound.

Still, he didn't answer her. He stared at her, feeling hurt and angry. Deserted. Betrayed. She'd sworn never to leave him. And yet, where was she now?

She seemed to know his thoughts. At least, she answered them. "Please. Try to understand. I didn't want to leave you. I swear to you. I had no choice." Hesitantly she approached, her hands outstretched. "Erik, please . . ."

He looked her up and down. He knew what he wanted. He made his demand. "I'll have those secrets now. All of them."

She dropped her hands. "You sound . . . so strange."

"I'm angry. And afraid. I don't know where you are. And besides . . ."

"What?"

"This is only a dream."

He felt cruel somehow, saying the truth right out loud like that. And more so, when she backed up a step.

"Don't say that. Let's pretend, please? Let's pretend that it's real."

He shook his head, not feeling he could allow that lie. "But it isn't real, Evangeline."

She fell back a second step. "How did you know that name?"

Then he felt more sad than angry. "I always knew. Since that day in your shop, when I touched you. And everything changed. You remember that day."

"Oh, yes. I do. I'll never forget it."

"Good." Impatience rose in him. "The secrets, then."

Even here, in this dream place, she hesitated to tell him. "What good will it do, to tell you now?"

He shook his head, aware by some means he couldn't explain that somewhere, in a windowless locked room, a fevered woman slept fitfully, racked by chills. "This might be the only chance you'll get to tell me the truth."

She knew what he meant. "Yes," she said, then added, "but will it do any good? Will you remember? Will it be real to you?"

"Probably not. But do it anyway."

"It does *feel* as if it will matter. And there's that old cliché, isn't there? About confession being good for the soul. Do you think it counts, even in dreams?"

He asked, "Are you stalling?"

She looked down at the wild grasses that grew at their feet. "Yes. I guess I am."

"Stop it, then. Tell me."

"What?"

"Everything."

She looked up and smiled, a beautiful, shy smile. Then she asked, with great formality, "Won't you sit in the flowers with me?"

He thought about that. There seemed no harm in it. "Yes. All right."

She reached out her hand.

His remained at his side. He looked down at it, wondering why he couldn't extend it to her. Then it came to him. Dreams were so tricky. They had their own rules.

He told her, "Here, we can't touch."

The longing in her eyes cut him like the sharpest of knives. "I see." She dropped her arm. "This way, then."

She led him to where the flowers grew thickest, then she sat. He followed suit. They looked at each other.

The silence grew painful. At last, she confessed, "I don't know... how to begin."

He considered for a moment. "Start when you were little, after your mother died."

"All right. If that's what you want."

He leaned back, half reclining on an elbow among the fragile flowers, and stretched his legs in their worn jeans out toward her.

She sighed as she watched him. "Oh, Erik. It's so hard to believe this is only a dream. You seem so big and solid and real." In her eyes, desire moved.

He responded to it, as he always had. He wanted nothing so much as to grab her and hold her, to cover her sweet mouth with his own. He tried to keep to the point. "You're stalling again."

"No. Listen. I want you to know."

"What?"

"Whatever happens, to have known your love has made all the difference to me. To have met you at last. It's made every lonely year worth living through..."

"Talk," he said, more gruffly than he should have.

"Yes. Of course. I will."

Yet still, she didn't speak for a moment. He sensed he shouldn't push her again right then, so he made himself wait until she could bring herself to begin the old story. As the seconds spun out, he found it unbearably painful, that he couldn't reach out and touch her. He had to do something. So he picked a yellow buttercup and rolled the stem between his thumb and forefinger.

At last, she spoke. "After our mother died, we—Nevada and Faith and I—lived with our father, Gideon. It was a rough life."

He chose a purple lupin. "You told me that." He felt her watching him as he picked more flowers, bleeding hearts and columbines and Queen Anne's lace, adding each one to the wild bouquet in his hand.

It came to him that she'd fallen silent again. He glanced up from the flowers. "Keep going."

"Yes. All right." She took in a breath and went on. "Gideon never seemed to make a go of anything. He worked odd jobs, when he could get them. And he gambled away most of his paychecks at cards. Sometimes he'd come up with wild money-making schemes. But none of them ever amounted to anything. We slept in his car a lot of the time, and we'd clean up at public rest rooms, and eat whatever he could scrape together for us. It seemed we were always hungry. And always moving west."

"From where you'd lived with your mother?"

"Yes. We started out in Kenosha, Wisconsin, where my mother's house was. And by the time I was ten, we were in Los Angeles."

"Five years of wandering."

"Yes."

"And then?"

"Then . . . things changed."

"Why?"

"Because of me."

"Explain."

"Because I . . . had an accident. In a public pool."

"What kind of accident?"

"A fatal one."

He looked up from the flowers then and right into her huge, soft eyes. He couldn't quite take in what she'd said. It had made no sense, even in this strange dream world. "*Fatal* means you died."

She closed her eyes then, and breathed deeply.

He saw again a cold, dank room. And he saw Evie, a prisoner there, shivering on a narrow bed.

She seemed to see what he saw. She whispered, her eyes still shut, "Tell me that *this* is real. You and me. Here in this meadow I've never seen in my life except in that picture of yours."

But he couldn't tell her that. That would have been a lie. He remembered the swimming pool. He wanted to get to the truth about that. "Evie. Go back. What did you say? You said a *fatal* accident."

With some effort, she opened her eyes and looked at him. "I'm saying I died. And came back to life. And when I came back, I was ... different than before."

Chapter Fifteen

"Erik? Erik, wake up." Someone shook him gently.

With a groan, Erik opened his eyes. Tawny was bending over him. "Erik?"

"Huh?" Every joint aching, he pulled himself upright on the couch. "Uh, what time is it?" He raised his wrist and looked at his watch.

Tawny confirmed what the watch told him. "Almost seven. Mom sent me over to see how you were doing."

"I'm fine." Out of the corner of his eye, he could see the painting of the mountain meadow. Strange. He must have been looking at it, when he dropped off to sleep. "I had . . . the weirdest dream."

Tawny had more important things than dreams on her mind. "I take it you haven't heard anything...from Evie?"

He combed through his hair with his fingers. "No."

Tawny watched him, shaking her head. "Erik, why didn't you go to bed?"

Because I couldn't take being in our bed without her, he thought. He said, "I wanted to be ready. In case she called or something."

Though Tawny was his baby sister, she gave him a look that reminded him of their mother. "How much sleep did you get?"

Groaning a little, he stood and stretched out the kinks in his back.

"Erik. Are you listening to me?"

His shirt had come partly out of his pants. He tucked it in a little better.

"Did you get any sleep at all?"

Erik made a face at his sister. "Come on, Tawn. Save the lectures, okay? Is there coffee?"

"I just got here. Give me a minute and I'll make some. Now answer my question."

He took her by the shoulders and gently moved her out of his path. Then he went to the door, pausing when he got there to explain to her, "I want to get something in my stomach and get the kids fed, too. And then would you take them to church?"

"You know I will."

"Good. Then I can call Jack and get together with him."

"For what?"

"To fill out a missing person's report."

Tawny just stared at him. "Oh, God," she said.

Erik knew he had to keep on the move. He headed for the kitchen, pausing along the way to check on each of the kids. They were all still sleeping right then, which was just fine with him. As soon as they woke, they'd want to know if Evie was home yet. He wasn't looking forward to answering them.

Tawny trailed after him, following him on a circuit of the kid's rooms and then down the stairs. In the kitchen, she took down the coffee and began spooning grounds into the white paper liner that fit in the top of the coffeemaker. Erik went to the cupboard and brought out a box of pancake mix, then he knelt to find the griddle in the cabinet by the sink.

"What are you doing?"

He sighed and looked up at her. "Making something to eat."

"I'll do that. You know you can't cook."

"Tawny, I have to keep moving."

She caught her lower lip between her teeth, her eyes suddenly much too bright. "Oh, Erik . . ."

He stood. "Don't. Just don't."

She looked away, collecting herself. Then she stepped over to him and shoved the coffee carafe at him. "Here. Finish the coffee. I've already measured the grounds."

He did as his little sister commanded. Once the coffee was brewing, he asked if she would eat, too.

"I'm dieting. Just coffee."

He set himself a place as Tawny heated the griddle and cracked eggs into the mixing bowl. As he'd feared was going to happen, he was finished with his short series of chores before she had the food ready.

There was nothing to do but sit down and wait. He stood behind his chair, to pull it out—and found himself looking across the breakfast table, to where Evie usually sat.

His gut clenched. And it was the hardest thing he'd ever done to draw air into his lungs.

"How many pancakes?" Tawny had turned. She saw his face. Saw the way he was clutching the back of the damn chair. Her face scrunched up in sympathy.

"Where the hell is she?" He hardly realized he was speaking until the words were already said.

"We'll find her," Tawny said, her pretty chin quivering. "She'll be all right."

"Seventeen hours. *Seventeen hours.* Since you left her at the shop."

Tawny's eyes were tearing up again. She reached out. Erik did the same. They met midway between the table and the counter, wrapping their arms around each other and holding on tight. Then he took her shoulders and put her at arm's length. "Six pancakes would be perfect."

She sniffed and lifted her chin high. "Six it is."

Just then the phone rang. Erik picked it up before it finished the first ring.

"Erik, it's Faith."

"Yeah?"

"Has she come home?"

"No."

He heard her draw in a breath. When she spoke, the words came fast, as if she wanted to get through what she had to say before he could start asking questions. "Listen, I've spoken with Nevada. There were some things Evie didn't explain to you. She was going to tell you, umm, in her own time. But now, with her disappearing like this, Faith and I really don't think we can keep quiet any longer."

Dread sent cold fingers walking up and down his spine. "What things?"

Tawny was looking at him expectantly. He shook his head and waved her away. She watched him a minute longer, then gave up and went back to mixing the pancake batter.

Faith was talking again. Erik listened, hardly daring to breathe, as Faith told him about their father, Gideon, who seemed to have some kind of obsession with his youngest daughter. Faith said Evie had been running from Gideon for years. And that just before Evie and Erik's marriage, Gideon had called Evie.

Feeling slow and stupid, Erik cut in. "Wait a minute. Go back a little here. Are you saying your father is still alive?"

Faith made a small noise of distress. "Did Evie say he wasn't?"

Erik tried to remember. "She told me he was 'gone.' But she knew how I'd take it. I thought she meant that he was dead."

"Oh, Erik. Please try to understand. She wanted time with you, time to adjust to married life. She didn't want you to be worrying—"

"Look. Just tell me what you're getting at here."

Faith didn't speak for a moment. He gave her the time to compose herself. Then she murmured, "All right. What I'm saying is, since Gideon called her, that means he'd found out where she lived. The way things have gone for fifteen years, that was her signal to move on. But she didn't move on. She stayed put."

"So?"

"Well, I just mean she broke the pattern, that's all. She didn't leave. And both Nevada and I are afraid that that might have set him off somehow. That he, umm, might be responsible for her disappearance yesterday."

In his mind's eye, he saw that strange, brief vision from his own dream: Evie, racked by fever, in a dark room on a narrow bed.

He shook his head. He had to get control here. He was really losing it, imagining that he might have dreamed of her where she was now.

"Hold on," he said. "Let's get this good and clear. What you're saying is that you believe your father has—" he had to swallow before he could say the ugly word "—kidnapped her."

Erik heard Tawny's startled gasp. He carefully avoided looking her way.

"I don't know," Faith said. "I just think it's likely that he's got something to do with her vanishing like this."

"Give me his address and phone number." Erik signaled Tawny for a pencil and some paper.

"That's just it," Faith said, as Tawny rushed over with the pad and a pen. "We don't know where he lives. We've spent our lives trying to put him completely behind us, so the last thing we've ever tried to find out is his address. And he's never stayed in one place for long anyway. He's a paranoid kind of man, Erik. When we were kids, he'd always get his driver's licenses under assumed names. He'd establish whole new identities for himself every year or two, just so he could never be found unless he wanted to be found."

"You have no idea where he lives." Erik repeated the information in a tone that sounded dead even to his own ears.

"No."

Erik clutched the phone harder, his anxiety and frustration growing, like a snowball rolling down a steep hill. "Tell me more about him. Why do you want him behind you? Why is he obsessed with Evie?"

Faith launched into a tale Erik could hardly believe, about how Evie had once been a famous psychic called Evangeline, and how her father had promoted his daughter's clairvoyant talents. Lost people had been found in ways no one could explain. And Gideon Jones had made a lot of money in the process. Then Evie had turned eighteen and her sisters had helped her run away. Ever since then, her father had been following her, tracking her down each new place she moved.

"Evie said Uncle Oggie got a postcard from our father, several months ago," Faith said at last.

"So Oggie might know where to reach him?"

"It's possible. Talk to him. I just don't know."

* * *

As his pancakes cooled on his plate and his sister tried to get him to explain what in the world was going on, Erik called Jack and asked him to come to his house at ten, when the kids would be at church.

Then Erik called Oggie Jones.

"Been meanin' to call you myself, son. You just beat me to the punch," Oggie declared. "Any word from Evie?"

"No. That's what I want to talk to you about."

The old man was silent for a moment. Then he muttered, "I figured this was comin'. But you know, Evie made me promise never to tell her secrets to a soul."

"I think it's a promise you're going to have to break."

"When and where?" Oggie's voice was resigned.

"Ten this morning. At my house."

"I'll be there." The line went dead.

"What is going on?" Tawny demanded, once he'd hung up.

Erik put his elbows on either side of his plate and rested his head in his hands. Tawny marched to his side. "Erik. What did you mean, *kidnapped?*"

There was nothing else to do but tell her. Briefly, in a low voice, he explained to her what Faith had told him. "We don't know for sure that Gideon took her," he added at the end. "It's just the only explanation that makes any sense. But don't say anything about it to the kids, all right?"

Tawny let out a little puff of air. "I'm eighteen years old, after all, Erik. I do have *some* sense."

He patted her arm. "I know. You're the greatest. Don't be mad."

Oggie arrived a few minutes before Jack. The old man was carrying a large clasp envelope under his arm. As soon as Jack arrived, Erik led both men to his studio, where he knew they wouldn't be disturbed if they were still at it when the kids came home.

Oggie stumped right over to the couch. He grunted and groaned as he settled down into it, laying the envelope he'd brought with him on the seat cushion next to him. Erik sat on his work stool. Jack declined a chair.

Once Oggie was settled, with his cane propped beside him, he pulled out a cigar. "Moments like these, a man needs a good smoke."

Jack, standing at his side, made a low noise. "Come on, Dad."

"It's all right," Erik said. He went to the worktable where he kept his supplies and found an empty soup can that he sometimes used for cleaning brushes. He handed it to the old man for an ashtray.

"Thanks, son."

Erik watched for a moment as Oggie made a big production of biting the end off his cigar and lighting up. Then Erik shook himself. Swiftly he related the information Faith had given him on the phone. Then he asked Oggie, "Do you have any idea where your brother lives—or how we can reach him? Faith says you received a postcard from him in August."

The smelly smoke from Oggie's cigar spiraled toward the ceiling. "Sorry. Not a clue. That card he sent was post-marked Las Vegas, but Evie said Giddy most likely only wants us to *think* that's where he lives."

Jack spoke up then. "I'll want to see that postcard, Dad."

Oggie patted the envelope beside him. "You'll get it in just a minute now."

Jack made a sort of growling noise in his throat. "Dad. What's going on? What's with the envelope? Just lay it out straight for once, will you?"

Oggie flicked his ash into the can. "I will, I will."

"Fine. So do it."

Oggie chewed the cigar a little. "Just like Faith, I got nothin' I can prove. But I can guess what's happened."

Erik had been sitting on the edge of his work stool, but he couldn't sit there anymore. He loomed over the old man. "*What's* happened?"

Oggie went on chewing his cigar, shifting it from left to right in his mouth. "Get calm. Listen up."

"I am."

Oggie looked at him doubtfully. Erik made himself sit on the stool again.

Oggie eyed him for a moment, as if weighing how calm he *really* was. Then he said it. "Her dad took her."

For a moment, no one spoke.

Then Erik said the ugly word once more. *"Kidnapped?"*

Oggie only nodded.

"What makes you so sure of that?" Jack asked.

Oggie blew more smoke and watched it float away. "All Evie's wanted for fifteen years is to be free of her dad. See, he made her life a misery. She's been tryin' to escape from him since she came of age. And in a way, even though he ain't *in* her life anymore, he's been runnin' it. He's had real power over her. Every breath she took, it was in fear of his catchin' up to her. She's lived on the edge of things, never settlin' down, never givin' her heart.

"But then, when she came here, she decided to stop runnin'. She put down roots, married, made a real life for herself. And I don't think Giddy can stand that. I get an awful feelin' he's gone over the edge about that."

The men were silent again. Then Jack asked, "What's in the envelope, Dad?"

Oggie gave the envelope a sideways glance. "It's clippings and stuff. From newspapers. All about Evie in the old days, when she was known as Evangeline. She saved them over the years and when she got married, she gave them to me, to keep for her, until she got up the nerve to show them to Erik here.''

"What about that postcard that Gideon sent you?"

"I stuck it in there, too."

Jack looked at Erik, then back at his father. "Well, let's see them, then."

Oggie picked up the envelope and held it out to his son, but it was Erik he spoke to. "She said she almost showed you these, the night you proposed to her."

Erik knew then where he'd seen that envelope before—on the morning after they'd first made love, as she was going out his front door. It had bumped his leg as they lingered over their goodbyes. He'd asked her about it and she'd told him it was only mail she'd collected from the post office on the way over.

It had never occurred to him that it might have been much more. He'd been blinded by his own happiness that morning. He hadn't even considered that there might be things she should tell him, things he should know.

Jack found the postcard inside the big envelope. He pulled it out by a corner and asked Erik for a small plastic bag to put it in.

An hour or so later, as Erik and Jack were reading the last of the yellowed clippings, Tawny returned with the kids. She promised to answer the phone and get lunch on the table so that Erik could go over to the sheriff's station and fill out a missing person's report on his wife.

Once the report was completed, Jack told Erik that with what they had now, he could probably get through an order for a DMV records check on Gideon Jones in California and the neighboring states, to see if they could come up with an address on the man.

"What about fingerprints?" Erik asked.

Jack lifted an eyebrow at him.

"I mean, couldn't you maybe check for prints on the postcard?"

"I plan to, though the chances of getting a decent print off of a card from a man who stuck it in the mail three months ago have to be almost nil."

"What about the store? Could you test for prints in there? Maybe match them up with what you get from the post-card?"

"Damn, Erik. You're really talking long shots now. But I'll look into it, okay?"

"Thanks."

"I'll call you by tomorrow evening, and let you know what we've dug up."

A feeling of hopelessness went through Erik. Soon, it would be twenty-four hours since Evie's disappearance. And here was Jack saying it would be another day before he had any more news about Gideon, the only real lead that they had.

Jack read Erik's expression. "Hey. I'm sorry, man."

Erik looked away. "I know you're doing what you can."

Since he'd already read all the clippings, Erik agreed to leave them at the station. He was a little stunned to think of the life Evie had once lived. Apparently, from what the clippings said, she had done a lot of good for a lot of people in thoroughly mysterious ways. And that made her se-crecy with him all the harder to understand.

If her father had been as mean and tyrannical a figure as Oggie and Faith had described, Erik could see why Evie had wanted to escape the man. He could even see how she might lie to her new husband and say that her father was dead.

But why should she want to hide what she'd been? From what he'd read, she'd done a lot more good than harm. And besides, she'd been little more than a child at the time, manipulated by her father. Not at fault at all. He just didn't get it.

He went home feeling as if he was no closer than he'd ever been to finding Evie—or to understanding why she'd felt she had to lie to him about her past.

At home, he found no peace. All three of his children were sitting in the living room, waiting for him.

"Dad," Pete said. "We really want to talk to you."

Darla, who must have come over and relieved Tawny while he was gone, gave him a sheepish look. "I didn't put them up to it."

Erik forced a smile for his mother. "I know you didn't, Mom."

"Good. Listen, I'm getting a pot roast started for dinner and—"

"Go on," he said before she could finish, thinking how damn lucky he was to have his mother and sister to count on. "This is my job and I'll do it."

Darla left them. Erik looked at his waiting children and didn't know how to begin.

"We want to know where Evie is," Jenny prompted.

Erik started to tell them how he was sure that Evie would be back soon.

Pete wasn't having any of that. "But where did she *go?*" the boy demanded. "No one's talking to us. And I got…things she needs to know about. Mark showed me how to use that bookkeeping program she bought. I been waiting to teach her all about it. But I can't teach her if she's not home."

Erik looked at his son pleadingly. He didn't have any idea what to say.

"Just tell us," Pete insisted. "Where *is* she?"

Feeling like the coward he knew he was, Erik looked away from Pete—and saw Becca, sitting curled up in Evie's favorite chair, clutching the stuffed toy she called Chippy. Becca was sucking her thumb, something he hadn't seen her do since right after Carolyn died.

"Becca, your thumb," he said sternly.

She'd been sucking so hard that it made a popping sound when she pulled it out of her mouth. She tucked it under her chin, as if she was going to stick it right back in the minute he stopped looking her way.

"Dad. Where's Evie?" Pete demanded again.

"Yeah." Jenny joined in. "We don't understand. She would never just leave without telling us."

"Something's wrong," Pete said. "Something bad's happened, hasn't it?"

Erik looked from one child to another and wondered if he was going to live through this—and much worse than that, if his children would.

"Dad?" Now Jenny sounded as if she might cry.

And Becca's thumb was back in her mouth. She sucked on it furiously.

Erik sank to the couch. He lowered his head and closed his eyes. He sent a wordless prayer to heaven for the right way to deal with this.

And then he felt a hand on his shoulder. He looked up. His son was standing over him. "Just tell us what happened, Dad. Just tell us like it is." Pete sat beside him, very close. Jenny, who'd been sitting a few feet away, scooted near on his other side. And Becca slid off Evie's chair and came to sit in his lap.

Erik took his son's advice. He told the facts he knew as simply as possible, about how Evie had disappeared yesterday afternoon from her shop and how he'd just been to the sheriff's station to fill out a missing person's report. He left out the stuff about Gideon Jones and the ugly possibility that Evie might have been kidnapped. That was all only speculation anyway, and not something they needed to know at this point.

When he was done, Jenny's eyes were teary-bright and Becca looked as if she might suck that thumb of hers right off, but at least they knew what was going on. They weren't much more in the dark than he was.

Erik spent the rest of the day with them, helping Pete with his homework on the computer, giving Jenny some ideas for an art project at school and holding Becca in his lap as much as he could. All day, the phone kept ringing, people wanting to know if Evie had shown up yet. He and Darla told everyone that they'd call them the minute they had news.

They ate dinner at six, and were cleaning up the dishes when there was a knock at the door.

Erik went to answer. He pulled back the door to find Nellie standing there, her thin face grim and determined in the spill of light from the room behind him.

Nellie didn't bother with any how-do-you-do's. "I hear no one has learned where she's gone."

Erik just shook his head.

"You look terrible, Erik." Nellie's tone came perilously close to being gentle.

"Grandma Nellie!" With a little cry, Becca slipped around her father and reached out her arms.

Nellie scooped her up and hugged her close.

"Evie's missing, Grandma," Becca said against Nellie's neck. "Come in my house. Read me a story."

Erik stepped back and Nellie carried Becca over the threshold. Darla came in from the kitchen, to see who it was. The two women looked at each other over Becca's blond head.

Then Darla said, "If you can stay, Nellie, I'll just finish the dishes and go on home now."

"Absolutely," Nellie said. "I'll visit with the children a-while, and see that they get tucked into bed."

A few hours later, when Nellie came downstairs after putting the kids to bed, she joined Erik in the kitchen.

He was sitting at the table, trying to read a weekly news-magazine when she came in. He set the magazine aside and looked up at her, thinking how strange life was sometimes. Here he was after all this time, alone with the woman who had hated him for just about the same number of years as Evie had been running from that terrible father of hers.

Nellie approached nervously. "Mind if I sit down?"

He gestured at a chair.

She pulled it out and sat. He waited, not knowing what to say himself, but trying to be receptive, in case she wanted to talk.

When she remained silent, he reached for his magazine again.

She spoke then. "Erik?"

He left the magazine where it lay. "Yeah?"

"Could you tell me...what has happened to her?"

He felt a headache coming on, behind his eyes. "We don't know for sure."

"Could you tell me what you do know?"

He looked at Nellie probingly. She was noted for her gossipy ways. Whatever he told her could be all over town within twenty-four hours.

She seemed to realize the direction of his thoughts. "Yes, Erik. I do love to talk. But in this case, I will guard my tongue. As God is my witness, I promise you."

For some reason, he believed her. "All right," he said. "Give me a minute."

He rose and went to the cupboard where a bottle of as-pirin waited. He shook two into his hand and washed them down with tap water.

"Erik?" Nellie said from behind him, as he set his empty glass on the drain board.

"Hmm?" He turned to look at her.

"You're a good man." Her voice sounded strange and tight, as if the words hurt coming out.

Erik said, "Thank you," because he couldn't think of anything else to say. He understood that things were going to be all right between him and Nellie from now on. It didn't mean as much as it should have, not without Evie there to see it happening.

Erik took his seat once more and began to tell Nellie everything he and the others had pieced together.

After he'd told her what he knew, Nellie seemed reluctant to leave. She got up and made hot chocolate for the two of them and they sat in silence together for a time.

At last, after midnight, she went home, saying she'd check with Darla tomorrow, and take her turn with the Riggins women in helping out around the house.

It was after one when Erik finally closed himself into his studio again. He was tempted, the minute he'd shut the door, to look at the portrait he'd turned to the wall. He longed to stare into her eyes again, even if they were only painted eyes.

But he didn't do it. He might break down and sob like a baby if he did it. He couldn't afford to waste his energy in tears.

So he went to the cramped couch beneath the windows and stretched out as best he could. From there, he could see the painting of the mountain meadow. He stared at it a while, finding that it kind of relaxed him, to look at it, to pretend he was lying there, with Evie, among the wildflowers.

Chapter Sixteen

It happened again, as it had the night before.

Erik woke in the meadow, with Evie. He was still holding the bunch of wildflowers he'd been picking one by one. He stared at the flowers.

"Erik?" she said. "Please. Look at me."

Though he knew it would hurt, he did it; he raised his eyes. And there she was. Achingly beautiful, her skin like cream, her hair shining with red lights in the sun.

He cursed the rules of this cruel dream. Here, he couldn't reach out and put his hands on her, feel the softness of her, pull her close and know her sweet breath against his skin.

"Oh, Erik." She put out a hand.

He pulled back, remembering what had to be done here. "Tell me about that 'fatal' accident you had."

"Yes. I will."

"Well, then?"

"All right. But I want you to know first—"

"What?"

"That I know I was wrong. I know I should have told you everything. But we had so much. I couldn't bear to risk it."

He dropped the flowers to the ground. "So you lied."

She was silent then, her gaze cast down at the fallen bouquet.

"I want the truth now, Evie." His tone was cruel. But she couldn't blame him for that. He had to be cruel. Certain things must be said. And who could know how much time she would have to say them?

In the dark room, her fever raged while a madman kept watch. . . .

"Tell me the rest," Erik commanded.

"All right. I will. Where was I?"

"A public swimming pool, you said."

She tucked her legs to the side and leaned on an arm, remembering. And then she began.

"It was hot. A sweltering July day in L.A. Nevada had scraped together enough change to take us swimming. We all three went, in the pitiful bathing suits that Faith had managed to get us from a Goodwill store. The pool was crowded. It seemed like there was hardly room to get in a stroke or two before you ran into someone else. But we didn't care. The water felt so wonderful. We paddled around, laughing, saying 'Excuse me' to strangers every few seconds. It was a pretty big pool. I was doing my best imitation of a breaststroke, in the deep end. And somebody jumped off the diving board and kicked me in the head—or at least that's what we decided later must have happened."

"You were hurt?"

"Knocked out cold. There were so many kids, though, that the lifeguard didn't see I was in trouble for several minutes. They pulled me out, tried to get me breathing again. But I was dead. My heart had stopped. The lifeguard said, 'I can't get a pulse. My God, she's dead.' I heard it from far away, not with my ears. Like I was above the whole thing, looking down.

"And then Nevada shoved the lifeguard out of the way. She grabbed me and shook me and screamed at me not to leave. That we were all together, sisters. We'd lost our mom, and we had to stick together. We needed each other. 'Please, Evie,' she was crying. 'Evie, don't leave us. Evie, come back!' And then Faith was there, too, sobbing and saying the same things. And . . . I couldn't stay above them anymore.

"The next thing I remember, I was throwing up on the concrete on the side of the pool."

"So you lived?"

"I guess. Or . . . maybe I came *back* to life. And brought a few things with me."

"Like?"

"Like after that, I started . . . to know things other people didn't know. See things other people didn't see. And I could sometimes make people feel better, by touching them. And my father . . ."

"Your father what?"

"He caught on right away that these abilities I had could be useful. He'd always been a con artist. And he started teaching me things, like how to really observe people, to make them think I could read their minds, even the times I couldn't. Within two years after the accident, he was taking out ads in tabloid newspapers. He billed me as a 'psychic locator.' He'd give a post office box where people in *need*—that was how he put it—could write. And then he'd find out the ones who had money to spend."

"And did you help these people?"

"Sometimes. My . . . abilities were never too dependable. I picked up random impressions, like visions, more than anything else. And the problem was always how to interpret what I'd seen.''

''You're saying you made mistakes at times, is that it?''

''Yes. And people got hurt. People paid their money and got their hopes up and...I would let them down. I got to hate myself for that, over the years. But that wasn't the worst of it.''

''What was?''

''I, umm...''

''Come on, Evie, don't give up now. Tell it all.''

She looked at him again, and he felt that she was taking in the whole of him, gaining what strength she could from the sight of him. ''Yes. Yes, I do want to. I want you to know.''

''And I'm listening. Tell me.''

She made herself speak. ''At first, my father let me tell the clients whatever I could pick up. He'd set up a sort of séance room in whatever hotel we were living in. He'd turn the lights low and have me pretend I was in a trance. And whatever I came up with, that was that.

''But then, sometimes, I'd pick up things that he didn't like. Things that would make the client mad—or worse, make him decide there was no point in paying any more money. By then, my father had caught on that a lot of desperate people can be milked for a lot of money, over time, if you can string them along effectively.''

''So he started to make you lie about what you saw?''

She bent her head. ''Yes.''

''How?''

''He forbade me to tell anything I saw, until I'd told it all to him first and he'd decided which parts of it to use. So the séances really became nothing more than performances. They were all preplanned, according to what he wanted the client to know. That was when things got so awful.''

"Why?"

"Because I... sometimes I saw things those people had a right to know. Once, there was this little girl. She'd been missing for weeks and the police had gotten nowhere. Finally, her poor, desperate parents resorted to us. I touched her mother, trying to open myself, to pick up what I could. And I..." The words wouldn't come.

"Come on, Evie," Erik whispered low.

His voice seemed to give her just enough will to finish it. "...I saw the little girl. I saw her dead, buried in a shallow grave. I opened my mouth to say it, to tell them. And my father must have seen that something he wasn't going to like was on its way out of my mouth. He dragged me back against him and clapped a hand over my lips. And he pressed it there, hard, holding my arms against my sides so I couldn't move. He spoke really calmly to them, saying that sometimes I had these little fits. He'd get in touch with them real soon, the minute I was feeling up to taking on the *psychic forces* once again."

Evie reached out and took up one of the lupins Erik had dropped. She brought it to her nose. "Funny," she said. "It has no scent."

He let her have a moment more before prompting, "What happened then?"

She touched the purple cluster of blossoms, just a breath of a touch. "After they left, I told my father what I'd seen. I *begged* him to let me tell them. He said no. They had lots of money. They were good for a long run. That's how he said it, a *long run.* He reminded me how my sisters counted on me, how things were good for all of us, since he'd dug up this talent for fortune-telling I had."

"And what did you do?"

The confession came out in whisper. "I did what he wanted."

He felt her pain, then. And he understood. Everything. "Hell. Evie."

She looked across the crown of the lupin at him, blinking back tears. "Don't be kind. I don't deserve kindness. We strung those people along for months. Till the police finally found what was left of the little girl. Buried in a shallow grave."

He reached out a hand. She ducked back from it and went on.

"I was thirteen then. For five more years, I went on doing what he wanted. Both Nevada and Faith got old enough to go out on their own. But they stayed, they took the abuse he heaped on them—he never had much use for them—for my sake. And then, when I was eighteen, and old enough that legally he had no power over me, we ran away. All three of us. Late one night."

"And you've been running ever since."

She met his eyes then. "No. Not after I came to North Magdalene. From then on, I didn't run anymore." She stood then, and gestured widely. "But refusing to run has had its price. It's cost me everything. And maybe, after the way I let my gifts be used all those years ago, I deserve to lose everything. I deserve to go missing. Forever. Like that poor little girl."

"Evie..."

But she was vanishing, as the meadow was vanishing. For a moment, he saw black-painted brick walls, a narrow bed, a huddled form.

And then the dream faded to nothing at all.

Chapter Seventeen

Jack found Erik at the town hall late Monday afternoon. Erik was doing the window and door trim of the downstairs meeting room. Out of the corner of his eye, he saw Jack come in.

He laid his brush across the open can of paint and straightened to his full height. "Well?"

"A couple of things. First, we've dusted the postcard for prints."

"And?"

"The only usable ones we found were a thumb and a forefinger. Both were my father's."

"I see. Anything else?"

"Yeah. We called Faith and got a description of Gideon, so the report we put out now says to look for Evie in company with a man matching her father's description."

"Good. What about the DMV checks?"

"We ran them. Came up with zero."

Erik felt hollow inside at that news. "I see."

"And as far as dusting the store for prints . . ."

"What?"

"I can't get Pangborn to give me an okay on that right now." Pangborn was the sheriff.

"Why not?"

"We got nothing on Gideon. We ran a check to see if he'd ever been arrested. Nothing at all. We couldn't find him anywhere. If he's ever been fingerprinted, it wasn't under the name Gideon Jones. There are bound to be prints from a lot of people in that store. To try to run a check on every print we got would cost major bucks. Pangborn's not willing to authorize an expense like that at this point, when we have no prints of Gideon's to follow up on anyway."

Erik wondered if the news could possibly get any grimmer. With a sigh, he pulled off his cap and gave it a slap against his paint-spattered white overalls.

"Look," Jack said. "Why don't you lock up the store? Don't let anyone in there for a few days. Maybe some new piece of evidence will turn up, and I can talk Pangborn into dusting for prints in there after all."

Erik thought of the store, so empty now that Evie wasn't there to make it come alive. Locking it up and forgetting about it for a while would be just fine with him. "Sure."

"Erik, I . . ."

He put his cap back on. "Thanks, Jack. You've done all you could. And I . . . I should get back to work now."

Jack opened his mouth, and then closed it. "Yeah. I suppose so." He turned and went out the way he had come.

Erik picked up his brush again and doggedly returned to his task. All he wanted to do was get through the day somehow. Then he could go home, go through the motions of the evening—dinner, and a little time with the kids.

At last, he could retreat to his studio. He could lie down on the couch.

And maybe, just maybe, he could be with Evie in his dreams.

The week crawled past.

On Tuesday, Jack took the keys to Wishbook from Erik. He spent several hours in the store alone, going over every inch of the place. He found nothing useful at all, though he did formulate a theory of the motions Gideon might have gone through, had he really kidnapped Evie Saturday afternoon.

Jack proposed that Gideon had parked his vehicle on Rambling Lane, across that overgrown field from Main and the back of Evie's store. He'd gone in the rear door, overpowered Evie and rendered her unconscious. He'd stopped to turn the Open sign around, lock the front door and take her purse, so it would look as if she'd left on her own steam. Then he'd carried her out the back way, flipping the light switch at the back door—which would have turned off the hall lights but not the ones inside the store. No doubt, he'd decided time was too precious to go back and take care of those lights. He'd left them burning, as he'd left the back open, unwilling, probably, to fumble around trying to lock it with an unconscious woman slung over his shoulder. Luck had been with him, enough that he'd made it across the field carrying Evie and stowed her safely in his vehicle without anyone seeing him.

Coincidentally, Angie Leslie called Jack at the station late that afternoon. She said she had noticed a black van she'd never seen before, parked over on Rambling Lane last Saturday. Jack went to Angie's place, where he interviewed her in-depth as to what she'd seen. But all she remembered was that the van had been there. She'd seen no one get in or out of it and she'd paid no attention at all to the license plate.

So Jack's theory reached a dead end right there.

Erik tried his best to keep going through the motions of living his life. On Wednesday, Pete had a soccer match in Nevada City. Erik took a little time off and the whole family went, with only Tawny staying at his place to watch the phone just in case. Pete played without much enthusiasm and his team lost.

Thursday was Thanksgiving. Erik went to dinner at his mother's. Darla outdid herself with a huge turkey and enough side dishes to make the table legs wobble supporting their weight. When they all bowed their heads to say grace, Erik found it damn hard to drum up any thankfulness.

Each night, Erik retreated to his studio a little earlier. He made no pretense of painting anything in there. He stretched out on the couch and looked at the painting of the mountain meadow and waited for sleep.

Friday night, after Nellie put the kids to bed, he and his former mother-in-law sat at the kitchen table over twin cups of hot chocolate, something that had become a sort of nightly ritual with them the past few days. Erik was counting the minutes, thinking that very soon Nellie would go home and he could go up to the studio.

But then someone pounded on the front door.

"Who's that?" Nellie asked.

Erik shrugged.

"I'll see." Nellie stood.

Erik watched her leave the room. Outside, the wind was up. He listened to it whooshing around under the eaves, making the panes rattle in the windows, as he waited without much interest for Nellie to find out who was there.

After a few minutes, when she didn't return, he decided he'd probably better see what was going on.

He found Nellie at the front door, blocking Oggie Jones from entering the house.

"I gotta see him, woman. Now," Oggie said.

Nellie stood firm. "Ogden, I asked you why."

"It ain't none of your business."

"The man is very tired. You know the kind of stress he's been under. And yet you refuse, as you always do, to explain what you're up to. And as long as you refuse to explain, I see no reason why poor Erik should have to converse with the likes of you in the middle of the night."

Oggie caught sight of Erik. "It's freezin' out here, boy. Tell this old bat to let me in."

Nellie puffed up her flat chest. "Well, I never . . ."

"It's all right, Nellie," Erik said gently. "I'll talk to him. Let him in."

Disapproval evident in every line of her gaunt form, Nellie stepped aside. Oggie stumped in on his cane and Nellie shut the door, closing out the biting wind.

Erik said, "Thanks for everything, Nellie. Why don't you go ahead and go home now?"

Nellie looked as if she'd just sucked a lemon. "Very well. If that's your wish." She softened a little. "I'll see you tomorrow."

"I'd appreciate that."

The two men waited as Nellie put on her coat and hat and went out into the blustery cold.

Once she was gone, Erik said, "Let's go upstairs, to my studio. We can talk there."

Upstairs, Oggie took the couch as he had that other time, when he and Jack were there. "This won't take long," he declared in a bleak voice.

"Okay. What can I do for you?"

Oggie grunted. "For me? That ain't the question. The question is, what can you do for Evie, gone missin' nigh on a week now."

Erik had started to sit, but instead he drew himself stiffly erect. "What are you getting at?"

"You know I was the one who talked Evie into stayin' put?"

"No, I—"

"I got that postcard from Giddy and I went and showed it to her. And then I told her that here, she would be safe. Here, she'd have her people all around her. And that it was time she learned that an old man like Giddy had no power over her that she didn't give him of her own free will."

"So? You were wrong."

"Yeah." There was bottomless self-disgust in the old man's voice. "In the end, her people didn't protect her. *We* didn't protect her. And I'm gonna live with that knowledge for the rest of my days."

Erik didn't know what to say. "Look, I—"

Oggie threw up a hand. "Wait. Let me say my piece here."

"All right."

"I'm gonna talk from my heart. And I'm sorry if it hurts you to hear what I got to say."

"Say it."

"I got me a hunch, a strong, awful feelin', that if we don't find Evie soon, we ain't never gonna see her alive again."

Erik stared at the old man. What he'd said was only what Erik himself secretly feared. But to hear it out loud that way stole the breath from his body.

Oggie tapped his cane on the floor. "Time's wastin', boy."

Erik found his voice. "I know that."

"And you done gone numb on us."

Erik frowned, not quite following.

Oggie elaborated. "You gotta face what you can do about this here situation."

"*What* can I do?"

"I don't know. Only you know."

"You're talking in riddles."

"I'm talkin' as clear as I know how, about somethin' no one can explain."

Erik turned from Oggie then, and found himself staring at the painting of the high mountain meadow.

"Evie ain't Carolyn, boy," Oggie said from behind him.

The words struck a chord deep inside Erik. He turned on the old man. "What the hell are you talking about?"

Oggie didn't flinch. His beady eyes met Erik's eyes, straight and true.

"Carolyn got lost, lost inside her mind," Oggie said. "And maybe she never found a way to really get back to you before she died. Maybe you feel that she abandoned you. But Evie is different than that. Stronger. More determined. She didn't go away. She was *taken*. And I personally believe that there was more to all those people she found in the old days than a bag of con artist's tricks."

"So?"

"So I believe Evie's got somethin'. Somethin' special. And I believe if you love her enough, you can reach out to that somethin' and bring her home safe."

Erik stared at the old man, torn between desperate belief and absolute denial. Then he sank to the stool and stared at the floor between his shoes. The logical, down-to-earth part of him completely rejected what Oggie said. His rational mind told him that the old man was babbling, at his wit's end from worry over Evie.

But a deeper part of him, the heart of him, wasn't so sure. He looked up. "What do I have to do?"

Oggie stood once more and leaned on his cane. "I believe you know. Just follow your heart, boy. Just follow your heart. That's all I gotta say. I can see myself out."

Feeling lost and a little bit dazed, Erik trailed the old man to the door anyway. Then he returned to his studio and sat for a time, staring at the painting of the high mountain meadow.

Soon enough, he rose and took the painting from the easel, replacing it with a blank canvas. Then he went to his worktable and got a pallet and a clean brush.

He stood before the easel for a long time, but nothing came to him. So he set down the pallet and lay on the couch.

Erik woke at dawn, his eyes turning immediately to the canvas he'd set up last night in place of the mountain meadow. It was just as he'd left it. Blank.

He felt like a fool. He didn't know what he'd expected.

He went to his bathroom and showered and changed. Then he headed downstairs to make coffee. Darla showed up soon after that. She cooked a big breakfast for everyone.

It was Saturday, exactly a week since the day Evie had disappeared. Erik decided to take the day off. Yesterday, he'd finished the interior of the new town hall. He had another job lined up, painting Cathy Quail's newly remodeled kitchen and bathrooms. But Cathy wasn't expecting him to start until Monday, so that could wait until then.

He spent the morning with the kids. Since the windy night had turned to rain overnight, they stayed indoors, playing Monopoly and computer games. He made the family's lunch himself, slapping sandwiches together and heating up canned soup. Everyone looked relieved when they came to the table and saw he hadn't attempted to cook anything more complicated.

All morning, his mind had kept returning to what Oggie had said the night before. Right after lunch, he asked his mother if she'd mind if he went upstairs for a little nap.

She shooed him off, just as if he were one of the kids, promising that she'd see to it he wasn't disturbed for as long as he wanted to rest.

He returned to his studio and the blank canvas that waited there. Again, he had no urge to paint anything. He felt that his mind was circling. Circling a certain impossible idea.

He lay down on the couch. Outside, the rain beat against the panes, as it had done on the day he and Evie were married.

He closed his eyes.

Evie was ill. Far gone in it now.

The dark place was alive with phantoms of her confused mind's creating. She lay in a shadowland between dream and waking. Occasionally some small object would pick itself up from the bureau or the bed stand and hurl itself through the air.

Telekinesis. Her psychic energy out of control.

Her father, grown kinder now that she seemed to truly be fading from the world, came to her with more tenderness than she ever remembered receiving from him before.

He bathed her hot face and begged her to come out of this, to do his will and all would be well. He talked of the old days, of all the incredible things she'd done then. And sometimes he would shake his head, mumble how she shouldn't hold it against him, that once in a while he'd made her lie.

"The lies were necessary, Evangeline. We had to tell them. We had to get what we could, while the money was there."

It seemed to her, as she listened to his disjointed babbling, that he had suffered guilt, too, for the deceptions he had orchestrated.

He took to sitting in a chair at the foot of the narrow bed, just being there with her, bringing a magazine to study, or the piles of junk mail he received, which he would read through completely, as if each form letter were a special message from someone he loved.

His sitting there was a vigil, really, and Evie knew it.

Once in a while, she'd ask for water or a cool cloth against her skin. Gideon always gave them, tenderly. He dosed her with aspirin and cold remedies. But he wouldn't go out and hunt down the antibiotics she really needed. In the end, he either refused to admit to himself how ill she was—or his fear of discovery was stronger than his desire to save her life.

Evie forgave him. Who was she to judge him? And who could know the agonies he'd suffered in his life, who could say what had been done to him, to make him the lonely, twisted man he had become?

And, also, within this darkness and suffering, there was great beauty. Sometimes, when her father left her alone, she would go to meet Erik, in the meadow with the mountains all around. Of course, she knew that she was only dreaming. But the dreams felt so real, so comforting.

And ever since she'd told Erik the painful old truths of the way she'd once abused her gifts, they could touch in the dreams. He would hold her and love her among the wildflowers. And for a time, she would forget all the pain.

Like now. She could see him right now.

With a glad cry, Evie reached out her arms. "I've been waiting for you. Where have you been?"

"Trying to get back to you." Erik moved out of the swirling shadows, whole and real. He came down onto the tiny bed with her, and enfolded her in his strong arms.

They kissed, a long, searching kiss. His skin felt cool and good, against her own fevered heat. His scent was a clean scent, his breath sweet with health.

He smoothed back her lank hair. "Your eyes are burning. You're like an oven, so dry, so hot."

"I know, I know. Hold me. Pretend you won't have to let me go."

In answer, he cradled her closer. She nuzzled his chest, feeling cherished, loved as she had never been loved until he came into her life.

She felt his lips in her hair. "So," he whispered. "This is it, this dark place?"

She burrowed her head against his shoulder. "Yes. I liked the meadow better."

"The meadow was a dream."

"Yes. But so is this. How are the children?"

"They're getting through it, somehow."

"Pete really loves the computer, huh?"

"Yeah. Where are we, Evie?"

"Huh?"

"I said, where are we?"

She pulled back a little and looked around, wondering if the dream had taken them to someplace she'd never seen before. But it hadn't. She explained patiently, "We're in the room where my father keeps me."

"No." There was an urgency in his voice, now. "What state? What town?"

She burrowed close to him again and shook her head against his chest. "He won't tell me. I've asked a thousand times."

"Have you tried . . . looking into his mind?"

She closed her eyes, a little ashamed to confess that she'd used the abilities she'd sworn never to use again, even in a desperate circumstance such as this one.

Erik wouldn't let it go. "Did you?"

She sighed. "Yes, I did—at first, when I wasn't so weak."

"And?"

"I got nothing. It's always been like that with him. A blank wall."

"But there must be something, some clue, something he's said..."

"There isn't. I swear. If there had been, I'd remember." At the thought of the total hopelessness of her situation, despair rolled through Evie, like a big black train through a dark tunnel, thundering, with frightening speed.

She would never get back to them. Erik would suffer terribly. Losing Carolyn had nearly destroyed his belief in love. But then he'd met Evie, and he'd learned to love again. How would he bear it, to lose her, too?

And the children. What of the children? Jenny and Becca, who were so glad she had married their dad. And Petey, just beginning to trust her. Little by little, one day at a time, Evie had been building faith with the children. And now that she had disappeared, where would that faith go? How would they pick up the pieces, after first losing their mother—and then losing the woman who'd presumed to try to fill the void their mother had left?

"Evie, you can't give up," Erik said.

But she didn't want to talk anymore. Words meant nothing now. She reached up with hungry arms. "Love me, Erik. Love me, now. This is all I have, these dreams of you..."

"Evie..."

She pressed her lips to his in a desperate caress.

He froze for a moment, and she feared he would pull away. But then he groaned. His mouth went soft on hers. His big hands, so cool and good, caressed her.

He laid her down on the wrinkled sheets and touched her everywhere, so she forgot the black walls that surrounded them, the illness that was taking her down to oblivion, the sad old man who kept her here—everything, all of it, except for Erik and his loving touch.

He came into her, murmuring love words. She clutched him close. Together, they left that dark place. They soared among the stars.

And when it was over, when they lay intertwined, he whispered, "Don't give in, Evie. Don't give up."

"Oh, Erik." She tried to hide her head against his shoulder.

He wouldn't let her. He captured her face in his hands and made her look at him. "No. I mean it. We need you, Evie."

"But there's nothing I can do now."

"Yes, there is. There has to be. Help me find the way to bring you back to me. The kids need you. *I* need you. More than I even know how to say."

She felt a single hot tear slide out of the corner of her eye. "I don't know..." she strove to explain, though it hurt so much to talk of her shame "...if I deserve to live..."

He brushed the tear away with a tender thumb. "No. Don't say that. You're brave. And good. Let the past go now. Forgive yourself."

"I don't know...if I can."

"You can. You have to. You will."

He seemed so sure. She could almost believe him. Another tear fell. He kissed the place where it trailed down her cheek.

"Don't give up..."

"Don't give up..." She repeated the words, feverishly, over and over, as Erik seemed to fade from her arms.

She was alone again.

She closed her eyes. The hot tears kept coming, burning her skin as they trailed down her cheeks.

When she looked again, her father was bending over her. "Evangeline, Evangeline. What will I do with you?"

She realized, in a far-off way, that somehow she had fallen off the bed onto the cold concrete floor.

Gideon had bound her with long chains, two of them, attached to manacles at her wrists and bolted to the black-painted brick walls above the bed. They were very light chains, but also very strong. And now, they were all tangled around her, hurting her.

She watched, semiconscious, as Gideon pulled a little key from a back pocket. He unlocked the manacles, untangled the chains, and threw them off to either side of the bed. Then he scooped her up and put her back on the mattress.

Dazed, she held up her unbound wrists. They were red where the manacles had chafed them.

"It's all right," he said. "I guess we don't need those anymore."

He didn't say why. He didn't have to. She was too ill to plot an escape now, and too weak to carry it out. She knew that—and he did, too.

"You'll be more comfortable now, I'm sure of it." His voice was sad and gentle. She turned her head and saw the envelopes. His junk mail, on the bed stand where he'd tossed it when he saw her on the floor. He put a hand on her forehead, a cold hand. He must have been outside, getting the mail.

"There, now," he said. "You rest while I go through my letters."

Don't give up, Erik's voice whispered in her mind.

Gideon reached across her, to scoop up the envelopes once more. She only got one glimpse, but it was enough. In her mind, she captured the address on the top envelope.

Her father smiled at her. "Rest, now. Just rest." He carried the mail to the chair by the door and began to sort through it, humming.

Evangeline pressed her eyes closed. She pictured that envelope. Every detail of it. She let it fill her mind.

Erik swam to consciousness to find himself standing in front of a painting he had never seen before.

Outside, the rain still beat against the windowpanes. But Erik hardly heard it. He stared at the painting for a long time, planning how to use what he knew without being called a lunatic.

When the plan was solid in his mind, he went to his bedroom, closed the door and called Nevada. He'd chosen her over Faith because, since Evie's disappearance, Jack had been in contact with Faith. The deputy would be less suspicious if Nevada came forward with new information at this point.

Nevada didn't hesitate. She said she'd back Erik one hundred percent. They spoke for a while longer, going over her story in detail, so it would sound convincing when she told it.

Next Erik called Jack. He explained how he'd just hung up from talking with Nevada, how Nevada had been going through some old correspondence of hers, searching for anything that might lead to the whereabouts of her father, and possibly Evie.

"She's found an address for him, in Oregon," Erik said. "She scribbled it on the back of an envelope a few years ago. Apparently Gideon had called her, to try to harass her into revealing Evie's whereabouts. And she'd managed to get his address out of him before he hung up."

Jack said nothing for a moment. Then he sighed. "That stinks, Erik."

"What do you mean?"

"I mean, it doesn't fit what we know about Gideon. That man wouldn't give his address to *anyone,* especially not one of his daughters. He'd be too afraid they might use it to track him down, turn the tables on him and make him stop bothering Evie. And why would a bright woman like Nevada have mislaid such an important piece of information for all this time?"

"Look. I only know what she told me."

Jack was silent again. Then he grudgingly agreed, "All right. Have you got the address—and Nevada's phone number?"

Erik gave them to him.

"I'll call Nevada right now and talk to her about her story. And if it checks out, I'll contact the Oregon authorities and have them look into it."

"And how long is that going to take?" Erik made no attempt to hide his impatience.

"Erik, look—"

"No, Jack. You look. I'm going there. Myself. Right away."

"Erik—"

"Come on. What do we have, really? We have nothing, no shred of evidence that Gideon Jones is the one responsible for Evie's disappearance. From what you've been able to dig up, Gideon has no record anywhere of trouble with the law. There's nothing for the Oregon authorities to go on. The most they're going to do is stroll on over to the address Nevada gave me and have a talk with Gideon—*if* he's there and *when* they get around to it."

"Erik—"

"I'm not through. The point is, *I* can do that. I can get myself to that address in Oregon in, say, eight hours tops.

And I can have a little talk with my father-in-law. And that is exactly what I'm going to do."

"Erik."

"What?"

"I see your point."

"Damn right you do. You're a smart man, Jack."

"One thing."

"I'm listening."

"I'm going with you."

For the first time in a week, Erik felt himself smile. "That's what I hoped you'd say."

Since Erik couldn't find a flight that would get them there faster than driving, they took Evie's van.

They left North Magdalene at 2:00 p.m. and crossed the border into Oregon at eight that night. It took them three more hours to find the house. It was fairly isolated, as they'd expected, on a narrow road several miles from a town called Prineville.

The mailbox with the address painted on it stood on a wood pole by the road, and a dirt driveway led between a gap in a barbed wire fence up to a run-down-looking clapboard house. In the bare yard stood a single scraggly leafless elm and an ancient black van very much like the one Angie Leslie had described to Jack.

"Well, what do you know?" Jack muttered.

"What now?" asked Erik.

"Hell," Jack said, reaching over the seat and grabbing his police-issue revolver, all snug in its holster. "Park. Let's go knock on the door." Jack strapped on the gun as soon as he got down from the van. "Just hang tight here for a minute, all right? I'll check things out around back."

Erik nodded and Jack disappeared around the side of the house. He returned shortly thereafter. "Everything looks sealed up tight. There *is* a back door. I tried it."

"And?"

"Locked. But I probably should keep an eye on it, in case he tries to get out that way." He touched the handle of the revolver. "You want this?"

"No, thanks."

"Okay, then. Give me a minute to get in position on the side of the house, where I can see how you're doing *and* keep an eye on the back door. See that pine over there?" He pointed to a tree several yards to their left. "I'll get behind that. Then you go for it." Jack moved away.

Erik counted to sixty, then started for the porch.

The old boards creaked as he tread on them. And then he was standing at the door. He glanced to the left and then right. All the windows had dark curtains on them. Sealed tight, as Jack had said.

Feeling strange, as if this whole thing wasn't really happening, Erik lifted his hand and knocked on the door. Then he waited. He heard no movement inside the house. Just the hoot of an owl, far off somewhere.

He knocked again. Still nothing.

There was a small diamond-shaped window at the top of the door. He peered into it. All he saw was darkness.

He tried the door and found it locked.

He was just thinking he was going to have to put his shoulder to it, see if he could break it in, when Jack materialized at his side.

"Looks like no one's going out the back way," Jack said.

"No one's answering, period," Erik said.

The two men looked at each other. Then Jack said, "I know what you're thinking. It's called breaking and entering."

"Jack. I know she's in there. I can feel it." He turned his shoulder to the door.

Jack put his hand on Erik's arm. "Hold on."

"What?"

"I used to be a private investigator, you know?"

"I heard."

"Got me all kinds of questionable skills doing that kind of work."

Erik watched in amazement as Jack pulled a couple of wires from his pocket and set to work picking the lock on the door. Within thirty seconds, there was a click. Jack's white teeth flashed in the darkness.

But there was still the dead bolt to deal with. Jack handled that, too, with a some kind of plastic card.

And then at last, the door swung back onto a dark foyer. Erik stepped inside and felt for a light switch. He found it within seconds. He flipped it on.

Light bathed the small space. And just beyond it, on the floor of the barren living room, a woman lay, her back to them, her body tucked tight in a fetal curl.

"Evie," Erik breathed, hardly aware that, beside him, Jack had drawn his gun.

"Careful, easy," Jack was saying.

But Erik paid him little heed. Five steps and he was standing over her. He dropped to his knees at her back. "Evie. Sweetheart . . ."

She didn't move.

"I'll look around," Jack said.

Erik waved him away. Nothing mattered but the thin, curled-up body before him.

"Evie. I'm here." He touched her shoulder. She neither moved toward his hand nor pulled tighter into herself.

He gave a tug. She fell back against his knees, like a husk of herself, an empty shell.

"Oh. Evie..." He didn't want to do it. He didn't want to know.

But he had to. He put two fingers against her throat, seeking a pulse.

There was nothing.

She was gone.

A keening cry came from him then, a cry that should have shamed him, it was so desperate and full of pain. He grabbed at her empty, lifeless body, gathering her into his arms and rocking her, his mind screaming, crying out, over and over, in a litany of lost hope.

Too late, too late, too late, too late...

He hated himself, for all those nights in the meadow, those nights of his numbness, when he didn't believe. When they talked of the past, and then when they just clung together, doing nothing to find out where her father had brought her.

Precious time, wasted. That's what it had been. And he would never forgive himself for this. Never, in a hundred thousand years.

"Evie, oh Evie," he moaned as he rocked her. The words came out of him of their own accord. "Evie, don't leave now. Evie, please. Come back. We need you, Evie. The kids. Me. We love you and need you. Please. Stay with us...."

And above him, looking down, someone heard. And answered.

And that was when he felt her lips move against his neck.

He pulled back, smoothed her filthy hair off her forehead. "Evie...?"

Her lips moved again, forming his name. "Erik." She tried a smile, a ghastly thing, her face was so pale.

But to him, she had never looked more beautiful. He pulled her, tenderly, against him once again. "It's all right," he whispered. "All right now. We'll get you to a hospital, right away."

Chapter Eighteen

Evie woke in the hospital forty-eight hours later. Erik was there, sitting in a chair in the corner of the room. He told her what she already knew—that she would be all right now—before calling the nurse to say she had awakened at last.

They let her go home four days after that, and for a while she stayed in the king-size bed upstairs, while Darla and Tawny and Nellie treated her like a queen. They even moved the computer up there, so Pete could show her a thing or two about it while she got her strength back.

By mid-December, she was much better, able to open her store again and work half days. Will Bacon, who ran the local clinic, warned her to take it easy, though. Pneumonia, Will said, could ruin a person's stamina for quite some time.

For years after that, Evie always felt that Jack Roper looked at her strangely. Jack had gone down into the basement of that old house. And he'd seen her father on the floor, knocked out by one of the bricks from the wall.

What Jack could never figure out, he said, was how Evie, in her condition, managed to work that brick free of the wall, let alone heft it and hit the old man with it.

Once or twice, Evie was tempted to explain to him about telekinesis. But she never did. Jack was such a practical soul. She doubted he'd believe her anyway. And that whole time was such a blur to her now, anyway. She *thought* she'd willed that brick out of the wall and through the air. But she'd never be absolutely positive that was what she had done.

And she had no memory at all of crawling up the basement stairs and into the living room where Erik said he'd found her.

No, really. She thought it was probably best to just let the whole thing go. Let Jack look at her strangely. She could live with that.

A few days before Christmas, Erik and Evie flew to Oregon and paid a visit to the institution where Gideon had been confined. The old man didn't recognize her. The doctors said it was the way it often went, in cases like these.

During the flight home, Evie thought—as she had a hundred times since that day she woke in the Oregon hospital—that maybe they should talk about it all. But they didn't. They glanced now and then at each other, shared a loving smile, and listened to the low drone of the powerful engines that were taking them home.

Christmas was beautiful. "The best we ever had," Becca said. Nevada and Faith showed up in the afternoon. They all went for a huge dinner at Darla's. Even Nellie came for that.

New Year's Eve, Erik and Evie went to a party at Delilah Fletcher's house. At midnight, they kissed beneath the mistletoe in Delilah's living room. Then they went home and made long, wonderful love in their king-size bed.

Afterward, as they held each other, Evie thought again of talking to him of the miracle of her rescue five weeks before. She remembered the meadow, and the dreams of him. And the envelope she'd stared so hard at, with the address of the old house on it.

But she said nothing. Erik had already explained to her how he'd found her. Nevada had come up with the address at the last minute; she'd forgotten she had it, and then discovered it scrawled on an envelope after all hope was gone.

And really, as each day passed, Evie saw less and less need for talking about it anyway.

The strange dreams of Erik in the meadow had helped her. In them, she'd told the truth about herself and her past. And in them, Erik had accepted that truth, gone on loving her in spite of the wrong she'd done. It didn't matter that it hadn't been real. The important thing was that she *felt* forgiven for those years when she had told lies about her visions for her father's gain.

At last, nothing of the past bound her anymore; all the darkness had turned to light. She could lead a happy, normal life with her newfound family.

And as the weeks—and then the months—went by, Evie learned something else about herself. The strange powers that had haunted her for over twenty years of her life were gone now. No visions ever came to her, to be blocked out by the wall. She saw as others saw at last. No more. And no less.

She wondered, at times, how that had happened. Erik had told her that she'd died on the living room floor of that old house—and come back when he called to her. Just as she had died when she was ten years old, returning then because her sisters had needed her so.

Was it possible that when Erik had called her back, she'd left her gifts behind? For another time, perhaps, when she was more capable of using them well?

She'd never be sure. It was all speculation.

And in the grand scheme of things, she wasn't even positive that it mattered. What mattered, for Evie Jones Riggins, was that life in North Magdalene went on, full and rich and good.

In April, on a bright, clear morning after the kids had left for school and Erik was gone to work, Evie decided to put some of the family's outerwear away in the spare closet in Erik's studio before she headed over to Main Street to open her store.

She set the coats across a corner chair and stuck her head in the closet, planning to push the canvases in there out of the way. But a tricky ray of sunlight found its way into the dark space and played upon the image of a pale, gnarled hand.

Curious, Evie pulled that canvas out into the light.

It was a painting she'd never seen before—a painting of her father's hand, scooping up a stack of mail, the address of the old house where her father had imprisoned her printed clearly on the top envelope.

Evie set the painting on an easel. She stared at it for a long time.

And then she decided she needed her husband. Right now.

She went out and found him, at his brother Joshua's house. Erik was just getting ready to paint the house a hideous green color that Joshua's wife, Wilma, had picked out herself. Evie marched into the yard and took her husband by the hand.

"Evie, what's going on?"

"Come with me, please."

"Sweetheart, I have work to do."

"This won't take long. An hour, tops, and you'll be back here slathering that stuff that looks like pea soup all over Joshua's house."

"Shh." He shot a look toward the front door. "Wilma will hear you."

"Then come with me and I'll shut up."

With a put-upon sigh, he let her lead him out the front gate and back home, where she pulled him up the stairs and pushed him into his studio.

He saw the painting then. He turned to meet her eyes. "Evie, I..."

She felt as if she just might cry. "It all really happened, didn't it? It happened for you, as much as for me?"

He looked at her for a long moment. Then he nodded.

"You really do know. Everything. All my secrets. All my...sins?"

"Evie..."

She cast her gaze down. "I suppose I should be grateful, shouldn't I? Because what happened between us was a miracle, wasn't it?"

"Naw."

She looked up at him then. "What do you mean?"

"It was just love, Evie. Love. That's all."

"Oh, Erik..."

He held out his arms to her. With a glad cry, she ran to him.

Their kiss was long and sweet. Soon enough, she was helping him out of his painter's overalls. They fell on the couch together, the sunlight streaming in to bathe their bodies in warm gold.

Evie clutched her husband's back as she cried out in love and joy.

And afterward, when they lay holding each other close on that couch, waiting for their heartbeats to slow a little, Evie thought of the miracle that was her life. Somehow, she had become what she'd never dared to dream she might be: an ordinary woman, loving and loved.

Evie snuggled closer to Erik and his arms tightened around her in response. Sighing in contentment, she recalled one of the visions she'd had, that day in her shop when Erik had grabbed her arm: a vision of the two of them, making love right here, in the sun. Until now, it had been the only vision from that day that remained unfulfilled.

Wonder stole through Evie. She knew then that the chains of the past had fallen away for good and all. What endured was love. Evangeline's final unexplained vision had found its true meaning at last.

* * * * *

COMING NEXT MONTH

#1015 SISTERS—Penny Richards
That Special Woman!
Cash Benedict's return meant seeing the woman he'd always wanted but felt he had no right to love. Skye Herder had never forgotten Cash, and now he was about to find out that Skye wasn't the only person he left behind all those years ago....

#1016 THE RANCHER AND HIS UNEXPECTED DAUGHTER—Sherryl Woods
And Baby Makes Three
Harlan Adams was used to getting his way, but feisty Janet Runningbea and her equally spunky daughter weren't making it easy for him. Janet sent Harlan's heart into a tailspin, until he was sure of only one thing—he wanted her as his wife!

#1017 BUCHANAN'S BABY—Pamela Toth
Buckles & Broncos
Not only had Donovan Buchanan been reunited with Bobbie McBride after five years, but he'd just discovered he was the father of her four-year-old daughter! Now that he'd found her, the handsome cowboy was determined to be the best father he could be—as well as future husband to his lost love.

#1018 FOR LOVE OF HER CHILD—Tracy Sinclair
Erica Barclay always put the needs of her son first. But when she fell for Michael Smith, she was torn between passion and her child. Could she still protect her son and listen to the needs of her own heart?

#1019 THE REFORMER—Diana Whitney
The Blackthorn Brotherhood
Strong, loving Letitia Cervantes was just the kind of woman Larkin McKay had been waiting for all his life. And when her son's rebellious spirit called out to the father in him, he wanted to bring them together into a ready-made family.

#1020 PLAYING DADDY—Lorraine Carroll
Cable McRay wasn't interested in taking on fatherhood and marriage. But Sara Nelson made those thoughts near impossible, and her son was proving irresistible—and Cable was soon playing daddy....

Silhouette

SPECIAL ✦ EDITION®

™

Special Edition is proud to announce the arrival of our newest edition

THAT'S MY BABY!

Beginning in February, and due to arrive every other month, THAT'S MY BABY! will feature stories of bringing up baby—and finding romance and love—by some of your favorite authors:

**Sherryl Woods
Laurie Paige
Barbara Faith**

Plus many more!

Don't miss the wonderful stories THAT'S MY BABY! will deliver. Sometimes bringing up baby can bring surprises...and showers of love! Only from Silhouette Special Edition!

**This March
come back to
where it all began with**

DESTINATION: CONARD COUNTY

Return to Conard County—where passions match the wild terrain under blue Wyoming skies.

Back by popular demand, the first two Conard County stories by Rachel Lee—all in one special collection!

**EXILE'S END
CHEROKEE THUNDER**

And don't forget to look for *A Conard County Reckoning*, the newest addition to the Conard County family. Available this March wherever books are sold.

Silhouette®